M000189666

The Dover
Anthology of
Cat Stories

Dover Publications, Inc.
Mineola, New York

Cats are having a moment. Internet cats like Grumpy Cat and Lil' Bub are veritable stars complete with agents and legal teams, Taylor Swift is rarely seen leaving her Manhattan apartment without one of her cats in her arms, and young women are now embracing the once-biting moniker of "cat lady." Looking at pop culture in 2015, one might think that cats are more popular, visible, and beloved than they've ever been. This is an illusion that fades as soon as one begins to look back in time, especially into literature.

You might not immediately call to mind any stories about cats, but as we found, once you begin looking for them, they're always there. It's worth mentioning that this volume is incomplete; like the street cats of Cairo, cat stories are innumerable. Rather than being comprehensive, our aim was to curate an anthology of classic stories that celebrate the essence of cats: their mystery, independence, beauty, fierceness, and, when we've earned it, their loyalty.

Bibliographical Note

The Dover Anthology of Cat Stories, first published by Dover Publications, Inc., in 2015, is a new compilation of works reprinted from standard editions. British and American spellings have been retained as in the original editions.

International Standard Book Number

ISBN-13: 978-0-486-79464-8
ISBN-10: 0-486-79464-4

Manufactured in the United States by Courier Corporation
79464401   2015
www.doverpublications.com

Contents

iv Contents

Tobermory
Saki

I<small>T</small> was a chill, rain-washed afternoon of a late August day, that indefinite season when partridges are still in the security of cold storage, and there is nothing to hunt—unless one is bounded on the north by the Bristol Channel, in which case one may lawfully gallop after fat red stags. Lady Blemley's house party was not bounded on the north by the Bristol Channel, hence there was a full gathering of her guests round the tea-table on this particular afternoon. And, in spite of the blankness of the season and the triteness of the occasion, there was no trace in the company of that fatigued restlessness which means a dread of the pianola and a subdued hankering for auction bridge. The undisguised, openmouthed attention of the entire party was fixed on the homely, negative personality of Mr. Cornelius Appin. Of all her guests, he was the one who had come to Lady Blemley with the vaguest reputation. Someone had said he was "clever," and he had got his invitation in the moderate expectation, on the part of his hostess, that some portion at least of his cleverness would be contributed to the general entertainment. Until teatime that day she had been unable to discover in what direction, if any, his cleverness lay. He was neither a wit nor a croquet champion, a hypnotic force nor a begetter of amateur theatricals. Neither did his exterior suggest the sort of man in whom women are willing to pardon a generous measure of mental deficiency. He had subsided into mere Mr. Appin, and the Cornelius seemed a piece of transparent baptismal bluff. And now he was claiming to have launched on the world a discovery beside which the invention of gun powder, of the printing press, and of steam locomotion were inconsiderable trifles. Science had made bewildering strides in many directions during recent decades, but this thing seemed to belong to the domain of miracle rather than to scientific achievement.

"And do you really ask us to believe," Sir Wilfrid was saying, "that you have discovered a means for instructing animals in the art of human speech and that dear old Tobermory has proved your first successful pupil?"

"It is a problem at which I have worked for the past seventeen years," said Mr. Appin, "but only during the last eight or nine months have I been rewarded with glimmerings of success. Of course I have experimented with thousands of animals, but latterly only with cats, those wonderful creatures which have assimilated themselves so marvellously with our civilization while retaining all their highly developed feral instincts. Here and there among cats one comes across an outstanding superior intellect, just as one does among the ruck of human beings, and when I made the acquaintance of Tobermory a week ago I saw at once that I was in contact with a "Beyond-cat" of extraordinary intelligence. I had gone far along the road to success in recent experiments; with Tobermory, as you call him, I have reached the goal."

Mr. Appin concluded his remarkable statement in a voice which he strove to divest of a triumphant inflexion. No one said "Rats," though Clovis's lips moved in a monosyllabic contortion which probably invoked those rodents of disbelief.

"And do you mean to say," asked Miss Resker, after a slight pause, "that you have taught Tobermory to say and understand easy sentences of one syllable?"

"My dear Miss Resker," said the wonder-worker patiently, "one teaches little children and savages and backward adults in that piecemeal fashion; when one has once solved the problem of making a beginning with an animal of highly developed intelligence one has no need for those halting methods. Tobermory can speak our language with perfect correctness."

This time Clovis very distinctly said, "Beyond-rats!" Sir Wilfrid was more polite, but equally sceptical.

"Hadn't we better have the cat in and judge for ourselves?" suggested Lady Blemley.

Sir Wilfrid went in search of the animal, and the company settled themselves down to the languid expectation of witnessing some more or less adroit drawing room ventriloquism.

In a minute Sir Wilfrid was back in the room, his face white beneath its tan and his eyes dilated with excitement.

"By Gad, it's true!"

His agitation was unmistakably genuine, and his hearers started forward in a thrill of awakened interest.

Collapsing into an armchair he continued breathlessly, "I found him dozing in the smoking room, and called after him to come for his tea. He blinked at me in his usual way, and I said, "Come on, Toby; don't keep us waiting;" and, by Gad! he drawled out in a most horribly natural voice, that he'd come when he dashed well pleased! I nearly jumped out of my skin!"

Appin had preached to absolutely incredulous hearers; Sir Wilfrid's statement carried instant conviction. A Babel-like chorus of startled exclamation arose, amid which the scientist sat mutely enjoying the first fruit of his stupendous discovery.

In the midst of the clamour Tobermory entered the room and made his way with velvet tread and studied unconcern across to the group seated round the tea-table.

A sudden hush of awkwardness and constraint fell on the company. Somehow there seemed an element of embarrassment in addressing on equal terms a domestic cat of acknowledged mental ability.

"Will you have some milk, Tobermory?" asked Lady Blemley in a rather strained voice.

"I don't mind if I do," was the response, couched in a tone of even indifference. A shiver of suppressed excitement went through the listeners, and Lady Blemley might be excused for pouring out the saucerful of milk rather unsteadily.

"I am afraid I have spilled a good deal of it," she said apologetically.

"After all, it's not my Axminster," was Tobermory's rejoinder.

Another silence fell on the group, and then Miss Resker, in her best district-visitor manner, asked if the human language had been difficult to learn. Tobermory looked squarely at her for a moment and then fixed his gaze serenely on the middle distance. It was obvious that boring questions lay outside his scheme of life.

"What do you think of human intelligence?" asked Mavis Pellington lamely.

"Of whose intelligence in particular?" asked Tobermory coldly.

"Oh, well, mine for instance," said Mavis, with a feeble laugh.

"You put me in an embarrassing position," said Tobermory, whose tone and attitude certainly did not suggest a shred of embarrassment. "When your inclusion in this house party was suggested, Sir Wilfrid protested that you were the most brainless woman of his acquaintance, and that there was a wide distinction between hospitality and the care of the feeble-minded. Lady Blemley replied that your lack of brain power was the precise quality which had earned you your invitation, as you were the only person she could think of who might be idiotic enough to buy their old car. You know, the one they call "The Envy of Sisyphus," because it goes quite nicely uphill if you push it."

Lady Blemley's protestations would have had greater effect if she had not casually suggested to Mavis only that morning that the car in question would be just the thing for her down at her Devonshire home.

Major Barfield plunged in heavily to effect a diversion.

"How about your carryings-on with the tortoiseshell puss up at the stables, eh?"

The moment he had said it everyone realized the blunder.

"One does not usually discuss these matters in public," said Tobermory frigidly. "From a slight observation of your ways since you've been in this house I should imagine you'd find it inconvenient if I were to shift the conversation onto your own little affairs."

The panic which ensued was not confined to the Major.

"Would you like to go and see if cook has got your dinner ready?" suggested Lady Blemley hurriedly, affecting to ignore the fact that it wanted at least two hours to Tobermory's dinnertime.

"Thanks," said Tobermory, "not quite so soon after my tea. I don't want to die of indigestion."

"Cats have nine lives, you know," said Sir Wilfrid heartily.

"Possibly," answered Tobermory; "but only one liver."

"Adelaide!" said Mrs. Cornett, "do you mean to encourage that cat to go out and gossip about us in the servants' hall?"

The panic had indeed become general. A narrow ornamental balustrade ran in front of most of the bedroom windows at the Towers, and it was recalled with dismay that this had formed a favourite promenade for Tobermory at all hours, whence he could watch the pigeons—and heaven knew what else besides. If he intended to become reminiscent in his present outspoken strain the effect would be something more than disconcerting. Mrs. Cornett, who spent much time at her toilet table, and whose complexion was reputed to be of a nomadic though punctual disposition, looked as ill at ease as the Major. Miss Scrawen, who wrote fiercely sensuous poetry and led a blameless life, merely displayed irritation; if you are methodical and virtuous in private you don't necessarily want everyone to know it. Bertie van Tahn, who was so depraved at seventeen that he had long ago given up trying to be any worse, turned a dull shade of gardenia white, but he did not commit the error of dashing out of the room like Odo Finsberry, a young gentleman who was understood to be reading for the Church and who was possibly disturbed at the thought of scandals he might hear concerning other people. Clovis had the presence of mind to maintain a composed exterior; privately he was calculating how long it would take to procure a box of fancy mice through the agency of the *Exchange and Mart* as a species of hush-money.

Even in a delicate situation like the present, Agnes Resker could not endure to remain too long in the background.

"Why did I ever come down here?" she asked dramatically. Tobermory immediately accepted the opening.

"Judging by what you said to Mrs. Cornett on the croquet lawn yesterday, you were out for food. You described the Blemleys as the dullest people to stay with that you knew, but said they were clever enough to employ a first-rate cook; otherwise they'd find it difficult to get anyone to come down a second time."

"There's not a word of truth in it! I appeal to Mrs. Cornett—" exclaimed the discomfitted Agnes.

"Mrs. Cornett repeated your remark afterwards to Bertie van Tahn," continued Tobermory, "and said, 'That woman is a regular Hunger Marcher; she'd go anywhere for four square meals a day' and Bertie van Tahn said—"

At this point the chronicle mercifully ceased. Tobermory had caught a glimpse of the big yellow Tom from the Rectory working his way through the shrubbery towards the stable wing. In a flash he had vanished through the open French window.

With the disappearance of his too brilliant pupil Cornelius Appin found himself beset by a hurricane of bitter upbraiding, anxious inquiry, and frightened entreaty. The responsibility for the situation lay with him, and he must prevent matters from becoming worse. Could Tobermory impart his dangerous gift to other cats? was the first question he had to answer. It was possible, he replied, that he might have initiated his intimate friend the stable puss into his new accomplishment, but it was unlikely that his teaching could have taken a wider range as yet.

"Then," said Mrs. Cornett, "Tobermory may be a valuable cat and a great pet; but I'm sure you'll agree, Adelaide, that both he and the stable cat must be done away with without delay."

"You don't suppose I've enjoyed the last quarter of an hour, do you?" said Lady Blemley bitterly. "My husband and I are very fond of Tobermory—at least, we were before this horrible accomplishment was infused into him; but now, of course, the only thing is to have him destroyed as soon as possible."

"We can put some strychnine in the scraps he always gets at dinnertime," said Sir Wilfrid, "and I will go and drown the stable cat myself. The coachman will be very sore at losing his pet, but I'll say a very catching form of mange has broken out in both cats and we're afraid of it spreading to the kennels."

"But my great discovery!" expostulated Mr. Appin; "after all my years of research and experiment—"

"You can go and experiment on the short-horns at the farm, who are under proper control," said Mrs. Cornett, "or the elephants at the Zoological Gardens. They're said to be highly intelligent, and they have this recommendation, that they don't come creeping about our bedrooms and under chairs, and so forth."

An archangel ecstatically proclaiming the Millennium, and then finding that it clashed with Henley and would have to be indefinitely postponed, could hardly have felt more crestfallen than Cornelius Appin at the reception of his wonderful achievements. Public opinion, however, was against him—in fact, had the general voice been consulted on the subject it is probable that a strong minority vote would have been in favour of including him in the strychnine diet.

Defective train arrangements and a nervous desire to see matters brought to a finish prevented an immediate dispersal of the party, but dinner that evening was not a social success. Sir Wilfrid had had rather a trying time with the stable cat and subsequently with the coachman. Agnes Resker ostentatiously limited her repast to a morsel of dry toast, which she bit as though it were a personal enemy, while Mavis Pellington maintained a vindictive silence throughout the meal. Lady Blemley kept up a flow of what she hoped was conversation, but her attention was fixed on the doorway. A plateful of carefully dosed fish scraps was in readiness on the sideboard, but sweets and savoury and dessert went their way, and no Tobermory appeared either in the dining room or kitchen.

The sepulchral dinner was cheerful compared with the subsequent vigil in the smoking room. Eating and drinking had at least supplied a distraction and cloak to the prevailing embarrassment. Bridge was out of the question in the general tension of nerves and tempers, and after Odo Finsberry had given a lugubrious rendering of "Melisande in the Wood" to a frigid audience, music was tacitly avoided. At eleven the servants went to bed, announcing that the small window in the pantry had been left open as usual for Tobermory's private use. The guests read steadily through the current batch of magazines, and fell back gradually on the "Badminton Library" and bound volumes of *Punch*. Lady Blemley made periodic visits to the pantry, returning each time with an expression of listless depression which forestalled questioning.

At two o'clock Clovis broke the dominating silence.

"He won't turn up tonight. He's probably in the local newspaper office at the present moment, dictating the first instalment of his reminiscences. Lady What's-her-name's book won't be in it. It will be the event of the day."

Having made this contribution to the general cheerfulness, Clovis went to bed. At long intervals the various members of the house party followed his example.

The servants taking round the early tea made a uniform announcement in reply to a uniform question. Tobermory had not returned.

Breakfast was, if anything, a more unpleasant function than dinner had been, but before its conclusion the situation was relieved. Tobermory's corpse was brought in from the shrubbery, where a gardener had just discovered it. From the bites on his throat and the yellow fur which coated his claws it was evident that he had fallen in unequal combat with the big Tom from the Rectory.

By midday most of the guests had quitted the Towers, and after lunch Lady Blemley had sufficiently recovered her spirits to write an extremely nasty letter to the Rectory about the loss of her valuable pet.

Tobermory had been Appin's one successful pupil, and he was destined to have no successor. A few weeks later an elephant in the Dresden Zoological Garden, which had shown no previous signs of irritability, broke loose and killed an Englishman who had apparently been teasing it. The victim's name was variously reported in the papers as Oppin and Eppelin, but his front name was faithfully rendered Cornelius.

"If he was trying German irregular verbs on the poor beast," said Clovis, "he deserved all he got."

The Cat that Walked by Himself
Rudyard Kipling

Hear and attend and listen; for this befell and behappened and became and was, O my Best Beloved, when the Tame animals were wild. The Dog was wild, and the Horse was wild, and the Cow was wild, and the Sheep was wild, and the Pig was wild—as wild as wild could be—and they walked in the Wet Wild Woods by their wild lones. But the wildest of all the wild animals was the Cat. He walked by himself, and all places were alike to him.

Of course the Man was wild too. He was dreadfully wild. He didn't even begin to be tame till he met the Woman, and she told him that she did not like living in his wild ways. She picked out a nice dry Cave, instead of a heap of wet leaves, to lie down in; and she strewed clean sand on the floor; and she lit a nice fire of wood at the back of the Cave; and she hung a dried wild-horse skin, tail-down, across the opening of the Cave; and she said, "Wipe your feet, dear, when you come in, and now we'll keep house."

That night, Best Beloved, they ate wild sheep roasted on the hot stones, and flavoured with wild garlic and wild pepper; and wild duck stuffed with wild rice and wild fenugreek and wild coriander; and marrowbones of wild oxen; and wild cherries, and wild grenadillas. Then the Man went to sleep in front of the fire ever so happy; but the Woman sat up, combing her hair. She took the bone of the shoulder of mutton—the big flat bladebone—and she looked at the wonderful marks on it, and she threw more wood on the fire, and she made a Magic. She made the First Singing Magic in the world.

Out of the Wet Wild Woods all the wild animals gathered together where they could see the light of the fire a long way off, and they wondered what it meant.

Then Wild Horse stamped with his wild foot and said, "O my Friends and O my Enemies, why have the Man and the Woman made that great light in that great Cave, and what harm will it do us?"

Wild Dog lifted up his wild nose and smelled the smell of the roast mutton, and said, "I will go up and see and look, and say; for I think it is good. Cat, come with me."

"Nenni!" said the Cat. "I am the Cat who walks by himself, and all places are alike to me. I will not come."

"Then we can never be friends again," said Wild Dog, and he trotted off to the Cave. But when he had gone a little way the Cat said to himself, "All places are alike to me. Why should I not go too and see and look and come away at my own liking?" So he slipped after Wild Dog softly, very softly, and hid himself where he could hear everything.

When Wild Dog reached the mouth of the Cave he lifted up the dried horse skin with his nose and sniffed the beautiful smell of the roast mutton, and the Woman, looking at the blade-bone, heard him, and laughed, and said, "Here comes the first. Wild Thing out of the Wild Woods, what do you want?"

Wild Dog said, "O my Enemy and Wife of my Enemy, what is this that smells so good in the Wild Woods?"

Then the Woman picked up a roasted mutton-bone and threw it to Wild Dog and said, "Wild Thing out of the Wild Woods, taste and try." Wild Dog gnawed the bone, and it was more delicious than anything he had ever tasted, and he said, "O my Enemy and Wife of my Enemy, give me another."

The Woman said, "Wild Thing out of the Wild Woods, help my Man to hunt through the day and guard this Cave at night, and I will give you as many roast bones as you need."

"Ah!" said the Cat, listening. "This is a very wise Woman, but she is not so wise as I am."

Wild Dog crawled into the Cave and laid his head on the Woman's lap, and said, "O my Friend and Wife of my Friend, I will help your Man to hunt through the day, and at night I will guard your Cave."

"Ah!" said the Cat, listening. "That is a very foolish Dog." And he went back through the Wet Wild Woods waving his wild tail, and walking by his wild lone. But he never told anybody.

When the Man waked up he said, "What is Wild Dog doing here?" And the Woman said, "His name is not Wild Dog anymore, but the First Friend, because he will be our friend for always and always and always. Take him with you when you go hunting."

Next night the Woman cut great green armfuls of fresh grass from the water meadows, and dried it before the fire, so that it smelt like new-mown hay, and she sat at the mouth of the Cave and plaited a halter out of horsehide, and she looked at the shoulder-of-mutton bone—at the big broad bladebone—and she made a Magic. She made the Second Singing Magic in the world.

Out of the Wild Woods all the wild animals wondered what had happened to Wild Dog, and at last Wild Horse stamped with his foot and said, "I will go and see and say why Wild Dog has not returned. Cat, come with me."

"Nenni!" said the Cat. "I am the Cat who walks by himself, and all places are alike to me. I will not come." But all the same he followed Wild Horse softly, very softly, and hid himself where he could hear everything.

When the Woman heard Wild Horse tripping and stumbling on his long mane, she laughed and said, "Here comes the second. Wild Thing out of the Wild Woods, what do you want?"

Wild Horse said, "O my Enemy and Wife of my Enemy, where is Wild Dog?"

The Woman laughed, and picked up the bladebone and looked at it, and said, "Wild Thing out of the Wild Woods, you did not come here for Wild Dog, but for the sake of this good grass."

And Wild Horse, tripping and stumbling on his long mane, said, "That is true; give it to me to eat."

The Woman said, "Wild Thing out of the Wild Woods, bend your wild head and wear what I give you, and you shall eat the wonderful grass three times a day."

"Ah!" said the Cat, listening. "This is a clever Woman, but she is not so clever as I am."

Wild Horse bent his wild head, and the Woman slipped the plaited-hide halter over it, and Wild Horse breathed on the Woman's feet and said, "O my Mistress, and Wife of my Master, I will be your servant for the sake of the wonderful grass."

"Ah!" said the Cat, listening. "That is a very foolish Horse." And he went back through the Wet Wild Woods, waving his wild tail and walking by his wild lone. But he never told anybody.

When the Man and the Dog came back from hunting, the Man said, "What is Wild Horse doing here?" And the Woman said, "His name is not Wild Horse anymore, but the First Servant, because he will carry us from place to place for always and always and always. Ride on his back when you go hunting."

Next day, holding her wild head high that her wild horns should not catch in the wild trees, Wild Cow came up to the Cave, and the Cat followed, and hid himself just the same as before; and everything happened just the same as before; and the Cat said the same things as before; and when Wild Cow had promised to give her milk to the Woman every day in exchange for the wonderful grass, the Cat went back through the Wet Wild Woods waving his wild tail and walking by his wild lone, just the same as before. But he never told anybody And when the Man and the Horse and the Dog came home from hunting and asked the same questions same as before, the Woman said, "Her name is not Wild Cow anymore, but the Giver of Good Food. She will give us the warm white milk for always and always and always, and I will take care of her while you and the First Friend and the First Servant go hunting."

Next day the Cat waited to see if any other Wild Thing would go up to the Cave, but no one moved in the Wet Wild Woods, so the Cat walked there by himself; and he saw the Woman milking the Cow, and he saw the light of the fire in the Cave, and he smelt the smell of the warm white milk.

Cat said, "O my Enemy and Wife of my Enemy, where did Wild Cow go?"

The Woman laughed and said, "Wild Thing out of the Wild Woods, go back to the Woods again, for I have braided up my hair, and I have put away the magic bladebone and we have no more need of either friends or servants in our Cave."

Cat said, "I am not a friend, and I am not a servant. I am the Cat who walks by himself, and I wish to come into your Cave."

Woman said, "Then why did you not come with First Friend on the first night?"

Cat grew very angry and said, "Has Wild Dog told tales of me?"

Then the Woman laughed and said, "You are the Cat who walks by himself, and all places are alike to you. You are neither a friend nor a servant. You have said it yourself. Go away and walk by yourself in all places alike."

Then Cat pretended to be sorry and said, "Must I never come into the Cave? Must I never sit by the warm fire? Must I never drink the warm white milk? You are very wise and very beautiful. You should not be cruel even to a Cat."

Woman said, "I knew I was wise, but I did not know I was beautiful. So I will make a bargain with you. If ever I say one word in your praise, you may come into the Cave."

"And if you say two words in my praise?" said the Cat.

"I never shall," said the Woman, "but if I say two words in your praise, you may sit by the fire in the Cave."

"And if you say three words?" said the Cat.

"I never shall," said the Woman, "but if I say three words in your praise, you may drink the warm white milk three times a day for always and always and always."

Then the Cat arched his back and said, "Now let the Curtain at the mouth of the Cave, and the Fire at the back of the Cave, and the Milkpots that stand beside the Fire, remember what my Enemy and the Wife of my Enemy has said." And he went away through the Wet Wild Woods waving his wild tail and walking by his wild lone.

That night when the Man and the Horse and the Dog came home from hunting, the Woman did not tell them of the bargain that she had made with the Cat, because she was afraid that they might not like it.

Cat went far and far away and hid himself in the Wet Wild Woods by his wild lone for a long time till the Woman forgot all about him. Only the Bat—the little upside-down Bat—that hung inside the Cave knew where Cat hid; and every evening Bat would fly to Cat with news of what was happening.

One evening Bat said, "There is a Baby in the Cave. He is new and pink and fat and small, and the Woman is very fond of him."

"Ah," said the Cat, listening. "But what is the Baby fond of?"

"He is fond of things that are soft and tickle," said the Bat. "He is fond of warm things to hold in his arms when he goes to sleep. He is fond of being played with. He is fond of all those things."

"Ah," said the Cat, listening. "Then my time has come."

Next night Cat walked through the Wet Wild Woods and hid very near the Cave till morning-time, and Man and Dog and Horse went hunting. The Woman was busy cooking that morning, and the Baby cried and interrupted. So she carried him outside the Cave and gave him a handful of pebbles to play with. But still the Baby cried.

Then the Cat put out his paddy paw and patted the Baby on the cheek, and it cooed; and the Cat rubbed against its fat knees and tickled it under its fat chin with his tail. And the Baby laughed; and the Woman heard him and smiled.

Then the Bat—the little upside-down Bat—that hung in the mouth of the Cave said, "O my Hostess and Wife of my

Host and Mother of my Host's Son, a Wild Thing from the Wild Woods is most beautifully playing with your Baby."

"A blessing on that Wild Thing whoever he may be," said the Woman, straightening her back, "for I was a busy woman this morning and he has done me a service."

That very minute and second, Best Beloved, the dried horse-skin Curtain that was stretched tail-down at the mouth of the Cave fell down—*woosh!*—because it remembered the bargain she had made with the Cat; and when the Woman went to pick it up—lo and behold!—the Cat was sitting quite comfy inside the Cave.

"O my Enemy and Wife of my Enemy and Mother of my Enemy," said the Cat, "it is I: for you have spoken a word in my praise, and now I can sit within the Cave for always and always and always. But still I am the Cat who walks by himself, and all places are alike to me."

The Woman was very angry, and shut her lips tight and took up her spinning wheel and began to spin.

But the Baby cried because the Cat had gone away, and the Woman could not hush it, for it struggled and kicked and grew black in the face.

"O my Enemy and Wife of my Enemy and Mother of my Enemy," said the Cat, "take a strand of the thread that you are spinning and tie it to your spindle-whorl and drag it along the floor, and I will show you a Magic that shall make your Baby laugh as loudly as he is now crying."

"I will do so," said the Woman, "because I am at my wits' end; but I will not thank you for it."

She tied the thread to the little clay spindle-whorl and drew it across the floor, and Cat ran after it and patted it with his paws and rolled head over heels, and tossed it backward over his shoulder and chased it between his hind legs and pretended to lose it, and pounced down upon it again, till the Baby laughed as loudly as it had been crying, and scrambled after the Cat and frolicked all over the Cave till it grew tired and settled down to sleep with the Cat in its arms.

"Now," said Cat, "I will sing the Baby a song that shall keep him asleep for an hour." And he began to purr, loud and low, low and loud, till the Baby fell fast asleep. The Woman smiled as she looked down upon the two of them, and said, "That was wonderfully done. No question but you are very clever, O Cat."

That very minute and second, Best Beloved, the smoke of the Fire at the back of the Cave came down in clouds from the roof—*puff!*—because it remembered the bargain she had made with the Cat; and when it had cleared away—lo and behold!—the Cat was sitting quite comfy close to the fire.

"O my Enemy and Wife of my Enemy and Mother of my Enemy," said the Cat, "it is I: for you have spoken a second word in my praise, and now I can sit by the warm fire at the back of the Cave for always and always and always. But still I am the Cat who walks by himself, and all places are alike to me."

Then the Woman was very very angry, and let down her hair and put more wood on the fire and brought out the broad blade-bone of the shoulder of mutton and began to make a Magic that should prevent her from saying a third word in praise of the Cat. It was not a Singing Magic, Best Beloved, it was a Still Magic; and by and by the Cave grew so still that a little wee-wee mouse crept out of a corner and ran across the floor.

"O my Enemy and Wife of my Enemy and Mother of my Enemy," said the Cat, "is that little mouse part of your Magic?"

"Ouh! Chee! No indeed!" said the Woman, and she dropped the bladebone and jumped upon the footstool in front of the fire and braided up her hair very quick for fear that the mouse should run up it.

"Ah," said the Cat, watching. "Then the mouse will do me no harm if I eat it?"

"No," said the Woman, braiding up her hair, "eat it quickly and I will ever be grateful to you."

Cat made one jump and caught the little mouse, and the Woman said, "A hundred thanks. Even the First Friend is not quick enough to catch little mice as you have done. You must be very wise."

That very minute and second, O Best Beloved, the Milkpot that stood by the fire cracked in two pieces—*ffft!*—because it remembered the bargain she had made with the Cat; and when the Woman jumped down from the footstool—lo and behold!—the Cat was lapping up the warm white milk that lay in one of the broken pieces.

"O my Enemy and Wife of my Enemy and Mother of my Enemy," said the Cat, "it is I: for you have spoken three words in my praise, and now I can drink the warm white milk three times a day for always and always and always. But *still* I am the Cat who walks by himself, and all places are alike to me."

Then the Woman laughed and set the Cat a bowl of the warm white milk and said, "O Cat, you are as clever as a man, but remember that your bargain was not made with the Man or the Dog, and I do not know what they will do when they come home."

"What is that to me?" said the Cat. "If I have my place in the Cave by the fire and my warm white milk three times a day I do not care what the Man or the Dog can do."

That evening when the Man and the Dog came into the Cave, the Woman told them all the story of the bargain, while the Cat sat by the fire and smiled. Then the Man said, "Yes, but he has not made a bargain with *me* or with all proper Men after me." Then he took off his two leather boots and he took up his little stone axe (that makes three) and he fetched a piece of wood and a hatchet (that is five altogether), and he set them out in a row and he said, "Now we will make *our* bargain. If you do not catch mice when you are in the Cave for always and always and always, I will throw these five things at you whenever I see you, and so shall all proper Men do after me."

"Ah!" said the Woman, listening. "This is a very clever Cat, but he is not as clever as my Man."

The Cat counted the five things (and they looked very knobby) and he said, "I will catch mice when I am in the Cave for always and always and always; but *still* I am the Cat who walks by himself, and all places are alike to me."

"Not when I am near," said the Man. "If you had not said that last I would have put all these things away for always and always and always; but now I am going to throw my two boots and my little stone axe (that makes three) at you whenever I meet you. And so shall all proper Men do after me!"

Then the Dog said, "Wait a minute. He has not made a bargain with *me* or with all proper Dogs after me." And he showed his teeth and said, "If you are not kind to the Baby while I am in the Cave for always and always and always, I will hunt you till I catch you, and when I catch you I will bite you. And so shall all proper Dogs do after me."

"Ah!" said the Woman, listening. "This is a very clever Cat, but he is not so clever as the Dog."

Cat counted the Dog's teeth (and they looked very pointed) and he said, "I will be kind to the Baby while I am in the cave, as long as he does not pull my tail too hard, for always and always and always. But *still* I am the Cat who walks by himself, and all places are alike to me."

"Not when I am near," said the Dog. "If you had not said that last I would have shut my mouth for always and always and always; but *now* I am going to hunt you up a tree whenever I meet you. And so shall all proper Dogs do after me."

Then the Man threw his two boots and his little stone axe (that makes three) at the Cat, and the Cat ran out of the Cave and the Dog chased him up a tree; and from that day to this, Best Beloved, three proper Men out of five will always throw things at a Cat whenever they meet him, and all proper Dogs will chase him up a tree. But the Cat keeps his side of the bargain too. He will kill mice, and he will be kind to Babies when he is in the house, just as long as they do not pull his tail too hard. But when he has done that, and between times, and when the moon gets up and night comes, he is the Cat that walks by himself, and all places are alike to him. Then he goes out to the Wet Wild Woods or up the Wet Wild Trees or on the Wet Wild Roofs, waving his wild tail and walking by his wild lone.

The Cats of Ulthar

H. P. Lovecraft

IT is said that in Ulthar, which lies beyond the river Skai, no man may kill a cat; and this I can verily believe as I gaze upon him who sitteth purring before the fire. For the cat is cryptic, and close to strange things which men cannot see. He is the soul of antique Aegyptus, and bearer of tales from forgotten cities in Meroe and Ophir. He is the kin of the jungle's lords, and heir to the secrets of hoary and sinister Africa. The Sphinx is his cousin, and he speaks her language; but he is more ancient than the Sphinx, and remembers that which she hath forgotten.

In Ulthar, before ever the burgesses forbade the killing of cats, there dwelt an old cotter and his wife who delighted to trap and slay the cats of their neighbors. Why they did this I know not; save that many hate the voice of the cat in the night, and take it ill that cats should run stealthily about yards and gardens at twilight. But whatever the reason, this old man and woman took pleasure in trapping and slaying every cat which came near to their hovel; and from some of the sounds heard after dark, many villagers fancied that the manner of slaying was exceedingly peculiar. But the villagers did not discuss such things with the old man and his wife; because of the habitual expression on the withered faces of the two, and because their cottage was so small and so darkly hidden under spreading oaks at the back of a neglected yard. In truth, much as the owners of cats hated these odd folk, they feared them more; and instead of berating them as brutal assassins, merely took care that no cherished pet or mouser should stray toward the remote hovel under the dark trees. When through some unavoidable oversight a cat was missed, and sounds heard after dark, the loser would lament impotently; or console himself by thanking Fate that it was not one of his children who had thus vanished. For the people of Ulthar were simple, and knew not whence it is all cats first came.

One day a caravan of strange wanderers from the South entered the narrow, cobbled streets of Ulthar. Dark wanderers they were, and unlike the other roving folk who passed through the village twice every year. In the marketplace they told fortunes for silver, and bought gay beads from the merchants. What was the land of these wanderers none could tell; but it was seen that they were given to strange prayers, and that they had painted on the sides of their wagons strange figures with human bodies and the heads of cats, hawks, rams, and lions. And the leader of the caravan wore a headdress with two horns and a curious disk betwixt the horns.

There was in this singular caravan a little boy with no father or mother, but only a tiny black kitten to cherish. The plague had not been kind to him, yet had left him this small furry thing to mitigate his sorrow; and when one is very young, one can find great relief in the lively antics of a black kitten. So the boy whom the dark people called Menes smiled more often than he wept as he sat playing with his graceful kitten on the steps of an oddly painted wagon.

On the third morning of the wanderers' stay in Ulthar, Menes could not find his kitten; and as he sobbed aloud in the marketplace certain villagers told him of the old man and his wife, and of sounds heard in the night. And when he heard these things his sobbing gave place to meditation, and finally to prayer. He stretched out his arms toward the sun and prayed in a tongue no villager could understand; though indeed the villagers did not try very hard to understand, since their attention was mostly taken up by the sky and the odd shapes the clouds were assuming. It was very peculiar, but as the little boy uttered his petition there seemed to form overhead the shadowy, nebulous figures of exotic things; of hybrid creatures crowned with horn-flanked disks. Nature is full of such illusions to impress the imaginative.

That night the wanderers left Ulthar, and were never seen again. And the householders were troubled when they noticed that in all the village there was not a cat to be found. From each hearth the familiar cat had vanished; cats large and small, black, grey, striped, yellow, and white. Old Kranon, the burgomaster, swore that the dark folk had taken the cats away in revenge for the killing of Menes' kitten; and cursed the caravan and the little boy. But Nith, the lean notary, declared that the old cotter and his wife were more likely persons to suspect; for their hatred of cats was notorious and increasingly bold. Still, no one durst complain to the sinister couple; even when little Atal, the innkeeper's son, vowed that he had at twilight seen all the cats of Ulthar in that accursed yard under the trees, pacing very slowly and solemnly in a circle around the cottage, two abreast, as if in performance of some unheard-of rite of beasts. The villagers did not know how much to believe from so small a boy; and though they feared that the evil pair had charmed the cats to their death, they preferred not to chide the old cotter till they met him outside his dark and repellent yard.

So Ulthar went to sleep in vain anger, and when the people awakened at dawn—behold! every cat was back at his accustomed hearth! Large and small, black, grey, striped, yellow, and white, none was missing. Very sleek and fat did the cats appear, and sonorous with purring content. The citizens talked with one another of the affair, and marveled not a little. Old Kranon again insisted that it was the dark folk who had taken them, since cats did not return alive from the cottage of the ancient man and his wife. But all agreed on one thing: that the refusal of all the cats to eat their portions of meat or drink their saucers of milk was exceedingly curious. And for two whole days the sleek, lazy cats of Ulthar would touch no food, but only doze by the fire or in the sun.

It was fully a week before the villagers noticed that no lights were appearing at dusk in the windows of the cottage under the trees. Then the lean Nith remarked that no one had seen the old man or his wife since the night the cats were away. In another week the burgomaster decided to overcome his fears and call at the strangely silent dwelling as a matter of duty, though in so doing he was careful to take with him Shang the blacksmith and Thul the cutter of stone as witnesses. And when they had broken down the frail door they found only this: two cleanly picked human skeletons on the earthen floor, and a number of singular beetles crawling in the shadowy corners.

There was subsequently much talk among the burgesses of Ulthar. Zath, the coroner, disputed at length with Nith, the lean notary; and Kranon and Shang and Thul were overwhelmed with questions. Even little Atal, the innkeeper's son, was closely questioned and given a sweetmeat as reward. They talked of the old cotter and his wife, of the caravan of dark wanderers, of small Menes and his black kitten, of the prayer of Menes and of the sky during that prayer, of the doings of the cats on the night the caravan left, and of what was later found in the cottage under the dark trees in the repellent yard.

And in the end the burgesses passed that remarkable law which is told of by traders in Hatheg and discussed by travelers in Nir; namely, that in Ulthar no man may kill a cat.

Cats' Paradise
Émile Zola

A<small>N</small> aunt left me an Angora cat that is the stupidest beast I know. This is the story he told me one winter evening in front of the fire.

I

I was then two years old, the fattest and most naïve cat you've ever seen. At that tender age, I presumptuously disdained all the pleasures of the house, and did not even give thanks to Providence for having placed me with your aunt. That wonderful woman adored me! At the bottom of a wardrobe I had a real bedroom, fitted out with a comforter and three blankets. The food was as good as the bed: no bread, no soup, nothing but meat, lovely red meat.

Ah well! In the midst of all this sweetness, I had but one desire, one dream—to slip out of a half-opened window and escape over the rooftops. Caresses seemed insipid, the softness of my bed made me feel ill, I was fat and I disgusted myself. I was bored with being happy all day long.

I must tell you that by stretching my neck I had been able to see a roof just outside the window. On that day, four cats played there on the blue tiles in the warm sun, fur bristling and tails erect, with every appearance of joy. I had never seen anything so extraordinary. From then on, I was fixed in the notion that happiness was to be found on the roofs, beyond that window so carefully closed—closed in fact, just as carefully as the doors of the cupboard where the meat was kept.

I decided to run away. There had to be other things in life besides juicy flesh. Out there was the unknown, the ideal existence. One day, someone forgot to push the kitchen window shut. I escaped onto a small roof that I found just beneath it.

II

How beautiful were the rooftops! The large gutters along the edge exhaled delicious odors, and I stalked voluptuously down them. My paws were immersed in the fine mud, which had a certain infinite sweetness and warmth. I felt as though I was walking over velvet. The pleasant heat of the sun seemed to be dissolving my fat.

I cannot hide from you the fact that I was trembling in every limb. There was something terrifying in my joy. I remember above all the terrible shock I felt—it actually made me lose my footing on the tiles—when three cats rolled down from the top of a house and came up to me meowing frightfully. I practically fainted, but they simply called me a fat scaredy-cat and explained that all the meowing was just a joke. So I joined in. It was delightful. These bravos weren't as fat as I was, however, and made fun of me when I slipped and rolled like a ball across the tin roof heated by the sun. One old tom was particularly friendly. He offered to educate me, and I accepted the offer eagerly.

Ah, the ease of life with your aunt was now far away. I drank from the gutters, and milk with sugar had never tasted so sweet. Everything struck me as good and beautiful. A cat passed by, a gorgeous cat, and simply the sight of her touched off in me a deep and unfamiliar emotion. Only in my dreams had I ever seen such an exquisite creature, with so adorably supple a back. My three companions and I dashed forward to greet her, and I was actually slightly ahead of the others in offering my compliments to this ravishing creature when one of my comrades gave me a savage bite in the neck. I emitted a howl of pain. "Bah," said the old tom, dragging me away. "You'll see plenty more of those."

III

After strolling for an hour or so, I developed a ferocious appetite.

"What do you eat up here on the rooftops?" I asked my friend the tom.

"Whatever you can find," he replied wisely.

This reply perplexed me, because hunt as I might I found nothing. Finally, however, I spotted a young workman preparing his lunch in an attic room. On the table, just under the window, was a lovely cutlet, appetizingly red.

"That's the answer," I told myself in all innocence.

At that I leaped on the table and snatched the cutlet. But the workman had seen me first, and gave me a terrific blow on the back with a broom. I dropped the cutlet and scurried away, cursing under my breath.

"What kind of an idiot are you?" the old tom asked. "Food on a table is supposed to be admired only from a distance. What we've got to do is hunt in the gutters."

I have never understood why food in a kitchen is off-limits to cats. My stomach had begun growling seriously. The tom put the finishing touch to my despair by saying that we needed to wait until night, when we could go down into the street and scavenge in the garbage heaps. Wait until night! He said this calmly and philosophically. As for me, I was faint at the very thought of prolonging my fast even a moment more.

IV

The night came on slowly, a night of fog that made me rigid with cold. Soon it began to rain, a fine, penetrating downpour blown about by brisk gusts of wind. We descended by way of a glassed skylight over a stairway. How shabby the street appeared! Here there was none of that pleasant heat of the sun, the roofs gleaming white where we had languished so deliciously. My paws slipped on the greasy pavement. I thought sadly of my three blankets and my comforter.

No sooner were we in the street than my friend the old tom began to tremble. He crouched down and crept craftily along the house wall, telling me to follow quickly behind him. Arriving at a doorway, he lost no time in hiding himself, simultaneously purring with satisfaction. When I asked him what was going on, he said, "Did you see that man with the basket and the hook?"

"Yes."

"Well, if he had seen us, we would have been caught and roasted on a spit!"

"Roasted on a spit!" I cried. "The street is no place for us. You can't eat, but you can be eaten!"

V

Meanwhile, rubbish was being put out in front of doors. I rummaged through it hopelessly. Two or three skinny bones that had been dragged through ashes made me realize just how succulent fresh meat can be. My friend the tom pawed through the garbage with enormous artistry and made me do the same all the night long, examining every paving stone without the least sign of hurry. After nearly ten hours of rain I was shivering all over. Damned street! Damned liberty! How I missed my prison!

In the morning the tom, noticing my shaky state, asked in an odd voice, "Have you had enough?"

"Oh, yes," I replied.

"Do you want to go back home?"

"I certainly do. But how can I find it?"

"Come on. The morning I saw you come out I knew that a fat cat like you is not cut out for the joys of liberty. I know where you live, I'll show you to the door."

He said all this with simple dignity. And when we arrived at the house, he bade me adieu without the least show of emotion.

"No," I cried, "we cannot take leave of each other like this. Come with me. We will share the same bed and the same food. My mistress is a wonderful woman..."

He didn't let me finish.

"Shut up," he said brusquely. "You are a fool. I'd die in your warm softness. Your life of abundance is fine for spoiled cats. Free cats will never buy your ease and your comforter for the price of being imprisoned.... Good-bye."

He climbed back onto his rooftops. I saw his great thin shadow shudder with pleasure at the caresses of the rising sun.

When I went back in, your aunt played the disciplinarian and punished me. I received my punishment with extreme joy. It produced in me a kind of voluptuous pleasure, being warm and being beaten at the same time. And even as I was being struck I could dream about the delicious snacks that would surely follow.

VI

So you see—thus concluded my cat, stretched out in front of the fire—the true happiness, the paradise, my dear master, is to be locked up and beaten in a place where there is meat.

I speak for cats.

The Cat's Grave

Natsume Sōseki

Translated by *Matt Treyvaud*

AFTER our move to Waseda, the cat began to grow thinner and thinner. He no longer showed any interest in playing with the children. Whenever the sun was out, all he would do was lie on the *engawa*,[1] not moving a muscle, square chin on his neatly arranged paws as he stared out at the bushes in the garden. No matter how rowdily the children played nearby, he did not deign to notice them. The children, for their part, had long since given up on the cat. Obviously finding him no fun anymore, they treated this old friend of theirs like a stranger. Nor were they the only ones: the maid put out food for the cat three times a day in the corner of the kitchen, but had little time for him otherwise. Worse yet, most of what she put out was gobbled up by a big calico who lived nearby and visited just for this purpose. Our cat did not seem particularly angered by this. I never saw a fight. He just lay there. There was, however, a certain joylessness in his repose. He did not look like someone stretching out to luxuriate in the sun's rays; rather, he seemed to lack any *way* to move—no, this does not fully describe it. It appeared that his listlessness had grown so great that, as lonely as it was to stay unmoving, to move would have been still lonelier, leaving him with no choice but to stay where he was, enduring things as best he could. His gaze was always fixed on the garden, but I doubt he saw the leaves on the bushes, or the shapes in which they grew. That was just

---

[1] A wooden veranda running around the edge of a traditional Japanese house.

where his greenish-yellow eyes happened to be resting. Just as the children no longer recognized his existence, he did not seem to clearly register the existence of the world around him either.

Still, he did go out from time to time, apparently with business to attend to. Every time he did so, however, the calico cat that lived nearby would give chase. Terrified, our cat would leap back up onto our veranda and burst through the paper of the closed *shōji*[2] screens to take refuge by the hearth inside. Those were the only times that we noticed his existence. No doubt they were also the only times that he was fully aware that he was alive.

As these things went on, the fur began to fall out of the cat's long tail. At first it just seemed dimpled here and there, but then patches of raw skin began to spread, and the whole thing drooped in a way that was pitiful to see. He took to twisting and straining his body, already weary enough with everything, to lick at his sore spots.

—Hey, I grunted to my wife. Looks like something's wrong with the cat.—Yes, I think he's just getting old, she replied, supremely indifferent. I let the matter pass as well. Not long afterwards, though, the cat began to bring up his food from time to time. His throat would pulse violently as he let out a painful-sounding noise somewhere between a sneeze and a hiccup. Painful as it sounded, though, I had no choice but to chase him outside whenever I noticed him like this. Otherwise, he would have soiled the *tatami*[3] or the *futon*[4] without a second thought. Most of the large *zabuton*[5] we had set aside for visitors were ruined this way.

---

[2] Translucent paper screens stretched over a light wooden framework and used in place of walls and partitions in Japanese architecture.

[3] Woven, stuffed mats used for flooring.

[4] A quilted mattress used for sleeping.

[5] Literally "seat *futon*," a smaller cushion used for sitting.

"We have to do something. It's probably a stomach bug—stir some Hōtan[6] in with his drinking water."

My wife didn't say anything. Two or three days later, I asked if she had given the cat any Hōtan to drink.—It's no use trying to make him drink, she replied. He won't open his mouth. He throws up whenever he eats fish bones, she added by way of explanation.—Well, why don't you stop giving them to him, then? I replied, rather roughly, before returning to my reading.

Nausea gone, the cat went back to quietly lying around as he had before. By now he was curling himself up tightly, huddled and still, as if he had nothing left to rely on but the *engawa* that held him up. The look in his eyes also began to change. In the beginning there had been a certain steadiness in the melancholy of his gaze, as if he were staring at something too far away to focus on. But this was giving way to an uncertain, incessant motion. Meanwhile, the color in his eyes was sinking deeper and deeper. It put me in mind of flickering lightning as the sun went down. But I let this pass too. Nor did my wife appear to pay it any mind. The children, of course, had forgotten that they ever had a cat.

One evening, the cat had been stretched out on its stomach at the edge of the children's bedding for a while when he suddenly let out a throaty groan, as if he had caught a fish only to suddenly have it snatched away. I thought it strange at the time, but no one else noticed it. The children were sound asleep. My wife was engrossed in her sewing. A short time later, the cat groaned again. My wife's hands finally paused.—What's wrong with him? I asked. We don't want him biting the children on the head or something during the night.—Oh, he would never, my wife said, and went back to sewing the sleeve of her *juban*.[7] The cat kept up his occasional groaning.

---

[6] A patent medicine for stomach ailments.
[7] An undergarment worn under kimono.

He then spent the entire following day groaning as he lay at the hearth. Tasks like making the tea and bringing in the kettle, I understand, were rather unsettling that day. But once night fell my wife and I both forgot about the cat entirely. In fact, that very evening was when the cat died. The maid found his body when she went to get some firewood from the shed in the yard the following morning, already stiff and lying on top of an old stove.

My wife made a point of going out to see the cat's body for herself. From that point on, her previous indifference was replaced by industrious concern. She sent one of our regular rickshaw boys out to buy a square grave marker, which she asked me to write something on. I wrote "HERE LIES THE CAT" on the front, and composed a short poem for the back: *Comes the lightning / Here beneath / As evening falls.*—Can I bury it as it is? asked the rickshaw boy.—What else are we going to do, have it cremated? said the maid witheringly.

The children, too, suddenly found a new fondness for the cat. They adorned his grave marker with glass bottles on either side, stuffed with bush clover. They also filled a small rice bowl with water to place before the grave. Both flowers and water were changed daily. On the evening of the third day, one of our girls, almost in her fourth year[8]—I was watching from the window of my study—approached the grave alone. After staring at the plain wooden marker for a while, she dipped a toy ladle she was carrying into the water that had been offered to the cat, scooping some up to drink. Nor was this the only time she did this. That little splash of water strewn with clover blossom petals quenched Aiko's thirst any number of times in the quiet of the evening.

---

[8] Almost in her fourth year by the traditional Japanese system of reckoning ages; as calculated by the Western system, she was just over two and a half years old at the time of this story.

Each month, on the anniversary of the cat's death, my wife makes sure to place a bowl of rice topped with dried bonito and salmon before his grave. She has yet to forget a single month. Lately, though, rather than taking the offering out to the garden, she seems content with leaving it on top of the chest of drawers in the living room.

The Black and White Dynasties
Théophile Gautier

A cat brought from Havana by Mademoiselle Aïta de la Penuela, a young Spanish artist whose studies of white angoras may still be seen gracing the printsellers' windows, produced the daintiest little kitten imaginable. It was just like a swan's-down powder-puff, and on account of its immaculate whiteness it received the name of Pierrot. When it grew big this was lengthened to Don Pierrot de Navarre as being more grandiose and majestic.

Don Pierrot, like all animals which are spoilt and made much of, developed a charming amiability of character. He shared the life of the household with all the pleasure which cats find in the intimacy of the domestic hearth. Seated in his usual place near the fire, he really appeared to understand what was being said, and to take an interest in it.

His eyes followed the speakers, and from time to time he would utter little sounds, as though he too wanted to make remarks and give his opinion on literature, which was our usual topic of conversation. He was very fond of books, and when he found one open on a table he would lie on it, look at the page attentively, and turn over the leaves with his paw; then he would end by going to sleep, for all the world as if he were reading a fashionable novel.

Directly I took up a pen he would jump on my writing-desk and with deep attention watch the steel nib tracing black spider legs on the expanse of white paper, and his head would turn each time I began a new line. Sometimes he tried to take part in the work, and would attempt to pull the pen out of my hand, no doubt in order to write himself, for he was an aesthetic cat, like Hoffman's Murr, and I strongly suspect him of having scribbled his memoirs at night on some housetop by the light of his phosphorescent eyes. Unfortunately these lucubrations have been lost.

Don Pierrot never went to bed until I came in. He waited for me inside the door, and as I entered the hall he would rub himself against my legs and arch his back, purring joyfully all the time. Then he proceeded to walk in front of me like a page, and if I had asked him, he would certainly have carried the candle for me. In this fashion he escorted me to my room and waited while I undressed; then he would jump on the bed, put his paws round my neck, rub noses with me, and lick me with his rasping little pink tongue, while giving vent to soft inarticulate cries, which clearly expressed how pleased he was to see me again. Then when his transports of affection had subsided, and the hour for repose had come, he would balance himself on the rail of the bedstead and sleep there like a bird perched on a bough. When I woke in the morning he would come and lie near me until it was time to get up. Twelve o'clock was the hour at which I was supposed to come in. On this subject Pierrot had all the notions of a concierge.

At that time we had instituted little evening gatherings among a few friends, and had formed a small society, which we called the Four Candles club, the room in which we met being, as it happened, lit by four candles in silver candlesticks, which were placed at the corners of the table.

Sometimes the conversation became so lively that I forgot the time, at the risk of finding, like Cinderella, my carriage turned into a pumpkin and my coachman into a rat.

Pierrot waited for me several times until two o'clock in the morning, but in the end my conduct displeased him, and he went to bed without me. This mute protest against my innocent dissipation touched me so much that ever after I came home regularly at midnight. But it was a long time before Pierrot forgave me. He wanted to be sure that it was not a sham repentance; but when he was convinced of the sincerity of my conversion, he deigned to take me into favour again, and he resumed his nightly post in the entrance hall.

To gain the friendship of a cat is not an easy thing. It is a philosophic, well-regulated, tranquil animal, a creature of habit and a lover of order and cleanliness. It does not give its affections indiscriminately. It will consent to be your friend if you are worthy of the honour, but it will not be your slave. With all its affection, it preserves its freedom of judgment, and it will not do anything for you which it considers unreasonable; but once it has given its love, what absolute confidence, what fidelity of affection! It will make itself the companion of your hours of work, of loneliness, or of sadness. It will lie the whole evening on your knee, purring and happy in your society, and leaving the company of creatures of its own kind to be with you. In vain the sound of caterwauling reverberates from the housetops, inviting it to one of those cats' evening parties where essence of red herring takes the place of tea. It will not be tempted, but continues to keep its vigil with you. If you put it down it climbs up again quickly, with a sort of crooning noise, which is like a gentle reproach. Sometimes, when seated in front of you, it gazes at you with such soft, melting eyes, such a human and caressing look, that you are almost awed, for it seems impossible that reason can be absent from it.

Don Pierrot had a companion of the same race as himself, and no less white. All the imaginable snowy comparisons it were possible to pile up would not suffice to give an idea of that immaculate fur, which would have made ermine look yellow.

I called her Seraphita, in memory of Balzac's Swedenborgian romance. The heroine of that wonderful story, when she climbed the snow peaks of the Falberg with Minna, never shone with a more pure white radiance. Seraphita had a dreamy and pensive character. She would lie motionless on a cushion for hours, not asleep, but with eyes fixed in rapt attention on scenes invisible to ordinary mortals.

Caresses were agreeable to her, but she responded to them with great reserve, and only to those of people whom she favoured with her esteem, which it was not easy to gain. She liked luxury, and it was always in the newest armchair or on the piece of furniture best calculated to show off her swan-like beauty, that she was to be found. Her toilette took an immense time. She would carefully smooth her entire coat every morning, and wash her face with her paw, and every hair on her body shone like new silver when brushed by her pink tongue. If anyone touched her she would immediately efface all traces of the contact, for she could not endure being ruffled. Her elegance and distinction gave one an idea of aristocratic birth, and among her own kind she must have been at least a duchess. She had a passion for scents. She would plunge her nose into bouquets, and nibble a perfumed handkerchief with little paroxysms of delight. She would walk about on the dressing table sniffling the stoppers of the scent-bottles, and she would have loved to use the violet powder if she had been allowed.

Such was Seraphita, and never was a cat more worthy of a poetic name.

Don Pierrot de Navarre, being a native of Havana, needed a hothouse temperature. This he found indoors, but the house was surrounded by large gardens, divided up by palings through which a cat could easily slip, and planted with big trees in which hosts of birds twittered and sang; and sometimes Pierrot, taking advantage of an open door, would go out hunting of an evening and run over the dewy grass and flowers. He would then have to wait till morning to be let in again, for although he might come mewing under the windows, his appeal did not always wake the sleepers inside.

He had a delicate chest, and one colder night than usual he took a chill which soon developed into consumption. Poor Pierrot, after a year of coughing, became wasted and thin, and his coat, which formerly boasted such a snowy glass, now put one in mind of the lustreless white of a shroud. His great limpid eyes looked enormous in his attenuated face. His pink nose had grown pale, and he would walk sadly along the sunny wall with slow steps, and watch the yellow autumn leaves whirling up in spirals. He looked as though he were reciting Millevoy's elegy.

There is nothing more touching than a sick animal; it submits to suffering with such gentle, pathetic resignation.

Everything possible was done to try and save Pierrot. He had a very clever doctor who sounded him and felt his pulse. He ordered him asses' milk, which the poor creature drank willingly enough out of his little china saucer. He lay for hours on my knee like the ghost of a sphinx, and I could feel the bones of his spine like the beads of a rosary under my fingers. He tried to respond to my caresses with a feeble purr which was like a death rattle.

When he was dying he lay panting on his side, but with a supreme effort he raised himself and came to me with dilated eyes in which there was a look of intense supplication. This look seemed to say: "Cannot you save me, you who are a man?" Then he staggered a short way with eyes already glazing, and fell down with such a lamentable cry, so full of despair and anguish, that I was pierced with silent horror.

He was buried at the bottom of the garden under a white rosebush which still marks his grave.

Seraphita died two or three years later of diphtheria, against which no science could prevail.

She rests not far from Pierrot. With her the white dynasty became extinct, but not the family. To this snow-white pair were born three kittens as black as ink.

Let him explain this mystery who can.

Just at that time Victor Hugo's *Misérables* was in great vogue, and the names of the characters in the novel were on everyone's lips. I called the two male kittens Enjolras and Gavroche, while the little female received the name of Eponine.

They were perfectly charming in their youth. I trained them like dogs to fetch and carry a bit of paper crumpled into a ball, which I threw for them. In time they learnt to fetch it from the tops of cupboards, from behind chests or from the

bottom of tall vases, out of which they would pull it very cleverly with their paws. When they grew up they disdained such
frivolous games, and acquired that calm philosophic temperament which is the true nature of cats.

To people landing in America in a slave colony all negroes
are negroes, and indistinguishable from one another. In the
same way, to careless eyes, three black cats are three black
cats; but attentive observers make no such mistake. Animal
physiognomy varies as much as that of men, and I could distinguish perfectly between those faces, all three as black as
Harlequin's mask, and illuminated by emerald disks shot with
gold.

Enjolras was by far the handsomest of the three. He was
remarkable for his great leonine head and big ruff, his powerful shoulders, long back and splendid feathery tail. There was
something theatrical about him, and he seemed to be always
posing like a popular actor who knows he is being admired.
His movements were slow, undulating and majestic. He put
each foot down with as much circumspection as if he were
walking on a table covered with Chinese bric-à-brac or
Venetian glass. As to his character, he was by no means a stoic,
and he showed a love of eating which that virtuous and sober
young man, his namesake, would certainly have disapproved.
Enjolras would undoubtedly have said to him, like the angel
to Swedenborg: "You eat too much."

I humoured this gluttony, which was as amusing as a gastro-
nomic monkey's, and Enjolras attained a size and weight seldom reached by the domestic cat. It occurred to me to have
him shaved poodle-fashion, so as to give the finishing touch to
his resemblance to a lion.

We left him his mane and a big tuft at the end of his tail,
and I would not swear that we did not give him mutton-chop
whiskers on his haunches like those Munito wore. Thus
tricked out, it must be confessed he was much more like a
Japanese monster than an African lion. Never was a more
fantastic whim carved out of a living animal. His shaven skin

took odd blue tints, which contrasted strangely with his black mane.

Gavroche, as though desirous of calling to mind his namesake in the novel, was a cat with an arch and crafty expression of countenance. He was smaller than Enjolras, and his movements were comically quick and brusque. In him absurd capers and ludicrous postures took the place of the banter and slang of the Parisian gamin. It must be confessed that Gavroche had vulgar tastes. He seized every possible occasion to leave the drawing room in order to go and make up parties in the backyard, or even in the street, with stray cats,

"De naissance quelconque et de sang peu prouvé,"

in which doubtful company he completely forgot his dignity as cat of Havana, son of Don Pierrot de Navarre, grandee of Spain of the first order, and of the aristocratic and haughty Doña Seraphita. Sometimes in his truant wanderings he picked up emaciated comrades, lean with hunger, and brought them to his plate of food to give them a treat in his good-natured, lordly way. The poor creatures, with ears laid back and watchful side-glances, in fear of being interrupted in their free meal by the broom of the housemaid, swallowed double, triple, and quadruple mouthfuls, and, like the famous dog, Siete-Aguas (seven waters) of Spanish *posadas* (inns), they licked the plate as clean as if it had been washed and polished by one of Gerard Dow's or Mieris's Dutch housewives.

Seeing Gavroche's friends reminded me of a phrase which illustrates one of Gavarni's drawings, "Ils son jolis les amis dont vous êtes susceptible d'aller avec!" ("Pretty kind of friends you like to associate with!")

But that only proved what a good heart Gavroche had, for he could easily have eaten all the food himself.

The cat named after the interesting Eponine was more delicate and slender than her brothers. Her nose was rather long, and her eyes slightly oblique, and green as those of Pallas Athene, to whom Homer always applied the epithet of γλαυχωπιζ. Her nose was of velvety black, with the grain of a fine Périgord truffle; her whiskers were in a perpetual state of agitation, all of which gave her a peculiarly expressive countenance. Her superb black coat was always in motion, and was watered and shot with shadowy markings. Never was there a more sensitive, nervous, electric animal. If one stroked her two or three times in the dark, blue sparks would fly crackling out of her fur.

Eponine attached herself particularly to me, like the Eponine of the novel to Marius, but I, being less taken up with Cosette than that handsome young man, could accept the affection of this gentle and devoted cat, who still shares the pleasure of my suburban retreat and is the inseparable companion of my hours of work.

She comes running up when she hears the front-door bell, receives the visitors, conducts them to the drawing room, talks to them—yes, talks to them—with little chirruping sounds, that do not in the least resemble the language cats use in taking to their own kind, but which simulate the articulate speech of man. What does she say? She says in the clearest way, "Will you be good enough to wait till monsieur comes down? Please look at the pictures, or chat with me in the meantime, if that will amuse you." Then when I come in she discreetly retires to an armchair or a corner of the piano, like a well-bred animal who knows what is correct in good society. Pretty little Eponine gave so many proofs of intelligence, good disposition and sociability, that by common consent she was raised to the dignity of a *person*, for it was quite evident that she was possessed of higher reasoning power than mere instinct. This dignity conferred on her the privilege of eating at table like a person instead of out of a saucer in a corner of the room like an animal.

So Eponine had a chair next to me at breakfast and dinner, but on account of her small size she was allowed to rest her two front paws on the edge of the table. Her place was laid, without spoon or fork, but she had her glass. She went right through dinner dish by dish, from soup to dessert, waiting for her turn to be helped, and behaving with such propriety and nice manners as one would like to see in many children. She made her appearance at the first sound of the bell, and on going into the dining room one found her already in her place, sitting up in her chair with her paws resting on the edge of the table-cloth, and seeming to offer you her little face to kiss, like a well-brought-up little girl who is affectionately polite towards her parents and elders.

As one finds flaws in diamonds, spots on the sun, and shadows on perfection itself, so Eponine, it must be confessed, had a passion for fish. She shared this in common with all other cats. Contrary to the Latin proverb,

"Catus amat pisces, sed non vult tingere plantas,"

she would willingly have dipped her paw into the water if by so doing she could have pulled out a trout or a young carp. She became nearly frantic over fish, and, like a child who is filled with the expectation of dessert, she sometimes rebelled at her soup when she knew (from previous investigations in the kitchen) that fish was coming. When this happened she was not helped, and I would say to her coldly: "Mademoiselle, a person who is not hungry for soup cannot be hungry for fish," and the dish would be pitilessly carried away from under her nose. Convinced that matters were serious, greedy Eponine would swallow her soup in all haste, down to the last drop, polishing off the last crumb of bread or bit of macaroni, and would then turn round and look at me with pride, like someone who has conscientiously done his duty. She was then given her portion, which she consumed with great satisfaction, and after tasting of every dish in turn, she would finish up by drinking a third of a glass of water.

When I am expecting friends to dinner Eponine knows there is going to be a party before she sees the guests. She looks at her place, and if she sees a knife and fork by her plate she decamps at once and seats herself on a music stool, which is her refuge on these occasions.

Let those who deny reasoning powers to animals explain if they can this little fact, apparently so simple, but which contains a whole series of inductions. From the presence near her plate of those implements which man alone can use, this observant and reflective cat concludes that she will have to give up her place for that day to a guest, and promptly proceeds to do so. She never makes a mistake; but when she knows the visitor well she climbs on his knee and tries to coax a tidbit out of him by her pretty caressing ways.

Midshipman, the Cat
John Coleman Adams

THIS is a true story about a real cat who, for aught I know, is still alive and following the sea for a living. I hope to be excused if I use the pronouns "who" and "he" instead of "which" and "it," in speaking of this particular cat; because although I know very well that the grammars all tell us that "he" and "who" apply to persons, while "it" and "which" apply to things, yet this cat of mine always seemed to us who knew him to be so much like a human being that I find it unsatisfactory to speak of him in any other way. There are some animals of whom you prefer to say "he," just as there are persons whom you sometimes feel like calling "it."

The way we met this cat was after this fashion: It was back somewhere in the seventies, and a party of us were cruising east from Boston in the little schooner-yacht *Eyvor*. We had dropped into Marblehead for a day and a night, and some of the boys had gone ashore in the tender. As they landed on the wharf, they found a group of small boys running sticks into a woodpile, evidently on a hunt for something inside.

"What have you in there?" asked one of the yachtsmen.

"Nothin' but a cat," said the boys.

"Well, what are you doing to him?"

"Oh, pokin' him up! When he comes out we'll rock him," was the answer, in good Marblehead dialect.

"Well, don't do it anymore. What's the use of tormenting a poor cat? Why don't you take somebody of your size?"

The boys slowly moved off, a little ashamed and a little afraid of the big yachtsman who spoke; and when they were well out of sight the yachtsmen went on, too, and thought no more about the cat they had befriended. But when they had wandered about the

tangled streets of the town for a little while, and paid the visits
which all good yachtsmen pay, to the grocery and the post office
and the apothecary's soda fountain, they returned to the wharf
and found their boat. And behold, there in the stern sheets sat
the little grey-and-white cat of the woodpile! He had crawled out
of his retreat and made straight for the boat of his champions. He
seemed in no wise disturbed or disposed to move when they
jumped on board, nor did he show anything but pleasure when
they stroked and patted him. But when one of the boys started to
put him ashore, the plucky little fellow showed his claws; and no
sooner was he set on his feet at the edge of the wharf than he
turned about and jumped straight back into the boat.

"He wants to go yachting," said one of the party, whom we
called "the Bos'n."

"Ye might as wal take the cat," said a grizzly old fisherman
standing on the wharf. "He doesn't belong to anybody, and ef
he stays here the boys'll worry him t'death."

"Let's take him aboard," said the yachtsmen. "It's good luck
to have a cat on board ship."

Whether it was good luck to the ship or not, it was very
clear that pussy saw it meant good luck to him, and curled
himself down in the bottom of the boat, with a look that meant
business. Evidently he had thought the matter all over and
made up his mind that this was the sort of people he wanted
to live with; and, being a Marblehead cat, it made no difference to him whether they lived afloat or ashore; he was going
where they went, whether they wanted him or not. He had
heard the conversation from his place in the woodpile, and
had decided to show his gratitude by going to sea with these
protectors of his. By casting in his lot with theirs he was paying
them the highest compliment of which a cat is capable. It
would have been the height of impoliteness not to recognize
his distinguished appreciation. So he was allowed to remain in
the boat, and was taken off to the yacht.

Upon his arrival there, a council was held, and it was unani-
mously decided that the cat should be received as a member

of the crew; and as we were a company of amateur sailors, sailing our own boat, each man having his particular duties, it was decided that the cat should be appointed midshipman, and should be named after his position. So he was at once and ever after known as "Middy." Everybody took a great interest in him, and he took an impartial interest in everybody— though there were two people on board to whom he made himself particularly agreeable. One was the quiet, kindly professor, the captain of the *Eyvor;* the other was Charlie, our cook and only hired hand. Middy, you see, had a seaman's true instinct as to the official persons with whom it was his interest to stand well.

It was surprising to see how quickly Middy made himself at home. He acted as if he had always been at sea. He was never seasick, no matter how rough it was or how uncomfortable any of the rest of us were. He roamed wherever he wanted to, all over the boat. At mealtimes he came to the table with the rest, sat up on a valise, and lapped his milk and took what bits of food were given him, as if he had eaten that way all his life. When the sails were hoisted it was his especial joke to jump upon the main gaff and be hoisted with it; and once he stayed on his perch till the sail was at the masthead. One of us had to go aloft and bring him down. When we had come to anchor and everything was snug for the night, he would come on deck and scamper out on the main boom, and race from there to the bowsprit end as fast as he could gallop, then climb, monkey-fashion, halfway up the masts, and drop back to the deck or dive down into the cabin and run riot among the berths.

One day, as we were jogging along, under a pleasant southwest wind, and everybody was lounging and dozing after dinner, we heard the Bos'n call out, "Stop that, you fellows!" and a moment after, "I tell you, quit! Or I'll come up and make you!"

We opened our lazy eyes to see what was the matter, and there sat the Bos'n, down in the cabin, close to the companionway, the tassel of his knitted cap coming nearly up to the combings of the hatch; and on the deck outside sat Middy, digging his claws into the tempting yarn, and occasionally going deep enough to scratch the Bos'n's scalp.

When night came and we were all settled down in bed, it was Middy's almost invariable custom to go the rounds of all the berths, to see if we were properly tucked in, and to end his inspection by jumping into the captain's bed, treading himself a comfortable nest there among the blankets, and curling himself down to sleep. It was his own idea to select the captain's berth as the only proper place in which to turn in.

But the most interesting trait in Middy's character did not appear until he had been a week or so on board. Then he gave us a surprise. It was when we were lying in Camden Harbor. Everybody was going ashore to take a tramp among the hills, and Charlie, the cook, was coming too, to row the boat back to the yacht.

Middy discovered that he was somehow "getting left." Being a prompt and very decided cat, it did not take him long to make up his mind what to do. He ran to the low rail of the yacht, put his forepaws on it, and gave us a long, anxious look. Then as the boat was shoved off he raised his voice in a plaintive mew. We waved him a good-bye, chaffed him pleasantly, and told him to mind the anchor, and have dinner ready when we got back.

That was too much for his temper. As quick as a flash he had dived overboard, and was swimming like a water spaniel, after the dinghy!

That was the strangest thing we had ever seen in all our lives! We were quite used to elephants that could play at see-saw, and horses that could fire cannon, to learned pigs and to educated dogs; but a cat that of his own accord would take to the water like a full-blooded Newfoundland was a little beyond anything we had ever heard of. Of course the boat was stopped, and Middy was taken aboard drenched and shivering, but perfectly happy to be once more with the crew. He had been ignored and slighted; but he had insisted on his rights, and as soon as they were recognized he was quite contented.

Of course, after that we were quite prepared for anything that Middy might do. And yet he always managed to surprise us by his bold and independent behavior. Perhaps his most brilliant performance was a visit he paid a few days after his swim in Camden Harbor.

We were lying becalmed in a lull of the wind off the entrance to Southwest Harbor. Near us, perhaps a cable's-length away, lay another small yacht, a schooner hailing from Lynn. As we drifted along on the tide, we noticed that Middy was growing very restless; and presently we found him running along the rail and looking eagerly toward the other yacht. What did he see—or smell—over there which interested him? It could not be the dinner, for they were not then cooking. Did he recognize any of his old chums from Marblehead? Perhaps there were some cat friends of his on the other craft. Ah, that was it! There they were on the deck, playing and frisking together— two kittens! Middy had spied them, and was longing to take a nearer look. He ran up and down the deck, mewing and snuffing the air. He stood up on his favorite position when on lookout, with his forepaws on the rail. Then, before we realized what he was doing, he had plunged overboard again, and was making for the other boat as fast as he could swim! He had attracted the attention of her company, and no sooner did he come up alongside than they prepared to welcome him. A fender was lowered, and when Middy saw it he swam toward it, caught it with his forepaws, clambered along it to the gunwale, and in a twinkling was over the side and on the deck scraping acquaintance with the strange kittens.

How they received him I hardly know, for by that time our boat was alongside to claim the runaway. And we were quite of the mind of the skipper of the *Winnie L.,* who said, as he handed our bold midshipman over the side, "Well, that beats all *my* going a-fishing!"

Only a day or two later Middy was very disobedient when we were washing decks one morning. He trotted about in the wet till his feet were drenched, and then retired to dry them on the white spreads of the berths below. That was quite too much for the captain's patience. Middy was summoned aft, and, after a sound rating, was hustled into the dinghy which was moored astern, and shoved off to the full length of her painter. The punishment was a severe one for Middy, who could bear anything better than exile from his beloved ship-mates. So of course he began to exercise his ingenious little brain to see how he could escape. Well under the overhang of the yacht he spied, just about four inches out of water, a little shoulder of the rudder. That was enough for him. He did not stop to think whether he would be any better off there. It was a part of the yacht, and that was home. So overboard he went, swam for the rudder, scrambled onto it, and began howling piteously to be taken on deck again; and, being a spoiled and much-indulged cat, he was soon rescued from his uncomfortable roosting place and restored to favor.

I suppose I shall tax your powers of belief if I tell you many more of Middy's doings. But truly he was a strange cat, and you may as well be patient, for you will not soon hear of his equal. The captain was much given to rifle practice, and used to love to go ashore and shoot at a mark. On one of his trips he allowed Middy to accompany him, for the simple reason, I suppose, that Middy decided to go, and got on board the dinghy when the captain did. Once ashore, the marksman selected a fine large rock as a rest for his rifle, and opened fire upon his target. At the first shot or two Middy seemed a little surprised, but showed no disposition to run away. After the first few rounds, however, he seemed to have made up his mind that since the captain was making all that racket it must be entirely right and proper, and nothing about which a cat need bother his head in the least. So, as if to show how entirely he confided in the captain's judgment and good intentions, that imperturbable cat calmly lay down, curled up, and went to sleep in the shade of the rock over which the captain's rifle was blazing and cracking about once in two minutes. If anybody was ever acquainted with a cooler or more self-possessed cat I should be pleased to hear the particulars.

I wish that this chronicle could be confined to nothing but our shipmate's feats of daring and nerve. But, unfortunately, he was not always blameless in his conduct. When he got hungry he was apt to forget his position as midshipman, and to behave just like any cat with an empty stomach. Or perhaps he may have done just what any hungry midshipman does under the circumstances; I do not quite know what a midshipman does under all circumstances and so I cannot say. But here is one of this cat midshipman's exploits. One afternoon, on our way home, we were working along with a head wind and sea toward Wood Island, a haven for many of the small yachts between Portland and the Shoals. The wind was light and we were a little late in making port. But as we were all agreed that it would be pleasanter to postpone our dinner till we were at anchor, the cook was told to keep things warm and wait till we were inside the port before he set the table. Now, his main dish that day was to be a fine piece of baked fish; and, unfortunately, it was nearly done when we gave orders to hold back the dinner. So he had closed the drafts of his little stove, left the door of the oven open, and turned into his bunk for a quiet doze—a thing which every good sailor does on all possible occasions; for a seafaring life is very uncertain in the matter of sleep, and one never quite knows when he will lose some, nor how much he will lose. So it is well to lay in a good stock of it whenever you can.

It seems that Middy was on watch, and when he saw Charlie fast asleep he undertook to secure a little early dinner for himself. He evidently reasoned with himself that it was very uncertain when we should have dinner and he'd better get his while he could. He quietly slipped down to the stove, walked coolly up to the oven, and began to help himself to baked haddock.

He must have missed his aim or made some mistake in his management of the business, and, by some lucky chance for the rest of us, waked the cook. For, the first we knew, Middy came flying up the cabin companionway, followed by a volley of shoes and spoons and pieces of coal, while we could hear Charlie, who was rather given to unseemly language when he was excited, using the strongest words in his dictionary about "that thief of a cat!"

"What's the matter?" we all shouted at once.

"Matter enough, sir!" growled Charlie. "That little cat's eaten up half the fish! It's a chance if you get any dinner tonight, sir."

You may be very sure that Middy got a sound wigging for that trick, but I am afraid the captain forgot to deprive him of his rations as he threatened. He was much too kindhearted.

The very next evening Middy startled us again by a most remarkable display of coolness and courage. After a weary thrash to windward all day, under a provokingly light breeze, we found ourselves under the lee of the little promontory at Cape Neddick, where we cast anchor for the night. Our supply of water had run very low, and so, just after sunset, two of the party rowed ashore in the tender to replenish our water keg, and by special permission Middy went with them.

It took some time to find a well, and by the time the jugs were filled it had grown quite dark. In launching the boat for the return to the yacht, by some ill luck a breaker caught her and threw her back upon the beach. There she capsized and spilled out the boys, together with their precious cargo. In the confusion of the moment, and the hurry of setting matters to rights, Middy was entirely forgotten, and when the boat again was launched, nobody thought to look for the cat. This time everything went well, and in a few minutes the yacht was sighted through the dusk. Then somebody happened to think of Middy! He was nowhere to be seen. Neither man remembered anything about him after the capsize. There was consternation in the hearts of those unlucky wights. To lose Middy was almost like losing one of the crew.

But it was too late and too dark to go back and risk another landing on the beach. There was nothing to be done but to leave poor Middy to his fate, or at least to wait until morning before searching for him.

But just as the prow of the boat bumped against the fender on the yacht's quarter, out from under the stern sheets came a wet, bedraggled, shivering cat, who leaped on board the yacht and hurried below into the warm cabin. In that moist adventure in the surf, Middy had taken care of himself, rescued himself from a watery grave, got on board the boat as soon as she was ready, and sheltered himself in the warmest corner. All this he had done without the least outcry, and without asking any help whatever. His self-reliance and courage were extraordinary.

Well, the pleasant month of cruising drew to a close, and it became a question what should be done with Middy. We could not think of turning him adrift in the cold world, although we had no fears but that so bright and plucky a cat would make a living anywhere. But we wanted to watch over his fortunes, and perhaps take him on the next cruise with us when he should have become a more settled and dignified Thomas. Finally, it was decided that he should be boarded for the winter with an artist, Miss Susan H———, a friend of one of our party. She wanted a studio cat, and would be particularly pleased to receive so accomplished and traveled a character as Middy. So when the yacht was moored to the little wharf at Annisquam, where she always ended her cruises, and we were packed and ready for our journey to Boston, Middy was tucked into a basket and taken to the train. He bore the confinement with the same good sense which had marked all his life with us, though I think his feelings were hurt at the lack of confidence we showed in him. And, in truth, we were a little ashamed of it ourselves, and when once we were on the cars somebody suggested that he be released from his prison just to see how he would behave. We might have known he would do himself credit. For when he had looked over his surroundings, peeped above the back of the seat at the passengers, taken a good look at the conductor, and counted the rest of the party to see that none of us was missing, Middy snuggled down upon the seat, laid his head upon the captain's knee, and slept all the way to Boston.

That was the last time I ever saw Middy. He was taken to his new boarding place in Boylston Street, where he lived very pleasantly for a few months, and made many friends by his pleasing manners and unruffled temper. But I suppose he found it a little dull in Boston. He was not quite at home in his aesthetic surroundings. I have always believed he sighed for the freedom of a sailor's life. He loved to sit by the open window when the wind was east, and seemed to be dreaming of faraway scenes. One day he disappeared. No trace of him was ever found. A great many things may have happened to him. But I never could get rid of the feeling that he went down to the wharves and the ships and the sailors, trying to find his old friends, looking everywhere for the stanch little *Eyvor;* and, not finding her, I am convinced that he shipped on some East Indiaman and is now a sailor cat on the high seas.

The Cat

Mary E. Wilkins Freeman

THE snow was falling, and the Cat's fur was stiffly pointed with it, but he was imperturbable. He sat crouched, ready for the death-spring, as he had sat for hours. It was night—but that made no difference—all times were as one to the Cat when he was in wait for prey. Then, too, he was under no constraint of human will, for he was living alone that winter. Nowhere in the world was any voice calling him; on no hearth was there a waiting dish. He was quite free except for his own desires, which tyrannized over him when unsatisfied as now. The Cat was very hungry—almost famished, in fact. For days the weather had been very bitter, and all the feebler wild things which were his prey by inheritance, the born serfs to his family, had kept, for the most part, in their burrows and nests, and the Cat's long hunt had availed him nothing. But he waited with the inconceivable patience and persistency of his race; besides, he was certain. The Cat was a creature of absolute convictions, and his faith in his deductions never wavered. The rabbit had gone in there between those low-hung pine boughs. Now her little doorway had before it a shaggy curtain of snow, but in there she was. The Cat had seen her enter, so like a swift grey shadow that even his sharp and practised eyes had glanced back for the substance following, and then she was gone. So he sat down and waited, and he waited still in the white night, listening angrily to the north wind starting in the upper heights of the mountains with distant screams, then swelling into an awful crescendo of rage, and swooping down with furious white wings of snow like a flock of fierce eagles into the valleys and ravines. The Cat was on the side of a mountain, on a wooded terrace. Above him a

54

few feet away towered the rock ascent as steep as the wall of a cathedral. The Cat had never climbed it—trees were the ladders to his heights of life. He had often looked with wonder at the rock, and miauled bitterly and resentfully as man does in the face of a forbidding Providence. At his left was the sheer precipice. Behind him, with a short stretch of woody growth between, was the frozen perpendicular wall of a mountain stream. Before him was the way to his home. When the rabbit came out she was trapped; her little cloven feet could not scale such unbroken steeps. So the Cat waited. The place in which he was looked like a maelstrom of the wood. The tangle of trees and bushes clinging to the mountainside with a stern clutch of roots, the prostrate trunks and branches, the vines embracing everything with strong knots and coils of growth, had a curious effect, as of things which had whirled for ages in a current of raging water, only it was not water, but wind, which had disposed everything in circling lines of yielding to its fiercest points of onset. And now over all this whirl of wood and rock and dead trunks and branches and vines descended the snow. It blew down like smoke over the rock-crest above; it stood in a gyrating column like some death-wraith of nature, on the level, then it broke over the edge of the precipice, and the Cat cowered before the fierce backward set of it. It was as if ice needles pricked his skin through his beautiful thick fur, but he never faltered and never once cried. He had nothing to gain from crying, and everything to lose; the rabbit would hear him cry and know he was waiting.

It grew darker and darker, with a strange white smother, instead of the natural blackness of night. It was a night of storm and death superadded to the night of nature. The mountains were all hidden, wrapped about, overawed, and tumultuously overborne by it, but in the midst of it waited, quite unconquered, this little, unswerving, living patience and power under a little coat of grey fur.

A fiercer blast swept over the rock, spun on one mighty foot of whirlwind athwart the level, then was over the precipice.

Then the Cat saw two eyes luminous with terror, frantic with the impulse of flight, he saw a little, quivering, dilating nose, he saw two pointing ears, and he kept still, with every one of his fine nerves and muscles strained like wires. Then the rabbit was out—there was one long line of incarnate flight and terror—and the Cat had her.

Then the Cat went home, trailing his prey through the snow.

The Cat lived in the house which his master had built, as rudely as a child's block house, but stanchly enough. The snow was heavy on the low slant of its roof, but it would not settle under it. The two windows and the door were made fast, but the Cat knew a way in. Up a pine tree behind the house he scuttled, though it was hard work with his heavy rabbit, and was in his little window under the eaves, then down through the trap to the room below, and on his master's bed with a spring and a great cry of triumph, rabbit and all. But his master was not there; he had been gone since early fall and it was now February. He would not return until spring, for he was an old man, and the cruel cold of the mountains clutched at his vitals like a panther, and he had gone to the village to winter. The Cat had known for a long time that his master was gone, but his reasoning was always sequential and circuitous; always for him what had been would be, and the more easily for his marvellous waiting powers so he always came home expecting to find his master.

When he saw that he was still gone, he dragged the rabbit off the rude couch which was the bed to the floor, put one little paw on the carcass to keep it steady, and began gnawing with head to one side to bring his strongest teeth to bear.

It was darker in the house than it had been in the wood, and the cold was as deadly, though not so fierce. If the Cat had not received his fur coat unquestioningly of Providence, he would have been thankful that he had it. It was a mottled grey, white on the face and breast, and thick as fur could grow.

The wind drove the snow on the windows with such force that it rattled like sleet, and the house trembled a little. Then all at once the Cat heard a noise, and stopped gnawing his rabbit and listened, his shining green eyes fixed upon a window. Then he heard a hoarse shout, a halloo of despair and entreaty; but he knew it was not his master come home, and he waited, one paw still on the rabbit. Then the halloo came again, and then the Cat answered. He said all that was essential quite plainly to his own comprehension. There was in his cry of response inquiry, information, warning, terror, and finally, the offer of comradeship; but the man outside did not hear him, because of the howling of the storm.

Then there was a great battering pound at the door, then another, and another. The Cat dragged his rabbit under the bed. The blows came thicker and faster. It was a weak arm which gave them, but it was nerved by desperation. Finally the lock yielded, and the stranger came in. Then the Cat, peering from under the bed, blinked with a sudden light, and his green eyes narrowed. The stranger struck a match and looked about. The Cat saw a face wild and blue with hunger and cold, and a man who looked poorer and older than his poor old master, who was an outcast among men for his poverty and lowly mystery of antecedents; and he heard a muttered, unintelligible voicing of distress from the harsh piteous mouth. There was in it both profanity and prayer, but the Cat knew nothing of that.

The stranger braced the door which he had forced, got some wood from the stock in the corner, and kindled a fire in the old stove as quickly as his half-frozen hands would allow. He shook so pitiably as he worked that the Cat under the bed felt the tremor of it. Then the man, who was small and feeble and marked with the scars of suffering which he had pulled down upon his own head, sat down in one of the old chairs and crouched over the fire as if it were the one love and desire of his soul, holding out his yellow hands like yellow claws, and he groaned. The Cat came out from under the bed and leaped up on his lap with the rabbit. The man gave a great shout and start of terror, and sprang, and the Cat slid clawing to the floor, and the rabbit fell inertly, and the man leaned, gasping with fright, and ghastly, against the wall. The Cat grabbed the rabbit by the slack of its neck and dragged it to the man's feet. Then he raised his shrill, insistent cry, he arched his back high, his tail was a splendid waving plume. He rubbed against the man's feet, which were bursting out of their torn shoes.

The man pushed the Cat away, gently enough, and began searching about the little cabin. He even climbed painfully the ladder to the loft, lit a match, and peered up in the darkness with straining eyes. He feared lest there might be a man, since there was a cat. His experience with men had not been pleasant, and neither had the experience of men been pleasant with him. He was an old wandering Ishmael among his kind; he had stumbled upon the house of a brother, and the brother was not at home, and he was glad.

He returned to the Cat, and stooped stiffly and stroked his back, which the animal arched like the spring of a bow.

Then he took up the rabbit and looked at it eagerly by the firelight. His jaws worked. He could almost have devoured it raw. He fumbled—the Cat close at his heels—around some rude shelves and a table, and found, with a grunt of self-gratulation, a lamp with oil in it. That he lighted; then he found a frying-pan and a knife, and skinned the rabbit, and prepared it for cooking, the Cat always at his feet.

When the odour of the cooking flesh filled the cabin, both the man and the Cat looked wolfish. The man turned the rabbit with one hand and stooped to pat the Cat with the other. The Cat thought him a fine man. He loved him with all his heart, though he had known him such a short time, and though the man had a face both pitiful and sharply set at variance with the best of things.

It was a face with the grimy grizzle of age upon it, with fever hollows in the cheeks, and the memories of wrong in the dim eyes, but the Cat accepted the man unquestioningly and loved him. When the rabbit was half cooked, neither the man nor the Cat could wait any longer. The man took it from the fire, divided it exactly in halves, gave the Cat one, and took the other himself. Then they ate.

Then the man blew out the light, called the Cat to him, got on the bed, drew up the ragged coverings, and fell asleep with the Cat in his bosom.

The man was the Cat's guest all the rest of the winter, and winter is long in the mountains. The rightful owner of the little hut did not return until May. All that time the Cat toiled hard, and he grew rather thin himself, for he shared everything except mice with his guest; and sometimes game was wary, and the fruit of patience of days was very little for two. The man was ill and weak, however, and unable to eat much, which was fortunate, since he could not hunt for himself. All day long he lay on the bed, or else sat crouched over the fire. It was a good thing that firewood was ready at hand for the picking up, not a stone's-throw from the door, for that he had to attend to himself.

The Cat foraged tirelessly. Sometimes he was gone for days together, and at first the man used to be terrified, thinking he would never return; then he would hear the familiar cry at the door, and stumble to his feet and let him in. Then the two would dine together, sharing equally; then the Cat would rest and purr, and finally sleep in the man's arms.

Towards spring the game grew plentiful; more wild little quarry were tempted out of their homes, in search of love as well as food. One day the Cat had luck—a rabbit, a partridge, and a mouse. He could not carry them all at once, but finally he had them together at the house door. Then he cried, but no one answered. All the mountain streams were loosened, and the air was full of the gurgle of many waters, occasionally pierced by a bird-whistle. The trees rustled with a new sound to the spring wind; there was a flush of rose and gold-green on the breasting surface of a distant mountain seen through an opening in the wood. The tips of the bushes were swollen and glistening red, and now and then there was a flower; but the Cat had nothing to do with flowers. He stood beside his booty at the house door, and cried and cried with his insistent triumph and complaint and pleading, but no one came to let him in. Then the cat left his little treasures at the door, and went around to the back of the house to the pine tree, and was up the trunk with a wild scramble, and in through his little window, and down through the trap to the room, and the man was gone.

The Cat cried again—that cry of the animal for human companionship which is one of the sad notes of the world; he looked in all the corners; he sprang to the chair at the window and looked out; but no one came. The man was gone and he never came again.

The Cat ate his mouse out on the turf beside the house; the rabbit and the partridge he carried painfully into the house, but the man did not come to share them. Finally, in the course of a day or two, he ate them up himself; then he slept a long time on the bed, and when he waked the man was not there.

Then the Cat went forth to his hunting grounds again, and came home at night with a plump bird, reasoning with his tireless persistency in expectancy that the man would be there; and there was a light in the window, and when he cried his old master opened the door and let him in.

His master had strong comradeship with the Cat, but not affection. He never patted him like that gentler outcast, but he had a pride in him and an anxiety for his welfare, though he had left him alone all winter without scruple. He feared lest some misfortune might have come to the Cat, though he was so large of his kind, and a mighty hunter. Therefore, when he saw him at the door in all the glory of his glossy winter coat, his white breast and face shining like snow in the sun, his own face lit up with welcome, and the Cat embraced his feet with his sinuous body vibrant with rejoicing purrs.

The Cat had his bird to himself, for his master had his own supper already cooking on the stove. After supper the Cat's master took his pipe, and sought a small store of tobacco which he had left in his hut over winter. He had thought often of it; that and the Cat seemed something to come home to in the spring. But the tobacco was gone; not a dust left. The man swore a little in a grim monotone, which made the profanity lose its customary effect. He had been, and was, a hard drinker; he had knocked about the world until the marks of its sharp corners were on his very soul, which was thereby calloused, until his very sensibility to loss was dulled. He was a very old man.

He searched for the tobacco with a sort of dull combativeness of persistency; then he stared with stupid wonder around the room. Suddenly many features struck him as being changed. Another stove-lid was broken; an old piece of carpet was tacked up over a window to keep out the cold; his firewood was gone. He looked and there was no oil left in his can. He looked at the coverings on his bed; he took them up, and again he made that strange remonstrant noise in his throat. Then he looked again for his tobacco.

Finally he gave it up. He sat down beside the fire, for May in the mountains is cold; he held his empty pipe in his mouth, his rough forehead knitted, and he and the Cat looked at each other across that impassable barrier of silence which has been set between man and beast from the creation of the world.

The Master Cat; or, Puss in Boots
Charles Perrault

T HERE was a miller who left no more estate to the three
sons he had than his mill his ass and his cat. The partition
was soon made. Neither scrivener nor attorney was sent for.
They would soon have eaten up all the poor patrimony. The
eldest had the mill, the second the ass, and the youngest nothing but the cat.

The poor young fellow was quite comfortless at having so
poor a lot.

"My brothers," said he, "may get their living handsomely
enough by joining their stocks together; but for my part, when
I have eaten up my cat, and made me a muff of his skin, I
must die of hunger."

The Cat, who heard all this, but made as if he did not, said
to him with a grave and serious air:

"Do not thus afflict yourself, my good master. You have
nothing else to do but to give me a bag and get a pair of boots
made for me that I may scamper through the dirt and the
brambles, and you shall see that you have not so bad a portion
in me as you imagine."

The Cat's master did not build very much upon what he
said. He had often seen him play a great many cunning tricks
to catch rats and mice, as when he used to hang by the heels,
or hide himself in the meal, and make as if he were dead; so
that he did not altogether despair of his affording him some
help in his miserable condition. When the Cat had what he
asked for he booted himself very gallantly, and putting his bag
about his neck, he held the strings of it in his two forepaws
and went into a warren where was great abundance of rabbits.
He put bran and sow thistle into his bag, and stretching out at

length, as if he had been dead, he waited for some young rabbits, not yet acquainted with the deceits of the world, to come and rummage his bag for what he had put into it.

Scarce was he lain down but he had what he wanted. A rash and foolish young rabbit jumped into his bag, and Monsieur Puss, immediately drawing close the strings, took and killed him without pity. Proud of his prey, he went with it to the palace and asked to speak with his majesty. He was shown upstairs into the King's apartment, and, making a low reverence, said to him:

"I have brought you, sir, a rabbit of the warren, which my noble lord the Marquis of Carabas" (for that was the title which puss was pleased to give his master) "has commanded me to present to your majesty from him."

"Tell thy master," said the king, "that I thank him and that he does me a great deal of pleasure."

Another time he went and hid himself among some standing corn, holding still his bag open, and when a brace of partridges ran into it he drew the strings and so caught them both. He went and made a present of these to the king, as he had done before of the rabbit that he took in the warren. The king, in like manner, received the partridges with great pleasure, and ordered him some money for drink.

The Cat continued for two or three months thus to carry his Majesty, from time to time, game of his master's taking. One day in particular, when he knew for certain that he was to take the air along the riverside, with his daughter, the most beautiful princess in the world, he said to his master:

"If you will follow my advice your fortune is made. You have nothing else to do but go and wash yourself in the river, in that part I shall show you, and leave the rest to me."

The Marquis of Carabas did what the Cat advised him to, without knowing why or wherefore. While he was washing the King passed by, and the Cat began to cry out:

"Help! help! My Lord Marquis of Carabas is going to be drowned."

At this noise the King put his head out of the coach window, and, finding it was the Cat who had so often brought him such good game, he commanded his guards to run immediately to the assistance of his Lordship the Marquis of Carabas.

While they were drawing the poor Marquis out of the river, the Cat came up to the coach and told the King that, while his master was washing, there came by some rogues, who went off with his clothes, though he had cried out: "Thieves! thieves!" several times, as loud as he could.

This cunning Cat had hidden them under a great stone. The King immediately commanded the officers of his wardrobe to run and fetch one of his best suits for the Lord Marquis of Carabas.

The King caressed him after a very extraordinary manner, and as the fine clothes he had given him extremely set off his good mien (for he was well made and very handsome in his person), the King's daughter took a secret inclination to him, and the Marquis of Carabas had no sooner cast two or three respectful and somewhat tender glances but she fell in love with him to distraction. The King would needs have him come into the coach and take part of the airing. The Cat, quite overjoyed to see his project begin to succeed, marched on before, and, meeting with some countrymen, who were mowing a meadow, he said to them:

"Good people, you who are mowing, if you do not tell the King that the meadow you mow belongs to my Lord Marquis of Carabas, you shall be chopped as small as herbs for the pot."

The King did not fail asking of the mowers to whom the meadow they were mowing belonged.

"To my Lord Marquis of Carabas," answered they altogether, for the Cat's threats had made them terribly afraid.

"You see, sir," said the Marquis, "this is a meadow which never fails to yield a plentiful harvest every year."

The Master Cat, who went still on before, met with some reapers, and said to them:

"Good people, you who are reaping, if you do not tell the King that all this corn belongs to the Marquis of Carabas, you shall be chopped as small as herbs for the pot."

The King, who passed by a moment after, would needs know to whom all that corn, which he then saw, did belong.

"To my Lord Marquis of Carabas," replied the reapers, and the King was very well pleased with it, as well as the Marquis, whom he congratulated thereupon. The Master Cat, who went always before, said the same words to all he met, and the King was astonished at the vast estates of my Lord Marquis of Carabas.

Monsieur Puss came at last to a stately castle, the master of which was an ogre, the richest had ever been known; for all the lands which the King had then gone over belonged to this castle. The Cat, who had taken care to inform himself who this ogre was and what he could do, asked to speak with him, saying he could not pass so near his castle without having the honor of paying his respects to him.

The ogre received him as civilly as an ogre could do, and made him sit down.

"I have been assured," said the Cat, "that you have the gift of being able to change yourself into all sorts of creatures you have a mind to; you can, for example, transform yourself into a lion, or elephant, and the like."

"That is true," answered the ogre very briskly; "and to convince you, you shall see me now become a lion."

Puss was so sadly terrified at the sight of a lion so near him that he immediately got into the gutter, not without abundance of trouble and danger, because of his boots, which were of no use at all to him in walking upon the tiles. A little while after, when Puss saw that the ogre had resumed his natural form, he came down, and owned he had been very much frightened.

"I have been, moreover, informed," said the Cat, "but I know not how to believe it, that you have also the power to take on you the shape of the smallest animals; for example, to change yourself into a rat or a mouse; but I must own to you I take this to be impossible."

"Impossible!" cried the ogre; "you shall see that presently."

And at the same time he changed himself into a mouse, and began to run about the floor. Puss no sooner perceived this but he fell upon him and ate him up.

Meanwhile the King, who saw, as he passed, this fine castle of the ogre's, had a mind to go into it. Puss, who heard the noise of his Majesty's coach running over the draw-bridge, ran out, and said to the King:

"Your Majesty is welcome to this castle of my Lord Marquis of Carabas."

"What! my Lord Marquis," cried the King, "and does this castle also belong to you? There can be nothing finer than this court and all the stately buildings which surround it; let us go into it, if you please."

The Marquis gave his hand to the Princess, and followed the King, who went first. They passed into a spacious hall, where they found a magnificent collation, which the ogre had prepared for his friends, who were that very day to visit him, but dared not to enter, knowing the King was there. His Majesty was perfectly charmed with the good qualities of my Lord Marquis of Carabas, as was his daughter, who had fallen violently in love with him, and, seeing the vast estate he possessed, said to him, after having drunk five or six glasses:

"It will be owing to yourself only, my Lord Marquis, if you are not my son-in-law."

The Marquis, making several low bows, accepted the honor which his Majesty conferred upon him, and forthwith, that very same day, married the Princess.

Puss became a great lord, and never ran after mice anymore but only for his diversion.

The Watchers
Bram Stoker

MY Dear Daughter:
I want you to take this letter as an instruction—absolute and imperative, and admitting of no deviation whatever—in case anything untoward or unexpected by you or by others should happen to me. If I should be suddenly and mysteriously stricken down—either by sickness, accident or attack—you must follow these directions implicitly. If I am not already in my bedroom when you are made cognizant of my state, I am to be brought there as quickly as possible. Even should I be dead, my body is to be brought there. Thenceforth, until I am either conscious and able to give instructions on my own account, or buried, I am never to be left alone—not for a single instant. From nightfall to sunrise at least two persons must remain in the room. It will be well that a trained nurse be in the room from time to time, and will note any symptoms, either permanent or changing, which may strike her. My solicitors, Marvin & Jewkes, of 27B Lincoln's Inn, have full instructions in case of my death; and Mr. Marvin has himself undertaken to see personally my wishes carried out. I should advise you, my dear Daughter, seeing that you have no relative to apply to, to get some friend whom you can trust to either remain within the house where instant communication can be made, or to come nightly to aid in the watching, or to be within call. Such friend may be either male or female; but, whichever it may be, there should be added one other watcher or attendant at hand of the opposite sex. Understand, that it is of the very essence of my wish that there should be, awake and exercising themselves to my purposes, both masculine and feminine intelligences. Once more, my dear Margaret, let

me impress on you the need for observation and just reasoning to conclusions, howsoever strange. If I am taken ill or
injured, this will be no ordinary occasion; and I wish to warn
you, so that your guarding may be complete.

Nothing in my room—I speak of the curios—must be
removed or displaced in any way, or for any cause whatever. I
have a special reason and a special purpose in the placing of
each; so that any moving of them would thwart my plans.

Should you want money or counsel in anything, Mr. Marvin
will carry out your wishes; to the which he has my full
instructions.

Abel Trelawny

...That night we were not yet regularly organized for watching, so that the early part of the evening showed an unevenly
balanced guard. Nurse Kennedy, who had been on duty all
day, was lying down, as she had arranged to come on again by
twelve o'clock. Doctor Winchester, who was dining in the
house, remained in the room until dinner was announced; and
went back at once when it was over. During dinner Mrs. Grant
remained in the room, and with her Sergeant Daw, who
wished to complete a minute examination which he had
undertaken of everything in the room and near it. At nine
o'clock Miss Trelawny and I went in to relieve the Doctor. She
had lain down for a few hours in the afternoon so as to be
refreshed for her work at night. She told me that she had
determined that for this night at least she would sit up
and watch. I did not try to dissuade her, for I knew that her
mind was made up. Then and there I made up my mind that
I would watch with her—unless, of course, I should see that
she really did not wish it. I said nothing of my intentions for
the present. We came in on tiptoe, so silently that the Doctor,
who was bending over the bed, did not hear us, and seemed a
little startled when suddenly looking up he saw our eyes upon
him. I felt that the mystery of the whole thing was getting on
his nerves, as it had already got on the nerves of some others

of us. He was, I fancied, a little annoyed with himself for having been so startled, and at once began to talk in a hurried manner as though to get over our idea of his embarrassment:

"I am really and absolutely at my wits' end to find any fit cause for this stupor. I have made again as accurate an examination as I know how, and I am satisfied that there is no injury to the brain, that is, no external injury. Indeed, all his vital organs seem unimpaired. I have given him, as you know, food several times and it has manifestly done him good. His breathing is strong and regular, and his pulse is slower and stronger than it was this morning. I cannot find evidence of any known drug, and his unconsciousness does not resemble any of the many cases of hypnotic sleep which I saw in the Charcot Hospital in Paris. And as to these wounds"—he laid his finger gently on the bandaged wrist which lay outside the coverlet as he spoke—"I do not know what to make of them. They might have been made by a carding machine; but that supposition is untenable. It is within the bounds of possibility that they might have been made by a wild animal if it had taken care to sharpen its claws. That too is, I take it, impossible. By the way, have you any strange pets here in the house; anything of an exceptional kind, such as a tiger cat or anything out of the common?" Miss Trelawny smiled a sad smile which made my heart ache, as she made answer:

"Oh no! Father does not like animals about the house, unless they are dead and mummied." This was said with a touch of bitterness—or jealousy, I could hardly tell which. "Even my poor kitten was only allowed in the house on sufferance; and though he is the dearest and best-conducted cat in the world, he is now on a sort of parole, and is not allowed into this room."

As she was speaking a faint rattling of the door handle was heard. Instantly Miss Trelawny's face brightened. She sprang up and went over to the door, saying as she went:

"There he is! That is my Silvio. He stands on his hind legs and rattles the door handle when he wants to come into a room." She opened the door, speaking to the cat as though he were a baby: "Did him want his movver? Come then; but he must stay with her!" She lifted the cat, and came back with him in her arms. He was certainly a magnificent animal. A chinchilla grey Persian with long silky hair; a really lordly animal with a haughty bearing despite his gentleness; and with great paws which spread out as he placed them on the ground. Whilst she was fondling him, he suddenly gave a wriggle like an eel and slipped out of her arms. He ran across the room and stood opposite a low table on which stood the mummy of an animal, and began to mew and snarl. Miss Trelawny was after him in an instant and lifted him in her arms, kicking and struggling and wriggling to get away; but not biting or scratching, for evidently he loved his beautiful mistress. He ceased to make a noise the moment he was in her arms; in a whisper she admonished him:

"O you naughty Silvio! You have broken your parole that mother gave for you. Now, say good night to the gentlemen, and come away to mother's room!" As she was speaking she held out the cat's paw to me to shake. As I did so I could not but admire its size and beauty. "Why," said I, "his paw seems like a little boxing glove full of claws." She smiled:

"So it ought to. Don't you notice that my Silvio has seven toes, see!" she opened the paw; and surely enough there were seven separate claws, each of them sheathed in a delicate, fine, shell-like case. As I gently stroked the foot the claws emerged and one of them accidentally—there was no anger now and the cat was purring—stuck into my hand. Instinctively I said as I drew back:

"Why, his claws are like razors!"

Doctor Winchester had come close to us and was bending over looking at the cat's claws; as I spoke he said in a quick, sharp way:

"Eh!" I could hear the quick intake of his breath. Whilst I was stroking the now quiescent cat, the Doctor went to the table and tore off a piece of blotting paper from the writing pad and came back. He laid the paper on his palm and, with a simple "pardon me!" to Miss Trelawny, placed the cat's paw on it and pressed it down with his other hand. The haughty cat seemed to resent somewhat the familiarity, and tried to draw its foot away. This was plainly what the Doctor wanted, for in the act the cat opened the sheaths of its claws and made several reefs in the soft paper. Then Miss Trelawny took her pet away. She returned in a couple of minutes; as she came in she said:

"It is most odd about that mummy! When Silvio came into the room first—indeed I took him in as a kitten to show to Father—he went on just the same way. He jumped up on the table, and tried to scratch and bite the mummy. That was what made Father so angry, and brought the decree of banishment on poor Silvio. Only his parole, given through me, kept him in the house."

Whilst she had been gone, Doctor Winchester had taken the bandage from her father's wrist. The wound was now quite clear, as the separate cuts showed out in fierce red lines. The Doctor folded the blotting paper across the line of punctures made by the cat's claws, and held it down close to the wound. As he did so, he looked up triumphantly and beckoned us over to him.

The cuts in the paper corresponded with the wounds in the wrist! No explanation was needed, as he said:

"It would have been better if master Silvio had not broken his parole!"

We were all silent for a little while. Suddenly Miss Trelawny said:

"But Silvio was not in here last night!"

"Are you sure? Could you prove that if necessary?"

She hesitated before replying:

"I am certain of it; but I fear it would be difficult to prove. Silvio sleeps in a basket in my room. I certainly put him to bed last night; I remember distinctly laying his little blanket over him, and tucking him in. This morning I took him out of the basket myself. I certainly never noticed him in here; though, of course, that would not mean much, for I was too concerned about poor father, and too much occupied with him, to notice even Silvio."

The Doctor shook his head as he said with a certain sadness:

"Well, at any rate it is no use trying to prove anything now. Any cat in the world would have cleaned blood marks—did any exist—from his paws in a hundredth part of the time that has elapsed."

Again we were all silent; and again the silence was broken by Miss Trelawny:

"But now that I think of it, it could not have been poor Silvio that injured Father. My door was shut when I first heard the sound; and Father's was shut when I listened at it. When I went in, the injury had been done; so that it must have been before Silvio could possibly have got in." This reasoning commended itself, especially to me as a barrister, for it was proof to satisfy a jury. It gave me a distinct pleasure to have Silvio acquitted of the crime—possibly because he was Miss Trelawny's cat and was loved by her. Happy cat! Silvio's mistress was manifestly pleased as I said:

"Verdict, 'not guilty!'" Doctor Winchester after a pause observed:

"My apologies to master Silvio on this occasion; but I am still puzzled to know why he is so keen against that mummy. Is he the same toward the other mummies in the house? There are, I suppose, a lot of them. I saw three in the hall as I came in."

"There are lots of them," she answered. "I sometimes don't know whether I am in a private house or the British Museum. But Silvio never concerns himself about any of them except that particular one. I suppose it must be because it is of an animal, not a man or a woman."

"Perhaps it is of a cat!" said the Doctor as he started up and went across the room to look at the mummy more closely. "Yes," he went on, "it is the mummy of a cat; and a very fine one, too. If it hadn't been a special favorite of some very special person it would never have received so much honor. See! A painted case and obsidian eyes—just like a human mummy. It is an extraordinary thing, that knowledge of kind to kind. Here is a dead cat—that is all; it is perhaps four or five thousand years old—and another cat of another breed, in what is practically another world, is ready to fly at it, just as it would if it were not dead. I should like to experiment a bit about that cat if you don't mind, Miss Trelawny." She hesitated before replying:

"Of course, do anything you may think necessary or wise; but I hope it will not be anything to hurt or worry my poor Silvio." The Doctor smiled as he answered:

"Oh, Silvio would be all right: it is the other one that my sympathies would be reserved for."

"How do you mean?"

"Master Silvio will do the attacking; the other one will do the suffering."

"Suffering?" There was a note of pain in her voice. The Doctor smiled more broadly:

"Oh, please make your mind easy as to that. The other won't suffer as we understand it; except perhaps in his structure and outfit."

"What on earth do you mean?"

"Simply this, my dear young lady, that the antagonist will be a mummy cat like this one. There are, I take it, plenty of them to be had in Museum Street. I shall get one and place it here instead of that one—you won't think that a temporary exchange will violate your Father's instructions, I hope. We shall then find out, to begin with, whether Silvio objects to all mummy cats, or only to this one in particular."

"I don't know," she said doubtfully. "Father's instructions seem very uncompromising." Then after a pause she went on: "But of course under the circumstances anything that is to be ultimately for his good must be done. I suppose there can't be anything very particular about the mummy of a cat."

Doctor Winchester said nothing. He sat rigid, with so grave a look on his face that his extra gravity passed on to me; and in its enlightening perturbation I began to realize more than I had yet done the strangeness of the case in which I was now so deeply concerned. When once this thought had begun there was no end to it. Indeed it grew, and blossomed, and reproduced itself in a thousand different ways. The room and all in it gave grounds for strange thoughts. There were so many ancient relics that unconsciously one was taken back to strange lands and strange times. There were so many mummies or mummy objects, round which there seemed to cling forever the penetrating odors of bitumen, and spices and gums—"Nard and Circassia's balmy smells"—that one was unable to forget the past. Of course, there was but little light in the room, and that carefully shaded; so that there was no glare anywhere. None of that direct light which can manifest itself as a power or an entity, and so make for companionship. The room was a large one, and lofty in proportion to its size. In its vastness was place for a multitude of things not often found in a bedchamber. In far corners of the room were shadows of uncanny shape. More than once as I thought, the multitudinous presence of the dead and the past took such hold on me that I caught myself looking round fearfully as though some strange personality or influence was present. Even the manifest presence of Doctor Winchester and Miss Trelawny could not altogether comfort or satisfy me at such moments. It was with a distinct sense of relief that I saw a new personality in the room in the shape of Nurse Kennedy. There was no doubt that that business-like, self-reliant, capable young woman added an element of security to such wild imaginings as my own. She had a quality of common sense that seemed to pervade everything around her, as though it were some kind of emanation. Up to that moment I had been building fancies around the sick man; so that finally all about him, including myself, had become involved in them, or enmeshed, or saturated, or . . . But now that she had come, he relapsed into his proper perspective as a patient; the room was a sickroom, and the shadows lost their fearsome quality. The only thing which it could not altogether abrogate was the strange Egyptian smell. You may put a mummy in a glass case and hermetically seal it so that no corroding air can get within; but all the same it will exhale its odor. One might think that four or five thousand years would exhaust the olfactory qualities of anything; but experience teaches us that these smells remain, and that their secrets are unknown to us. Today they are as much mysteries as they were when the embalmers put the body in the bath of natron . . .

All at once I sat up. I had become lost in an absorbing reverie. The Egyptian smell had seemed to get on my nerves—on my memory—on my very will.

At that moment I had a thought which was like an inspiration. If I was influenced in such a manner by the smell, might it not be that the sick man, who lived half his life or more in the atmosphere, had gradually and by slow but sure process taken into his system something which had permeated him to such degree that it had a new power derived from quantity— or strength—or . . .

I was becoming lost again in a reverie. This would not do. I must take such precaution that I could remain awake, or free from such entrancing thought. I had had but half a night's sleep last night; and this night I must remain awake. Without stating my intention, for I feared that I might add to the trouble and uneasiness of Miss Trelawny, I went downstairs and out of the house. I soon found a chemist's shop, and came away with a respirator. When I got back, it was ten o'clock; the Doctor was going for the night. The Nurse came with him to the door of the sickroom, taking her last instructions. Miss Trelawny sat still beside the bed. Sergeant Daw, who had entered as the Doctor went out, was some little distance off.

When Nurse Kennedy joined us, we arranged that she should sit up till two o'clock, when Miss Trelawny would relieve her. Thus, in accordance with Mr. Trelawny's instructions, there would always be a man and a woman in the room; and each one of us would overlap, so that at no time would a new set of watchers come on duty without someone to tell of what—if anything—had occurred. I lay down on a sofa in my own room, having arranged that one of the servants should call me a little before twelve. In a few moments I was asleep.

When I was waked, it took me several seconds to get back my thoughts so as to recognize my own identity and surroundings. The short sleep had, however, done me good, and I could look on things around me in a more practical light than I had been able to do earlier in the evening. I bathed my face, and thus refreshed went into the sickroom. I moved very softly. The Nurse was sitting by the bed, quiet and alert; the Detective sat in an armchair across the room in deep shadow. He did not move when I crossed, until I got close to him, when he said in a dull whisper:

"It is all right; I have not been asleep!" An unnecessary thing to say, I thought—it always is, unless it be untrue in spirit. When I told him that his watch was over; that he might go to bed till I should call him at six o'clock, he seemed relieved and went with alacrity. At the door he turned and, coming back to me, said in a whisper:

"I sleep lightly and I shall have my pistols with me. I won't feel so heavy-headed when I get out of this mummy smell."

He too, then, had shared my experience of drowsiness!

I asked the Nurse if she wanted anything. I noticed that she had a vinaigrette in her lap. Doubtless she, too, had felt some of the influence which had so affected me. She said that she had all she required, but that if she should want anything she would at once let me know. I wished to keep her from noticing my respirator, so I went to the chair in the shadow where her back was toward me. Here I quietly put it on, and made myself comfortable.

For what seemed a long time, I sat and thought and thought. It was a wild medley of thoughts, as might have been expected from the experiences of the previous day and night.

Again I found myself thinking of the Egyptian smell; and I remember that I felt a delicious satisfaction that I did not experience it as I had done. The respirator was doing its work.

It must have been that the passing of this disturbing thought made for repose of mind, which is the corollary of bodily rest, for, though I really cannot remember being asleep or waking from it, I saw a vision—I dreamed a dream, I scarcely know which.

I was still in the room, seated in the chair. I had on my respirator and knew that I breathed freely. The Nurse sat in her chair with her back toward me. She sat quite still. The sick man lay as still as the dead. It was rather like the picture of a scene than the reality; all were still and silent; and the stillness and silence were continuous. Outside, in the distance I could hear the sounds of a city, the occasional roll of wheels, the shout of a reveler, the far-away echo of whistles and the rumbling of trains. The light was very, very low; the reflection of it under the green-shaded lamp was a dim relief to the darkness, rather than light. The green silk fringe of the lamp had merely the color of an emerald seen in the moonlight. The room, for all its darkness, was full of shadows. It seemed in my whirling thoughts as though all the real things had become shadows—shadows which moved, for they passed the dim outline of the high windows. Shadows which had sentience. I even thought there was sound, a faint sound as of the mew of a cat—the rustle of drapery and a metallic clink as of metal faintly touching metal. I sat as one entranced. At last I felt, as in nightmare, that this was sleep, and that in the passing of its portals all my will had gone.

All at once my senses were full awake. A shriek rang in my ears. The room was filled suddenly with a blaze of light. There was the sound of pistol shots—one, two; and a haze of white smoke in the room. When my waking eyes regained their power, I could have shrieked with horror myself at what I saw before me.

Zut
Guy Wetmore Carryl

SIDE by side, on the avenue de la Grande Armée, stand the épicerie of Jean-Baptiste Caille and the salle de coiffure of Hippolyte Sergeot, and between these two there is a great gulf fixed, the which has come to be through the acerbity of Alexandrine Caille (according to Espérance Sergeot), through the duplicity of Espérance Sergeot (according to Alexandrine Caille). But the veritable root of all evil is Zut, and Zut sits smiling in Jean-Baptiste's doorway, and cares naught for anything in the world, save the sunlight and her midday meal.

When Hippolyte found himself in a position to purchase the salle de coiffure, he gave evidence of marked acumen by uniting himself in the holy—and civil—bonds of matrimony with the retiring patron's daughter, whose dot ran into the coveted five figures, and whose heart, said Hippolyte, was as good as her face was pretty, which, even by the unprejudiced, was acknowledged to be forcible commendation. The installation of the new establishment was a nine days' wonder in the quartier. It is a busy thoroughfare at its western end, is the avenue de la Grande Armée, crowded with bicyclists and with a multitude of creatures fearfully and wonderfully clad, who do incomprehensible things in connection with motor carriages. Also there are big cafés in plenty, whose waiters must be smoothly shaven: and moreover, at the time when Hippolyte came into his own, the porte Maillot station of the Métropolitain had already pushed its entrée and sortie up through the soil, not a hundred metres from his door, where they stood like atrocious yellow tulips, art nouveau, breathing people out and in by thousands. There was no lack of possible custom. The problem was to turn possible into probable, and probable into permanent; and here the seven wits and the ten thousand francs of Espérance came prominently to the fore. She it was who sounded the progressive note, which is half the secret of success.

"Pour attirer les gens," she said, with her arms akimbo, "il faut d'abord les épater."

In her creed all that was worth doing at all was worth doing gloriously. So, under her guidance, Hippolyte journeyed from shop to shop in the faubourg St. Antoine, and spent hours of impassioned argument with carpenters and decorators. In the end, the salle de coiffure was glorified by fresh paint without and within, and by the addition of a long mirror in a gilt frame, and a complicated apparatus of gleaming nickel-plate, which went by the imposing title of appareil antiseptique, and the acquisition of which was duly proclaimed by a special placard that swung at right angles to the door. The shop was rechristened, too, and the black and white sign across its front which formerly bore the simple inscription "Kilbert, Coiffeur," now blazoned abroad the vastly more impressive legend "Salon Malakoff." The window shelves fairly groaned beneath their burden of soaps, toilet waters, and perfumery, a string of bright yellow sponges occupied each corner of the window, and, through the agency of white enamel letters on the pane itself, public attention was drawn to the apparently contradictory facts that English was spoken and "schampoing" given within. Then Hippolyte engaged two assistants, and clad them in white duck jackets, and his wife fabricated a new blouse of blue silk, and seated herself behind the desk with an engaging smile. The enterprise was fairly launched, and experience was not slow in proving the theories of Espérance to be well founded. The quartier was épaté from the start, and took with enthusiasm the bait held forth. The affairs of the Salon Malakoff prospered prodigiously.

But there is a serpent in every Eden, and in that of the Sergeot this rôle was assumed by Alexandrine Caille. The worthy épicier himself was of too torpid a temperament to fall a victim to the gnawing tooth of envy, but in the soul of his wife the launch, and, what was worse, the immediate prosperity of the Salon Malakoff, bred dire resentment. Her own establishment had grown grimy with the passage of time, and the annual profits displayed a constant and disturbing tendency toward complete evaporation, since the coming of the big cafés, and the resultant subversion of custom to the wholesale dealers. This persistent narrowing of the former appreciable gap between purchase and selling price rankled in Alexandrine's mind, but her misguided efforts to maintain the percentage of profit by recourse to inferior qualities only made bad worse, and, even as the Sergeot were steering the Salon Malakoff forth upon the waters of prosperity, there were nightly conferences in the household next door, at which impending ruin presided, and exasperation sounded the keynote of every sentence. The resplendent façade of Hippolyte's establishment, the tide of custom which poured into and out of his door, the loudly expressed admiration of his ability and thrift, which greeted her ears on every side, and, finally, the sight of Espérance, fresh, smiling, and prosperous, behind her little counter—all these were as gall and wormwood to Alexandrine, brooding over her accumulating debts and her decreasing earnings, among her dusty stacks of jars and boxes. Once she had called upon her neighbour, somewhat for courtesy's sake, but more for curiosity's, and since then the agreeable scent of violet and lilac perfumery dwelt always in her memory, and mirages of scrupulously polished nickel and glass hung always before her eyes. The air of her own shop was heavy with the pungent odours of raw vegetables, cheeses, and dried fish, and no brilliance redeemed the sardine and biscuit boxes which surrounded her. Life became a bitter thing to Alexandrine Caille, for if nothing is more gratifying than one's own success, surely nothing is less so than that of one's neighbour. Moreover, her visit had never been returned, and this again was fuel for her rage.

But the sharpest thorn in her flesh—and even in that of her phlegmatic husband—was the base desertion to the enemy's camp of Abel Flique. In the days when Madame Caille was unmarried, and when her ninety kilos were fifty still, Abel had been youngest commis in the very shop over which she now held sway, and the most devoted suitor in all her train. Even after his prowess in the black days of '71 had won him the attention of the civil authorities, and a grateful municipality had transformed the grocer-soldier into a guardian of law and order, he still hung upon the favour of his heart's first love, and only gave up the struggle when Jean-Baptiste bore off the prize and enthroned her in state as presiding genius of his newly acquired épicerie. Later, an unwittingly kindly prefect had transferred Abel to the seventeenth arrondissement, and so the old friendship was picked up where it had been dropped, and the ruddy-faced agent found it both convenient and agreeable to drop in frequently at Madame Caille's on his way home, and exchange a few words of reminiscence or banter for a box of sardines or a minute package of tea. But, with the deterioration in his old friends' wares, and the almost simultaneous appearance of the Salon Malakoff, his loyalty wavered. Flique sampled the advantages of Hippolyte's establishment, and, being won over thereby, returned again and again. His hearty laugh came to be heard almost daily in the salle de coiffure, and because he was a brave homme and a good customer, who did not stand upon a question of a few sous, but allowed Hippolyte to work his will, and trim and curl and perfume him to his heart's content, there was always a welcome for him, and a smile from Madame Sergeot, and occasionally a little present of brillantine or perfumery, for friendship's sake, and because it is well to have the good will of the all-powerful police.

From her window Madame Caille observed the comings and goings of Abel with a resentful eye. It was rarely now that he glanced into the épicerie as he passed, and still more rarely that he greeted his former flame with a stiff nod. Once she had hailed him from the doorway, sardines in hand, but he had replied that he was pressed for time, and had passed rapidly on. Then indeed did blackness descend upon the soul of Alexandrine, and in her deepest consciousness she vowed to have revenge. Neither the occasion nor the method was as yet clear to her, but she pursed her lips ominously, and bided her time.

In the existence of Madame Caille there was one emphatic consolation for all misfortunes, the which was none other than Zut, a white angora cat of surpassing beauty and prodigious size. She had come into Alexandrine's possession as a kitten, and, what with much eating and an inherent distaste for exercise, had attained her present proportions and her superb air of unconcern. It was from the latter that she derived her name, the which, in Parisian argot, at once means everything and nothing, but is chiefly taken to signify complete and magnificent indifference to all things mundane and material: and in the matter of indifference Zut was past mistress. Even for Madame Caille herself, who fed her with the choicest morsels from her own plate, brushed her fine fur with excessive care, and addressed caressing remarks to her at minute intervals throughout the day, Zut manifested a lack of interest that amounted to contempt. As she basked in the warm sun at the shop door, the round face of her mistress beamed upon her from the little desk, and the voice of her mistress sent fulsome flattery winging toward her on the heavy air. Was she beautiful, mon Dieu! In effect, all that one could dream of the most beautiful! And her eyes, of a blue like the heaven, were they not wise and calm? Mon Dieu, yes! It was a cat among thousands, a mimi almost divine.

Jean-Baptiste, appealed to for confirmation of these statements, replied that it was so. There was no denying that this was a magnificent beast. And of a chic. And caressing—(which was exaggeration). And of an affection—(which was doubtful). And courageous—(which was wholly untrue). Mazette, yes! A cat of cats! And was the boy to be the whole afternoon in delivering a cheese, he demanded of her? And Madame Caille would challenge him to ask her that—but it was a good, great beast all the same!—and so bury herself again in her accounts, until her attention was once more drawn to Zut, and fresh flattery poured forth. For all of this Zut cared less than nothing. In the midst of her mistress's sweetest cajolery, she simply closed her sapphire eyes, with an inexpressibly eloquent air of weariness, or turned to the intricacies of her toilet, as who should say: "Continue. I am listening. But it is unimportant."

But long familiarity with her disdain had deprived it of any sting, so far as Alexandrine was concerned. Passive indifference she could suffer. It was only when Zut proceeded to an active manifestation of ingratitude that she inflicted an irremediable wound. Returning from her marketing one morning, Madame Caille discovered her graceless favourite seated complacently in the doorway of the Salon Malakoff, and, in a paroxysm of indignation, bore down upon her, and snatched her to her breast.

"Unhappy one!" she cried, planting herself in full view of Espérance, and, while raining the letter of her reproach upon the truant, contriving to apply its spirit wholly to her neighbour. "What hast thou done? Is it that thou desertest me for strangers, who may destroy thee? Name of a name, hast thou no heart? They would steal thee from me—and above all, *now!* Well then, no! One shall see if such things are permitted! Vagabond!" And with this parting shot, which passed harmlessly over the head of the offender, and launched itself full at Madame Sergeot, the outraged épicière flounced back into her own domain, where, turning, she threatened the empty air with a passionate gesture.

"Vagabond!" she repeated. "Good-for-nothing! Is it not enough to have robbed me of my friends, that you must steal my child as well? We shall see!"—then, suddenly softening— "Thou art beautiful, and good, and wise. Mon Dieu, if I should lose thee, and above all, *now!*"

Now there existed a marked, if unvoiced, community of feeling between Espérance and her resentful neighbour, for the former's passion for cats was more consuming even than the latter's. She had long cherished the dream of possessing a white angora, and when, that morning, of her own accord, Zut stepped into the Salon Malakoff, she was received with demonstrations even warmer than those to which she had long since become accustomed. And, whether it was the novelty of her surroundings, or merely some unwonted instinct which made her unusually susceptible, her habitual indifference then and there gave place to animation, and her satisfaction was vented in her long, appreciative purr, wherewith it was not once a year that she vouchsafed to gladden her owner's heart. Espérance hastened to prepare a saucer of milk, and, when this was exhausted, added a generous portion of fish, and Zut then made a tour of the shop, rubbing herself against the chair legs, and receiving the homage of customers and duck-clad assistants alike. Flique, his ruddy face screwed into a mere knot of features, as Hippolyte worked violet hair tonic into his brittle locks, was moved to satire by the apparition.

"Tiens! It is with the cat as with the clients. All the world forsakes the Caille."

Strangely enough, the wrathful words of Alexandrine, as she snatched her darling from the doorway, awoke in the mind of Espérance her first suspicion of this smouldering resentment. Absorbed in the launching of her husband's affairs, and constantly employed in the making of change and with the keeping of her simple accounts, she had had no time to bestow upon her neighbours, and, even had her attention been free, she could hardly have been expected to deduce the rancour of Madame Caille from the evidence at hand. But even if she had been able to ignore the significance of that furious outburst at her very door, its meaning had not been lost upon the others, and her own half-formed conviction was speedily confirmed.

"What has she?" cried Hippolyte, pausing in the final stage of his operations upon the highly perfumed Flique.

"Do I know?" replied his wife with a shrug. "She thinks I stole her cat—*I!*"

"Quite simply, she hates you," put in Flique. "And why not? She is old, and fat, and her business is taking itself off, like that! You are young and"—with a bow, as he rose—"beautiful, and your affairs march to a marvel. She is jealous, c'est tout! It is a bad character, that."

"But, mon Dieu!"—

"But what does that say to you? Let her go her way, she and her cat. Au r'voir, 'sieurs, 'dame."

And, rattling a couple of sous into the little urn reserved for tips, the policeman took his departure, amid a chorus of "Merci, m'sieu', au r'voir, m'sieu'," from Hippolyte and his duck-clad aids.

But what he had said remained behind. All day Madame Sergeot pondered upon the incident of the morning and Abel Flique's comments thereupon, seeking out some more plausible reason for this hitherto unsuspected enmity than the mere contrast between her material conditions and those of Madame Caille seemed to her to afford. For, to a natural placidity of temperament, which manifested itself in a reluctance to incur the displeasure of anyone, had been lately added in Espérance a shrewd commercial instinct, which told her that the fortunes of the Salon Malakoff might readily be imperilled by an unfriendly tongue. In the quartier, gossip spread quickly and took deep root. It was quite imaginably within the power of Madame Caille to circulate such rumours of Sergeot dishonesty as should draw their lately won custom from them and leave but empty chairs and discontent where now all was prosperity and satisfaction.

Suddenly there came to her the memory of that visit which she had never returned. Mon Dieu! and was not that reason enough? She, the youngest patronne in the quartier, to ignore deliberately the friendly call of a neighbour! At least it was not too late to make amends. So, when business lagged a little in the late afternoon, Madame Sergeot slipped from her desk, and, after a furtive touch to her hair, went in next door to pour oil upon the troubled waters.

Madame Caille, throned at her counter, received her visitor with unexampled frigidity.

"Ah, it is you," she said. "You have come to make some purchases, no doubt."

"Eggs, madame," answered her visitor, disconcerted, but tactfully accepting the hint.

"The best quality—or—?" demanded Alexandrine, with the suggestion of a sneer.

"The best, evidently, madame. Six, if you please. Spring weather at last, it would seem."

To this generality the other made no reply. Descending from her stool, she blew sharply into a small paper bag, thereby distending it into a miniature balloon, and began selecting the eggs from a basket, holding each one to the light, and then dusting it with exaggerated care before placing it in the bag. While she was thus employed Zut advanced from a secluded corner, and, stretching her fore legs slowly to their utmost length, greeted her acquaintance of the morning with a yawn. Finding in the cat an outlet for her embarrassment, Espérance made another effort to give the interview a friendly turn.

"He is beautiful, madame, your matou," she said.

"It is a female," replied Madame Caille, turning abruptly from the basket, "and she does not care for strangers."

This second snub was not calculated to encourage neighbourly overtures, but Madame Sergeot had felt herself to be in the wrong, and was not to be so readily repulsed.

"We do not see Monsieur Caille at the Salon Malakoff," she continued. "We should be enchanted"—

"My husband shaves himself," retorted Alexandrine, with renewed dignity.

"But his hair"—ventured Espérance.

"*I* cut it!" thundered her foe.

Here Madame Sergeot made a false move. She laughed. Then, in confusion, and striving, too late, to retrieve herself— "Pardon, madame," she added, "but it seems droll to me, that. After all, ten sous is a sum so small"—

"All the world, unfortunately," broke in Madame Caille, "has not the wherewithal to buy mirrors, and pay itself frescoes and appareils antiseptiques! The eggs are twenty-four sous—but we do not pride ourselves upon our eggs. Perhaps you had better seek them elsewhere for the future!"

For sole reply Madame Sergeot had recourse to her expressive shrug, and then laying two francs upon the counter, and gathering up the sous which Alexandrine rather hurled at than handed her, she took her way toward the door with all the dignity at her command. But Madame Caille, feeling her snub to have been insufficient, could not let her go without a final thrust.

"Perhaps your husband will be so amiable as to shampoo my cat!" she shouted. "She seems to like your 'Salon'!"

But Espérance, while for concord's sake inclined to tolerate all rudeness to herself, was not prepared to hear Hippolyte insulted, and so, wheeling at the doorway, flung all her resentment into two words.

"Mal élevée!"

"Gueuse!" screamed Alexandrine from the desk. And so they parted.

Now, even at this stage, an armed truce might still have been preserved, had Zut been content with the evil she had wrought, and not thought it incumbent upon her further to embitter a quarrel that was a very pretty quarrel as it stood. But, whether it was that the milk and fish of the Salon Malakoff lay sweeter upon her memory than any of the familiar dainties of the épicerie Caille, or that, by her unknowable feline instinct, she was irresistibly drawn toward the scent of violet and lilac brillantine, her first visit to the Sergeot was soon repeated, and from this visit other visits grew, until it was almost a daily occurrence for her to saunter slowly into the salle de coiffure, and there receive the food and homage which were rendered as her undisputed due. For, whatever was the bitterness of Espérance toward Madame Caille, no part thereof descended upon Zut. On the contrary, at each visit her heart was more drawn toward the sleek angora, and her desire but strengthened to possess her peer. But white angoras are a luxury, and an expensive one at that, and, however prosperous the Salon Malakoff might be, its proprietors were not as yet in a position to squander eighty francs upon a whim. So, until profits should mount higher, Madame Sergeot was forced to content herself with the voluntary visits of her neighbour's pet.

Madame Caille did not yield her rights of sovereignty without a struggle. On the occasion of Zut's third visit, she descended upon the Salon Malakoff, robed in wrath, and found the adored one contentedly feeding on fish in the very bosom of the family Sergeot. An appalling scene ensued.

"If," she stormed, crimson of countenance, and threatening Espérance with her fist, "if you *must* entice my cat from her home, at *least* I will thank you not to give her food. I provide all that is necessary; and, for the rest, how do I know what is in that saucer?"

And she surveyed the duck-clad assistants and the astounded customers with tremendous scorn.

"You others," she added, "I ask you, is it just? These people take my cat, and feed her—*feed* her—with I know not what! It is overwhelming, unheard of —and, above all, *now!*"

But here the peaceful Hippolyte played trumps.

"It is the privilege of the vulgar," he cried, advancing, razor in hand, "when they are at home, to insult their neighbours, but here—no! My wife has told me of you and of your sayings. Beware! or I shall arrange your affair for you! Go! you and your cat!"

And, by way of emphasis, he fairly kicked Zut into her astonished owner's arms. He was magnificent, was Hippolyte!

This anecdote, duly elaborated, was poured into the ears of Abel Flique an hour later, and that evening he paid his first visit in many months to Madame Caille. She greeted him effusively, being willing to pardon all the past for the sake of regaining this powerful friend. But the glitter in the agent's eye would have cowed a fiercer spirit than hers.

"You amuse yourself," he said sternly, looking straight at her over the handful of raisins which she tendered him, "by wearying my friends. I counsel you to take care. One does not sell inferior eggs in Paris without hearing of it sooner or later. I know more than I have told, but not more than I *can* tell, if I choose."

"Our ancient friendship"—faltered Alexandrine, touched in a vulnerable spot.

"—preserves you thus far," added Flique, no less unmoved. "Beware how you abuse it!"

And so the calls of Zut were no longer disturbed.

But the rover spirit is progressive, and thus short visits became long visits, and finally the angora spent whole nights in the Salon Malakoff, where a box and a bit of carpet were provided for her. And one fateful morning the meaning of Madame Caille's significant words "and above all, *now!*" was made clear.

The prosperity of Hippolyte's establishment had grown apace, so that, on the morning in question, the three chairs were occupied, and yet other customers awaited their turn. The air was laden with violet and lilac. A stout chauffeur, in a leather suit, thickly coated with dust, was undergoing a shampoo at the hands of one of the duck-clad, and, under the skilfully plied razor of the other, the virgin down slid from the lips and chin of a slim and somewhat startled youth, while from a vaporizer Hippolyte played a fine spray of perfumed water upon the ruddy countenance of Abel Flique. It was an eloquent moment, eminently fitted for some dramatic incident, and that dramatic incident Zut supplied. She advanced slowly and with an air of conscious dignity from the corner where was her carpeted box, and in her mouth was a limp something, which, when deposited in the immediate centre of the Salon Malakoff, resolved itself into an angora kitten, as white as snow!

"Epatant!" said Flique, mopping his perfumed chin. And so it was.

There was an immediate investigation of Zut's quarters, which revealed four other kittens, but each of these was marked with black or tan. It was the flower of the flock with which the proud mother had won her public.

"And they are all yours!" cried Flique, when the question of ownership arose. "Mon Dieu, yes! There was such a case not a month ago, in the eighth arrondissement—a concierge of the avenue Hoche who made a contrary claim. But the courts decided against her. They are all yours, Madame Sergeot. My felicitations!"

Now, as we have said, Madame Sergeot was of a placid temperament which sought not strife. But the unprovoked insults of Madame Caille had struck deep, and, after all, she was but human.

So it was that, seated at her little desk, she composed the following masterpiece of satire:

CHÈRE MADAME,—We send you back your cat, and the others—all but one. One kitten was of a pure white, more beautiful even than its mother. As we have long desired a white angora, we keep this one as a souvenir of you. We regret that we do not see the means of accepting the kind offer you were so amiable as to make us. We fear that we shall not find time to shampoo your cat, as we shall be so busy taking care of our own. Monsieur Flique will explain the rest.

We pray you to accept, madame, the assurance of our distinguished consideration,

HIPPOLYTE AND ESPÉRANCE SERGEOT.

It was Abel Flique who conveyed the above epistle, and Zut, and four of Zut's kittens, to Alexandrine Caille, and, when that wrathful person would have rent him with tooth and nail, it was Abel Flique who laid his finger on his lip, and said,—

"Concern yourself with the superior kitten, madame, and I concern myself with the inferior eggs!"

To which Alexandrine made no reply. After Flique had taken his departure, she remained speechless for five consecutive minutes for the first time in the whole of her waking existence, gazing at the spot at her feet where sprawled the white angora, surrounded by her mottled offspring. Even when the first shock of her defeat had passed, she simply heaved a deep sigh, and uttered two words—

"Oh, *Zut!*"

The which, in Parisian argot, at once means everything and nothing.

The Afflictions of an English Cat

Honoré de Balzac

Translated by *Carl Van Vechten*

WHEN the report of your first meeting arrived in London, O! French Animals, it caused the hearts of the friends of Animal Reform to beat faster. In my own humble experience, I have so many proofs of the superiority of Beasts over Man that in my character of an English Cat I see the occasion, long awaited, of publishing the story of my life, in order to show how my poor soul has been tortured by the hypocritical laws of England. On two occasions, already, some Mice, whom I have made a vow to respect since the bill passed by your august parliament, have taken me to Colburn's, where, observing old ladies, spinsters of uncertain years, and even young married women, correcting proofs, I have asked myself why, having claws, I should not make use of them in a similar manner. One never knows what women think, especially the women who write, while a Cat, victim of English perfidy, is interested to say more than she thinks, and her profuseness may serve to compensate for what these ladies do not say. I am ambitious to be the Mrs. Inchbald of Cats and I beg you to have consideration for my noble efforts, O! French Cats, among whom has risen the noblest house of our race, that of Puss in Boots, eternal type of Advertiser, whom so many men have imitated but to whom no one has yet erected a monument.

I was born at the home of a parson in Catshire, near the little town of Miaulbury. My mother's fecundity condemned nearly all her infants to a cruel fate, because, as you know, the cause of the maternal intemperance of English cats, who threaten to populate the whole world, has not yet been decided. Toms and females each insist it is due to their own amiability and respective virtues. But impertinent observers have remarked that Cats in England are required to be so boringly proper that this is their only distraction. Others pretend that herein may lie concealed great questions of commerce and politics, having to do with the English rule of India, but these matters are not for my paws to write of and I leave them to the *Edinburgh-Review.* I was not drowned with the others on account of the whiteness of my robe. Also I was named Beauty. Alas! the parson, who had a wife and eleven daughters, was too poor to keep me. An elderly female noticed that I had an affection for the parson's Bible; I slept on it all the time, not because I was religious, but because it was the only clean spot I could find in the house. She believed, perhaps, that I belonged to the sect of sacred animals which had already furnished the she-ass of Balaam, and took me away with her. I was only two months old at this time. This old woman, who gave evenings for which she sent out cards inscribed *Tea and Bible,* tried to communicate to me the fatal science of the daughters of Eve. Her method, which consisted in delivering long lectures on personal dignity and on the obligations due the world, was a very successful one. In order to avoid these lectures one submitted to martyrdom.

One morning I, a poor little daughter of Nature, attracted by a bowl of cream, covered by a muffin, knocked the muffin off with my paw, and lapped the cream. Then in joy, and perhaps also on account of the weakness of my young organs, I delivered myself on the waxed floor to the imperious need which young Cats feel. Perceiving the proofs of what she called my intemperance and my faults of education, the old woman seized me and whipped me vigorously with a birchrod, protesting that she would make me a lady or she would abandon me.

"Permit me to give you a lesson in gentility," she said. "Understand, Miss Beauty, that English Cats veil natural acts, which are opposed to the laws of English respectability,

in the most profound mystery, and banish all that is improper,
applying to the creature, as you have heard the Reverend
Doctor Simpson say, the laws made by God for the creation.
Have you ever seen the Earth behave itself indecently?
Learn to suffer a thousand deaths rather than reveal your
desires; in this suppression consists the virtue of the saints.
The greatest privilege of Cats is to depart with the grace that
characterizes your actions, and let no one know where you
are going to make your little toilets. Thus you expose yourself only when you are beautiful. Deceived by appearances,
everybody will take you for an angel. In the future when
such a desire seizes you, look out of the window, give the
impression that you desire to go for a walk, then run to a
copse or to the gutter."

As a simple Cat of good sense, I found much hypocrisy in
this doctrine, but I was so young!

"And when I am in the gutter?" thought I, looking at the old
woman.

"Once alone, and sure of not being seen by anybody, well,
Beauty, you can sacrifice respectability with much more
charm because you have been discreet in public. It is in the
observance of this very precept that the perfection of the
moral English shines the brightest: they occupy themselves
exclusively with appearances, this world being, alas, only illusion and deception."

I admit that these disguises were revolting to all my animal
good sense, but on account of the whipping, it seemed prefer-
able to understand that exterior propriety was all that was
demanded of an English Cat. From this moment I accustomed myself to conceal the titbits that I loved under the bed.
Nobody ever saw me eat, or drink, or make my toilet. I was
regarded as the pearl of Cats.

Now I had occasion to observe those stupid men who are
called savants. Among the doctors and others who were
friends of my mistress, there was this Simpson, a fool, a son of
a rich landowner, who was waiting for a bequest, and who, to

deserve it, explained all animal actions by religious theories. He saw me one evening lapping milk from a saucer and complimented the old woman on the manner in which I had been bred, seeing me lick first the edges of the saucer and gradually diminish the circle of fluid.

"See," he said, "how in saintly company all becomes perfection: Beauty understands eternity, because she describes the circle which is its emblem in lapping her milk."

Conscience obliges me to state that the aversion of Cats to wetting their fur was the only reason for my fashion of drinking, but we will always be badly understood by the savants who are much more preoccupied in showing their own wit, than in discovering ours.

When the ladies or the gentlemen lifted me to pass their hands over my snowy back to make the sparks fly from my hair, the old woman remarked with pride, "You can hold her without having any fear for your dress; she is admirably well-bred!" Everybody said I was an angel; I was loaded with delicacies, but I assure you that I was profoundly bored. I was well aware of the fact that a young female Cat of the neighbourhood had run away with a Tom. This word, Tom, caused my soul a suffering which nothing could alleviate, not even the compliments I received, or rather that my mistress lavished on herself.

"Beauty is entirely moral; she is a little angel," she said. "Although she is very beautiful she has the air of not knowing it. She never looks at anybody, which is the height of a fine aristocratic education. When she does look at anybody it is with that perfect indifference which we demand of our young girls, but which we obtain only with great difficulty. She never intrudes herself unless you call her; she never jumps on you with familiarity; nobody ever sees her eat, and certainly that monster of a Lord Byron would have adored her. Like a tried and true Englishwoman she loves tea, sits, gravely calm, while the Bible is being explained, and thinks badly of nobody, a fact which permits one to speak freely before her. She is simple, without affectation, and has no desire for jewels. Give her a ring and she will not keep it. Finally, she does not imitate the vulgarity of the hunter. She loves her home and remains there so perfectly tranquil that at times you would believe that she was a mechanical Cat made at Birmingham or Manchester, which is the *ne plus ultra* of the finest education."

What these men and old women call education is the custom of dissimulating natural manners, and when they have completely depraved us they say that we are well-bred. One evening my mistress begged one of the young ladies to sing. When this girl went to the piano and began to sing I recognized at once an Irish melody that I had heard in my youth, and I remembered that I also was a musician. So I merged my voice with hers, but I received some raps on the head while she received compliments. I was revolted by this sovereign injustice and ran away to the garret. Sacred love of country! What a delicious night! I at last knew what the roof was. I heard Toms sing hymns to their mates, and these adorable elegies made me feel ashamed of the hypocrisies my mistress had forced upon me. Soon some of the Cats observed me and appeared to take offence at my presence, when a Tom with shaggy hair, a magnificent beard, and a fine figure, came to look at me and said to the company, "It's only a child!" At these condescending words, I bounded about on the tiles, moving with that agility which distinguishes us; I fell on my paws in that flexible fashion which no other animal knows how to imitate in order to show that I was no child. But these calineries were a pure waste of time. "When will someone serenade me?" I asked myself. The aspect of these haughty Toms, their melodies, that the human voice could never hope to rival, had moved me profoundly, and were the cause of my inventing little lyrics that I sang on the stairs. But an event of tremendous importance was about to occur which tore me violently from this innocent life. I went to London with a niece of my mistress, a rich heiress who adored me, who kissed me, caressed me with a kind of madness, and who pleased me so

much that I became attached to her, against all the habits of
our race. We were never separated and I was able to observe
the great world of London during the season. It was there that
I studied the perversity of English manners, which have
power even over the beasts, that I became acquainted with
that cant which Byron cursed and of which I am the victim as
well as he, but without having enjoyed my hours of leisure.

Arabella, my mistress, was a young person like many others
in England; she was not sure whom she wanted for a husband.
The absolute liberty that is permitted girls in choosing a husband drives them nearly crazy, especially when they recall that
English custom does not sanction intimate conversation after
marriage. I was far from dreaming that the London Cats had
adopted this severity, that the English laws would be cruelly
applied to me, and that I would be a victim of the court at the
terrible Doctors' Commons. Arabella was charming to all the
men she met, and every one of them believed that he was
going to marry this beautiful girl, but when an affair threatened to terminate in wedlock, she would find some pretext for
a break, conduct which did not seem very respectable to me.
"Marry a bow-legged man! Never!" she said of one. "As to that
little fellow he is snub-nosed." Men were all so much alike to
me that I could not understand this uncertainty founded on
purely physical differences.

Finally one day an old English Peer, seeing me, said to her:
"You have a beautiful Cat. She resembles you. She is white,
she is young, she should have a husband. Let me bring her a
magnificent Angora that I have at home."

Three days later the Peer brought in the handsomest Tom of
the Peerage. Puff, with a black coat, had the most magnificent
eyes, green and yellow, but cold and proud. The long silky hair
of his tail, remarkable for its yellow rings, swept the carpet.
Perhaps he came from the imperial house of Austria, because,
as you see, he wore the colours. His manners were those of a
Cat who had seen the court and the great world. His severity,
in the matter of carrying himself, was so great that he would

not scratch his head were anybody present. Puff had travelled on the continent. To sum up, he was so remarkably handsome that he had been, it was said, caressed by the Queen of England. Simple and naïve as I was I leaped at his neck to engage him in play, but he refused under the pretext that we were being watched. I then perceived that this English Cat Peer owed this forced and fictitious gravity that in England is called respectability to age and to intemperance at table. His weight, that men admired, interfered with his movements. Such was the true reason for his not responding to my pleasant advances. Calm and cold he sat on his unnamable, agitating his beard, looking at me and at times closing his eyes. In the society world of English Cats, Puff was the richest kind of catch for a Cat born at a parson's. He had two valets in his service; he ate from Chinese porcelain, and he drank only black tea. He drove in a carriage in Hyde Park and had been to parliament.

My mistress kept him. Unknown to me, all the feline population of London learned that Miss Beauty from Catshire had married Puff, marked with the colours of Austria. During the night I heard a concert in the street. Accompanied by my lord, who, according to his taste, walked slowly, I descended. We found the Cats of the Peerage, who had come to congratulate me and to ask me to join their Ratophile Society. They explained that nothing was more common than running after Rats and Mice. The words, shocking, vulgar, were constantly on their lips. To conclude, they had formed, for the glory of the country, a Temperance Society. A few nights later my lord and I went on the roof of Almack's to hear a grey Cat speak on the subject. In his exhortation, which was constantly supported by cries of "Hear! Hear!" he proved that Saint Paul in writing about charity had the Cats of England in mind. It was then the special duty of the English, who could go from one end of the world to the other on their ships without fear of the sea, to spread the principles of the *morale ratophile*. As a matter of fact English Cats were already preaching the doctrines of the Society, based on the hygienic discoveries of science.

When Rats and Mice were dissected little distinction could be found between them and Cats; the oppression of one race by the other then was opposed to the Laws of Beasts, which are stronger even than the Laws of Men. "They are our brothers," he continued. And he painted such a vivid picture of the suffering of a Rat in the jaws of a Cat that I burst into tears.

Observing that I was deceived by this speech, Lord Puff confided to me that England expected to do an immense trade in Rats and Mice; that if the Cats would eat no more, Rats would be England's best product; that there was always a practical reason concealed behind English morality; and that the alliance between morality and trade was the only alliance on which England really counted.

Puff appeared to me to be too good a politician ever to make a satisfactory husband.

A country Cat made the observation that on the continent, especially at Paris, near the fortifications, Tom Cats were sacrificed daily by the Catholics. Somebody interrupted with the cry of "Question!" Added to these cruel executions was the frightful slander of passing the brave animals off for Rabbits, a lie and a barbarity which he attributed to an ignorance of the true Anglican religion which did not permit lying and cheating except in the government, foreign affairs, and the cabinet.

He was treated as a radical and a dreamer. "We are here in the interests of the Cats of England, not in those of continental Cats!" cried a fiery Tory Tom. Puff went to sleep. Just as the assembly was breaking up a young Cat from the French embassy, whose accent proclaimed his nationality, addressed me these delicious words:

"Dear Beauty, it will be an eternity before Nature forms another Cat as perfect as you. The cashmere of Persia and the Indies is like camel's hair when it is compared to your fine and brilliant silk. You exhale a perfume which is the concentrated essence of the felicity of the angels, an odour I have detected in the salon of the Prince de Talleyrand, which I left to come to this stupid meeting. The fire of your eyes illuminates the night!

Your ears would be entirely perfect if they would listen to my supplications. There is not a rose in England as rose as the rose flesh which borders your little rose mouth. A fisherman would search in vain in the depths of Ormus for pearls of the quality of your teeth. Your dear face, fine and gracious, is the loveliest that England has produced. Near to your celestial robe the snow of the Alps would seem to be red. Ah! those coats which are only to be seen in your fogs! Softly and gracefully your paws bear your body which is the culmination of the miracles of creation, but your tail, the subtle interpreter of the beating of your heart, surpasses it. Yes! never was there such an exquisite curve, more correct roundness. No Cat ever moved more delicately. Come away from this old fool of a Puff, who sleeps like an English Peer in parliament, who besides is a scoundrel who has sold himself to the Whigs, and who, owing to a too long sojourn at Bengal, has lost everything that can please a Cat."

Then, without having the air of looking at him, I took in the appearance of this charming French Tom. He was a careless little rogue and not in any respect like an English Cat. His cavalier manner as well as his way of shaking his ear stamped him as a gay bachelor without a care. I avow that I was weary of the solemnity of English Cats, and of their purely practical propriety. Their respectability, especially, seemed ridiculous to me. The excessive naturalness of this badly groomed Cat surprised me in its violent contrast to all that I had seen in London. Besides my life was so strictly regulated, I knew so well what I had to count on for the rest of my days, that I welcomed the promise of the unexpected in the physiognomy of this French Cat. My whole life appeared insipid to me. I comprehended that I could live on the roofs with an amazing creature who came from that country where the inhabitants consoled themselves for the victories of the greatest English general by these words:

Malbrouk s'en va-t-en guerre,
Mironton, TON, TON, MIRONTAINE!

Nevertheless I awakened my lord, told him how late it was, and suggested that we ought to go in. I gave no sign of having listened to this declaration, and my apparent insensibility petrified Brisquet. He remained behind, more surprised than ever because he considered himself handsome. I learned later that it was an easy matter for him to seduce most Cats. I examined him through a corner of my eye: he ran away with little bounds, returned, leaping the width of the street, then jumped back again, like a French Cat in despair. A true Englishman would have been decent enough not to let me see how he felt.

Some days later my lord and I were stopping in the magnificent house of the old Peer; then I went in the carriage for a drive in Hyde Park. We ate only chicken bones, fish bones, cream, milk, and chocolate. However heating this diet might prove to others my so-called husband remained sober. He was respectable even in his treatment of me. Generally he slept from seven in the evening at the whist table on the knees of his Grace. On this account my soul received no satisfaction and I pined away. This condition was aggravated by a little affection of the intestines occasioned by pure herring oil (the Port Wine of English Cats), which Puff used, and which made me very ill. My mistress sent for a physician who had graduated at Edinburgh after having studied a long time in Paris. Having diagnosed my malady he promised my mistress that he would cure me the next day. He returned, as a matter of fact, and took an instrument of French manufacture out of his pocket. I felt a kind of fright on perceiving a barrel of white metal terminating in a slender tube. At the sight of this mechanism, which the doctor exhibited with satisfaction, Their Graces blushed, became irritable, and muttered several fine sentiments about the dignity of the English: for instance that the Catholics of old England were more distinguished for their opinions of this infamous instrument than for their opinions of the Bible. The Duke added that at Paris the French unblushingly made an exhibition of it in their national theatre in a comedy by Molière, but that in London a watchman would not dare pronounce its name.

"Give her some calomel."

"But Your Grace would kill her!" cried the doctor.

"The French can do as they like," replied His Grace. "I do not know, no more do you, what would happen if this degrading instrument were employed, but what I do know is that a true English physician should cure his patients only with the old English remedies."

This physician, who was beginning to make a big reputation, lost all his practice in the great world. Another doctor was called in, who asked me some improper questions about Puff, and who informed me that the real device of the English was: *Dieu et mon droit conjugal!*

One night I heard the voice of the French Cat in the street. Nobody could see us; I climbed up the chimney and, appearing on the housetop, cried, "In the rain trough!" This response gave him wings; he was at my side in the twinkling of an eye. Would you believe that this French Cat had the audacity to take advantage of my exclamation. He cried, "Come to my arms," daring to become familiar with me, a Cat of distinction, without knowing me better. I regarded him frigidly and, to give him a lesson, I told him that I belonged to the Temperance Society.

"I see, sir," I said to him, "by your accent and by the looseness of your conversation, that you, like all Catholic Cats, are inclined to laugh and make sport, believing that confession will purge you, but in England we have another standard of morality. We are always respectable, even in our pleasures."

This young Cat, struck by the majesty of English cant, listened to me with a kind of attention which made me hope I could convert him to Protestantism. He then told me in purple words that he would do anything I wished provided I would permit him to adore me. I looked at him without being able to reply because his very beautiful and splendid eyes sparkled like stars; they lighted the night. Made bold by my silence, he cried, "Dear Minette!"

"What new indecency is this?" I demanded, being well aware that French Cats are very free in their references.

Brisquet assured me that on the continent everybody, even the King himself, said to his daughter, *Ma petite Minette,* to show his affection, that many of the prettiest and most aristocratic young wives called their husbands, *Mon petit chat,* even when they did not love them. If I wanted to please him I would call him, *Mon petit homme!* Then he raised his paws with infinite grace. Thoroughly frightened I ran away. Brisquet was so happy that he sang *Rule Britannia,* and the next day his dear voice hummed again in my ears.

"Ah! you also are in love, dear Beauty," my mistress said to me, observing me extended on the carpet, the paws flat, the body in soft abandon, bathing in the poetry of my memories.

I was astonished that a woman should show so much intelligence, and so, raising my dorsal spine, I began to rub up against her legs and to purr lovingly with the deepest chords of my contralto voice.

While my mistress was scratching my head and caressing me and while I was looking at her tenderly a scene occurred in Bond Street which had terrible results for me.

Puck, a nephew of Puff's, in line to succeed him and who, for the time being, lived in the barracks of the Life Guards, ran into my dear Brisquet. The sly Captain Puck complimented the *attaché* on his success with me, adding that I had resisted the most charming Toms in England. Brisquet, foolish, vain Frenchman that he was, responded that he would be happy to gain my attention, but that he had a horror of Cats who spoke to him of temperance, the Bible, etc.

"Oh!" said Puck, "she talks to you then?"

Dear French Brisquet thus became a victim of English diplomacy, but later he committed one of these impardonable faults which irritate all well-bred Cats in England. This little idiot was truly very inconsistent. Did he not bow to me in Hyde Park and try to talk with me familiarly as if we were well acquainted? I looked straight through him coldly and severely.

The coachman seeing this Frenchman insult me slashed him with his whip. Brisquet was cut but not killed and he received the blow with such nonchalance, continuing to look at me, that I was absolutely fascinated. I loved him for the manner in which he took his punishment, seeing only me, feeling only the favour of my presence, conquering the natural inclination of Cats to flee at the slightest warning of hostility. He could not know that I came near dying, in spite of my apparent coldness. From that moment I made up my mind to elope. That evening, on the roof, I threw myself tremblingly into his arms.

"My dear," I asked him, "have you the capital necessary to pay damages to old Puff?"

"I have no other capital," replied the French Cat, laughing, "than the hairs of my moustache, my four paws, and this tail." Then he swept the gutter with a proud gesture.

"Not any capital," I cried, "but then you are only an adventurer, my dear!"

"I love adventures," he said to me tenderly. "In France it is the custom to fight a duel in the circumstances to which you allude. French Cats have recourse to their claws and not to their gold."

"Poor country," I said to him, "and why does it send beasts so denuded of capital to the foreign embassies?"

"That's simple enough," said Brisquet. "Our new government does not love money—at least it does not love its employees to have money. It only seeks intellectual capacity."

Dear Brisquet answered me so lightly that I began to fear he was conceited.

"Love without money is nonsense," I said. "While you were seeking food you would not occupy yourself with me, my dear."

By way of response this charming Frenchman assured me that he was a direct descendant of Puss in Boots. Besides he had ninety-nine ways of borrowing money and we would have, he said, only a single way of spending it. To conclude, he knew music and could give lessons. In fact, he sang to me, in poignant tones, a national romance of his country, *Au clair de la lune....*

At this inopportune moment, when seduced by his reasoning, I had promised dear Brisquet to run away with him as soon as he could keep a wife comfortably, Puck appeared, followed by several other Cats.

"I am lost!" I cried.

The very next day, indeed, the bench of Doctors' Commons was occupied by a *procès-verbal* in criminal conversation. Puff was deaf; his nephews took advantage of his weakness. Questioned by them, Puff said that at night I had flattered him by calling him, *Mon petit homme!* This was one of the most terrible things against me, because I could not explain where I had learned these words of love. The judge, without knowing it, was prejudiced against me, and I noted that he was in his second childhood. His lordship never suspected the low intrigues of which I was the victim. Many little Cats, who should have defended me against public opinion, swore that Puff was always asking for his angel, the joy of his eyes, his sweet Beauty! My own mother, come to London, refused to see me or to speak to me, saying that an English Cat should always be above suspicion, and that I had embittered her old age. Finally the servants testified against me. I then saw perfectly clearly how everybody lost his head in England. When it is a matter of a criminal conversation, all sentiment is dead; a mother is no longer a mother, a nurse wants to take back her milk, and all the Cats howl in the streets. But the most infamous thing of all was that my old attorney who, in his time, would believe in the innocence of the Queen of England, to whom I had confessed everything to the last detail, who had assured me that there was no reason to whip a Cat, and to whom, to prove my innocence, I avowed that I did not even know the meaning of the words, "criminal conversation" (he told me that the crime was so called precisely because one spoke so little while committing it), this attorney, bribed by Captain Puck, defended me so badly that my case appeared to be lost. Under these circumstances I went on the stand myself.

"My Lords," I said, "I am an English Cat and I am innocent. What would be said of the justice of old England if . . ."

Hardly had I pronounced these words than I was interrupted by a murmur of voices, so strongly had the public been influenced by the *Cat-Chronicle* and by Puck's friends.

"She questions the justice of old England which has created the jury!" cried some one.

"She wishes to explain to you, My Lords," cried my adversary's abominable lawyer, "that she went on the rooftop with a French Cat in order to convert him to the Anglican faith, when, as a matter of fact, she went there to learn how to say, *Mon petit homme,* in French, to her husband, to listen to the abominable principles of papism, and to learn to disregard the laws and customs of old England!"

Such piffle always drives an English audience wild. Therefore the words of Puck's attorney were received with tumultuous applause. I was condemned at the age of twenty-six months, when I could prove that I still was ignorant of the very meaning of the word, Tom. But from all this I gathered that it was on account of such practices that Albion was called Old England.

I fell into a deep miscathropy which was caused less by my divorce than by the death of my dear Brisquet, whom Puck had had killed by a mob, fearing his vengeance. Also nothing made me more furious than to hear the loyalty of English Cats spoken of.

You see, O! French Animals, that in familiarizing ourselves with men, we borrow from them all their vices and bad institutions. Let us return to the wild life where we obey only our instincts, and where we do not find customs in conflict with the sacred wishes of Nature. At this moment I am writing a treatise on the abuse of the working classes of animals, in order to get them to pledge themselves to refrain from turning spits, to refuse to allow themselves to be harnessed to carriages, in order, to sum up, to teach them the means of protecting themselves against the oppression of the grand aristocracy. Although we are celebrated for our scribbling I believe that Miss Martineau would not repudiate me. You know that on the continent literature has become the haven of all Cats who protest against the immoral monopoly of marriage, who resist the tyranny of institutions, and who desire to encourage natural laws. I have omitted to tell you that, although Brisquet's body was slashed with a wound in the back, the coroner, by an infamous hypocrisy, declared that he had poisoned himself with arsenic, as if so gay, so light-headed a Cat could have reflected long enough on the subject of life to conceive so serious an idea, and as if a Cat whom I loved could have the least desire to quit this existence! But with Marsh's apparatus spots have been found on a plate.

Gipsy
Booth Tarkington

O
N a fair Saturday afternoon in November Penrod's little
old dog Duke returned to the ways of his youth and had
trouble with a strange cat on the back porch. This indiscretion, so uncharacteristic, was due to the agitation of a surprised moment, for Duke's experience had inclined him to a
peaceful pessimism, and he had no ambition for hazardous
undertakings of any sort. He was given to musing but not to
avoidable action, and he seemed habitually to hope for something which he was pretty sure would not happen. Even in his
sleep, this gave him an air of wistfulness.

Thus, being asleep in a nook behind the metal refuse can,
when the strange cat ventured to ascend the steps of the
porch, his appearance was so unwarlike that the cat felt
encouraged to extend its field of reconnaissance—for the
cook had been careless, and the backbone of a three-pound
whitefish lay at the foot of the refuse can.

This cat was, for a cat, needlessly tall, powerful, independent, and masculine. Once, long ago, he had been a roly-poly
pepper-and-salt kitten; he had a home in those days, and a
name, "Gipsy," which he abundantly justified. He was precocious in dissipation. Long before his adolescence, his lack of
domesticity was ominous, and he had formed bad companionships. Meanwhile, he grew so rangy, and developed such
length and power of leg and such traits of character, that the
father of the little girl who owned him was almost convincing
when he declared that the young cat was half broncho and
half Malay pirate—though, in the light of Gipsy's later career,
this seems bitterly unfair to even the lowest orders of bronchos and Malay pirates.

No; Gipsy was not the pet for a little girl. The rosy hearth-stone and sheltered rug were too circumspect for him. Surrounded by the comforts of middle-class respectability, and profoundly oppressed, even in his youth, by the Puritan ideals of the household, he sometimes experienced a sense of suffocation. He wanted free air and he wanted free life; he wanted the lights, the lights, and the music. He abandoned the *bourgeoisie* irrevocably. He went forth in a May twilight, carrying the evening beefsteak with him, and joined the underworld.

His extraordinary size, his daring, and his utter lack of sympathy soon made him the leader—and, at the same time, the terror—of all the loose-lived cats in a wide neighbourhood. He contracted no friendships and had no confidants. He seldom slept in the same place twice in succession, and though he was wanted by the police, he was not found. In appearance he did not lack distinction of an ominous sort; the slow, rhythmic, perfectly controlled mechanism of his tail, as he impressively walked abroad, was incomparably sinister. This stately and dangerous walk of his, his long, vibrant whiskers, his scars, his yellow eye, so ice-cold, so fire-hot, haughty as the eye of Satan, gave him the deadly air of a mousquetaire duellist. His soul was in that walk and in that eye; it could be read—the soul of a bravo of fortune, living on his wits and his valour, asking no favours and granting no quarter. Intolerant, proud, sullen, yet watchful and constantly planning—purely a militarist, believing in slaughter as in a religion, and confident that art, science, poetry, and the good of the world were happily advanced thereby—Gipsy had become, though technically not a wildcat, undoubtedly the most untamed cat at large in the civilized world. Such, in brief, was the terrifying creature which now elongated its neck, and, over the top step of the porch, bent a calculating scrutiny upon the wistful and slumberous Duke.

The scrutiny was searching but not prolonged. Gipsy muttered contemptuously to himself, "Oh, sheol; I'm not afraid o' *that!*" And he approached the fish bone, his padded feet making no noise upon the boards. It was a desirable fish bone, large, with a considerable portion of the fish's tail still attached to it.

It was about a foot from Duke's nose, and the little dog's dreams began to be troubled by his olfactory nerve. This faithful sentinel, on guard even while Duke slept, signalled that alarums and excursions by parties unknown were taking place, and suggested that attention might well be paid. Duke opened one drowsy eye. What that eye beheld was monstrous.

Here was a strange experience—the horrific vision in the midst of things so accustomed. Sunshine fell sweetly upon porch and backyard; yonder was the familiar stable, and from its interior came the busy hum of a carpenter shop, established that morning by Duke's young master, in association with Samuel Williams and Herman. Here, close by, were the quiet refuse can and the wonted brooms and mops leaning against the latticed wall at the end of the porch, and there, by the foot of the steps, was the stone slab of the cistern, with the iron cover displaced and lying beside the round opening, where the carpenters had left it, not half an hour ago, after lowering a stick of wood into the water, "to season it." All about Duke were these usual and reassuring environs of his daily life, and yet it was his fate to behold, right in the midst of them, and in ghastly juxtaposition to his face, a thing of nightmare and lunacy.

Gipsy had seized the fish bone by the middle. Out from one side of his head, and mingling with his whiskers, projected the long, spiked spine of the big fish: down from the other side of that ferocious head dangled the fish's tail, and from above the remarkable effect thus produced shot the intolerable glare of two yellow eyes. To the gaze of Duke, still blurred by slumber, this monstrosity was all of one piece—the bone seemed a living part of it. What he saw was like those interesting insect faces which the magnifying glass reveals to great M. Fabre. It was impossible for Duke to maintain the philosophic calm of

M. Fabre, however; there was no magnifying glass between him and this spined and spiky face. Indeed, Duke was not in a position to think the matter over quietly. If he had been able to do that, he would have said to himself: "We have here an animal of most peculiar and unattractive appearance, though, upon examination, it seems to be only a cat stealing a fish bone. Nevertheless, as the thief is large beyond all my recollection of cats and has an unpleasant stare, I will leave this spot at once."

On the contrary, Duke was so electrified by his horrid awakening that he completely lost his presence of mind. In the very instant of his first eye's opening, the other eye and his mouth behaved similarly, the latter loosing upon the quiet air one shriek of mental agony before the little dog scrambled to his feet and gave further employment to his voice in a frenzy of profanity. At the same time the subterranean diapason of a demoniac bass viol was heard; it rose to a wail, and rose and rose again till it screamed like a small siren. It was Gipsy's war-cry, and, at the sound of it, Duke became a frothing maniac. He made a convulsive frontal attack upon the hobgoblin—and the massacre began.

Never releasing the fish bone for an instant, Gipsy laid back his ears in a chilling way, beginning to shrink into himself like a concertina, but rising amidships so high that he appeared to be giving an imitation of that peaceful beast, the dromedary. Such was not his purpose, however, for, having attained his greatest possible altitude, he partially sat down and elevated his right arm after the manner of a semaphore. This sema-phore arm remained rigid for a second, threatening; then it vibrated with inconceivable rapidity, feinting. But it was the treacherous left that did the work. Seemingly this left gave Duke three lightning little pats upon the right ear, but the change in his voice indicated that these were no love taps. He yelled "help!" and "bloody murder!"

Never had such a shattering uproar, all vocal, broken out upon a peaceful afternoon. Gipsy possessed a vocabulary for

cat-swearing certainly second to none out of Italy, and probably equal to the best there, while Duke remembered and
uttered things he had not thought of for years.

The hum of the carpenter shop ceased, and Sam Williams
appeared in the stable doorway. He stared insanely.

"My gorry!" he shouted. "Duke's havin' a fight with the biggest cat you ever saw in your life! C'mon!"

His feet were already in motion toward the battlefield, with
Penrod and Herman hurrying in his wake. Onward they sped,
and Duke was encouraged by the sight and sound of these
reinforcements to increase his own outrageous clamours and
to press home his attack. But he was ill-advised. This time it
was the right arm of the semaphore that dipped—and Duke's
honest nose was but too conscious of what happened in
consequence.

A lump of dirt struck the refuse-can with violence, and
Gipsy beheld the advance of overwhelming forces. They
rushed upon him from two directions, cutting off the steps of
the porch. Undaunted, the formidable cat raked Duke's nose
again, somewhat more lingeringly, and prepared to depart
with his fish bone. He had little fear for himself, because he
was inclined to think that, unhampered, he could whip anything on earth; still, things seemed to be growing rather warm
and he saw nothing to prevent his leaving.

And though he could laugh in the face of so unequal an
antagonist as Duke, Gipsy felt that he was never at his best or
able to do himself full justice unless he could perform that
feline operation inaccurately known as "spitting." To his
notion, this was an absolute essential to combat; but, as all cats
of the slightest pretensions to technique perfectly understand,
it can neither be well done nor produce the best effects unless
the mouth be opened to its utmost capacity so as to expose the
beginnings of the alimentary canal, down which—at least that
is the intention of the threat—the opposing party will soon be
passing. And Gipsy could not open his mouth without relin-
quishing his fish bone.

Therefore, on small accounts he decided to leave the field to his enemies and to carry the fish bone elsewhere. He took two giant leaps. The first landed him upon the edge of the porch. There, without an instant's pause, he gathered his fur-sheathed muscles, concentrated himself into one big steel spring, and launched himself superbly into space. He made a stirring picture, however brief, as he left the solid porch behind him and sailed upward on an ascending curve into the sunlit air. His head was proudly up; he was the incarnation of menacing power and of self-confidence. It is possible that the whitefish's spinal column and flopping tail had interfered with his vision, and in launching himself he may have mistaken the dark, round opening of the cistern for its dark, round cover. In that case, it was a leap calculated and executed with precision, for as the boys clamoured their pleased astonishment, Gipsy descended accurately into the orifice and passed majestically from public view, with the fish bone still in his mouth and his haughty head still high.

There was a grand splash!

The Blue Dryad
G. H. Powell

"ACCORDING to that theory"—said a critical friend, *à propos* of the last story but one—"susceptibility of 'discipline' would be the chief test of animal character, which means that the best dogs get their character from men. If so—"

"You pity the poor brutes?"

"Oh no. I was going to say that on that principle cats should have next to no character at all."

"They have plenty," I said, "but it's usually bad—at least hopelessly unromantic. Who ever heard of a heroic or self-denying cat? Cats do what they like, not what you want them to do."

He laughed. "Sometimes they do what you like very much. You haven't heard Mrs. Warburton-Kinneir's cat-story?"

"The Warburton-Kinneirs! I didn't know they were back in England."

"Oh yes. They've been six months in Hampshire, and now they are in town. She has Thursday afternoons."

"Good," I said, "I'll go the very next Friday, and take my chance. . . ."

Fortunately only one visitor appeared to tea. And as soon as I had explained my curiosity, he joined me in petitioning for the story which follows:—

Stoffles was her name, a familiar abbreviation, and Mephistophelian was her nature. She had all the usual vices of the feline tribe, including a double portion of those which men are so fond of describing as feminine. Vain, indolent, selfish, with a highly cultivated taste for luxury and neatness in her personal appearance, she was distinguished by all those little irritating habits and traits for which nothing but an affectionate heart (a thing in her case conspicuous by its absence) can atone.

It would be incorrect, perhaps, to say that Stoffles did not care for the society of my husband and myself. She liked the best of everything, and these our circumstances allowed us to give her. For the rest, though in kitten days suspected of having caught a mouse, she had never been known in after life to do anything which the most lax of economists could describe as useful. She would lie all day in the best armchair enjoying real or pretended slumbers, which never affected her appetite at supper-time; although in that eventide which is the feline morn she would, if certain of a sufficient number of admiring spectators, condescend to amuse their dull human intelligence by exhibitions of her dexterity. But she was soon bored, and had no conception of altruistic effort. Abundantly cautious and prudent in all matters concerning her own safety and comfort, she had that feline celerity of vanishing like air or water before the foot, hand, or missile of irritated man; while on the other hand, when a sensitive specimen of the gentler sex (my grandmother, for example) was attentively holding the door open for her, she would stiffen and elongate her whole body, and, regardless of all exhibitions of kindly impatience, proceed out of the drawing room as slowly as a funeral *cortège* of crocodiles.

A good-looking Persian cat is an ornamental piece of furniture in a house; but though fond of animals, I never succeeded in getting up an affection for Stoffles until the occurrence of the incident here to be related. Even in this, however, I cannot conceal from myself that the share which she took was taken, as usual, solely for her own satisfaction.

We lived, you know, in a comfortable old-fashioned house facing the highroad, on the slope of a green hill from which one looked across the gleaming estuary (or the broad mud-flats) of Southampton Water on to the rich, rolling woodland of the New Forest. I say *we*, but in fact for some months I had been alone, and my husband had just returned from one of his sporting and scientific expeditions in South America. He had already won fame as a naturalist, and had succeeded in bringing home alive quite a variety of beasts, usually of the reptile order, whose extreme rarity seemed to me a merciful provision of Nature.

But all his previous triumphs were completely eclipsed, I soon learned, by the capture, alive, on this last expedition, of an abominably poisonous snake, known to those who knew it as the Blue Dryad, or more familiarly in backwoods slang, as the Half-hour Striker, in vague reference to its malignant and fatal qualities. The time in which a snakebite takes effect is, by the way, no very exact test of its virulence, the health and condition not only of the victim, but of the snake, having of course to be taken into account.

But the Blue Dryad, sometimes erroneously described as a variety of rattlesnake, is, I understand, supposed to kill the average man, under favourable circumstances, in less time even than the deadly Copperhead—which it somewhat resembles, except that it is larger in size, and bears a peculiar streak of faint peacock-blue down the back, only perceptible in a strong light. This precious reptile was destined for the Zoological Gardens.

Being in extremely delicate health at the time, I need hardly say that I knew nothing of these gruesome details until afterwards. Henry (that is my husband), after entering my room with a robust and sunburned appearance that did my heart good, merely observed—as soon as we had exchanged greetings—that he had brought home a pretty snake which "wouldn't (just as long, that is to say, as it couldn't) do the slightest harm,"—an evasive assurance which I accepted as became the nervous wife of an enthusiastic naturalist. I believe I insisted on its not coming into the house.

The cook, indeed, on my husband expressing a wish to put it in the kitchen, had taken up a firmer position: she had threatened to "scream" if "the vermin" were introduced into her premises; which ultimatum, coming from a stalwart young woman with unimpaired lungs, was sufficient.

Fortunately the weather was very hot (being in July of the ever-memorable summer of 1893), so it was decided that the Blue Dryad, wrapped in flannel and securely confined in a basket, should be left in the sun, on the farthest corner of the veranda, during the hour or so in the afternoon when my husband had to visit the town on business.

He had gone off with a cousin of mine, an officer of Engineers in India, stationed, I think, at Lahore, and home on leave. I remember that they were a long time, or what seemed to me a long time, over their luncheon; and the last remark of our guest as he came out of the dining room remained in my head as even meaningless words will run in the head of any idle invalid shut up for most of the day in a silent room. What he said was, in the positive tone of one emphasizing a curious and surprising statement, "D'you know, by the way, it's the *one* animal that doesn't care a rap for the cobra." And, my husband seeming to express disbelief and a desire to change the subject as they entered my boudoir, "It's a holy fact! Goes for it, so smart! Has the beggar on toast before you can say 'Jack Robinson!'"

The observation did not interest me, but simply ran in my head. Then they came into my room, only for a few moments, as I was not to be tired. The Engineer tried to amuse Stoffles, who was seized with such a fit of mortal boredom that he transferred his attentions to Ruby, the Gordon setter, a devoted and inseparable friend of mine, under whose charge I was shortly left as they passed out of the house. The Lieutenant, it appears, went last, and inadvertently closed without fastening the veranda door. Thereby hangs a tale of the most trying quarter of an hour it has been my lot to experience.

I suppose I may have been asleep for ten minutes or so when I was awakened by the noise of Ruby's heavy body jumping out through the open window. Feeling restless and seeing me asleep, he had imagined himself entitled to a short spell off guard. Had the door not been ostensibly latched he would have made his way out by it, being thoroughly used to opening doors and such tricks—a capacity which in fact proved fatal to him. That it was unlatched I saw in a few moments, for the dog on his return forced it open with a push and trotted up in a disturbed manner to my bedside. I noticed a tiny spot of blood on the black side of his nose, and naturally supposed he had scratched himself against a bush or a piece of wire. "Ruby," I said, "what have you been doing?" Then he whined as if in pain, crouching close to my side and shaking in every limb. I should say that I was myself lying with a shawl over my feet on a deep sofa with a high back. I turned to look at Stoffles, who was slowly perambulating the room, looking for flies and other insects (her favourite amusement) on the wainscot. When I glanced again at the dog his appearance filled me with horror; he was standing, obviously from pain, swaying from side to side and breathing hard. As I watched, his body grew more and more rigid. With his eyes fixed on the half-open door, he drew back as if from the approach of some dreaded object, raised his head with a pitiful attempt at a bark, which broke off into a stifled howl, rolled over sideways suddenly, and lay dead. The horrid stiffness of the body, almost resembling a stuffed creature overset, made me believe that he had died as he stood, close to my side, perhaps meaning to defend me—more probably, since few dogs would be proof against such a terror, trusting that I should protect him against the *thing coming in at the door*. Unable to resist the unintelligible idea that the dog had been frightened to death, I followed the direction of his last gaze, and at first saw nothing. The next moment I observed round the corner of the veranda door a small, dark, and slender object, swaying gently up and down like a dry bough in the wind. It had passed right into the room with the same slow, regular motion before I realized what it was and what had happened.

My poor, stupid Ruby must have nosed at the basket on the verandah till he succeeded somehow in opening it, and have been bitten in return for his pains by the abominable beast which had been warranted in this insufficient manner to do no harm, and which I now saw angrily rearing its head and hissing fiercely at the dead dog within three yards of my face.

I am not one of those women who jump on chairs or tables when they see a mouse, but I have a constitutional horror of the most harmless reptiles. Watching the Blue Dryad as it glided across the patch of sunlight streaming in from the open window, and knowing what it was, I confess to being as nearly frightened out of my wits as I ever hope to be. If I had been well, perhaps I might have managed to scream and run away. As it was, I simply dared not speak or move a finger for fear of attracting the beast's attention to myself. Thus I remained a terrified spectator of the astonishing scene which followed. The whole thing seemed to me like a dream. As the beast entered the room, I seemed again to hear my cousin making the remark above mentioned about the cobra. *What* animal, I wondered dreamily, could he have meant? Not Ruby! Ruby was dead. I looked at his stiff body again and shuddered. The whistle of a train sounded from the valley below, and then an errand boy passed along the road at the back of the house (for the second or third time that day) singing in a cracked voice the fragment of a popular melody, of which I am sorry to say I know no more—

"I've got a little cat,
And I'm very fond of that;
But daddy wouldn't buy me a bow, wow, wow;"

the *wow-wows* becoming fainter and further as the youth strode down the hill. If I had been "myself," as the poor folk say, this coincidence would have made me laugh, for at that very moment Stoffles, weary of patting flies and spiders on the back, appeared gently purring on the crest, so to speak, of the sofa.

It has often occurred to me since that if the scale of things had been enlarged—if Stoffles, for example, had been a Bengal tiger, and the Dryad a boa constrictor or crocodile—the tragedy which followed would have been worthy of the pen of any sporting and dramatic historian. I can only say that, being transacted in such objectionable proximity to myself, the thing was as impressive as any combat of mastodon and iguanodon could have been to primitive man.

Stoffles, as I have said, was inordinately vain and self-conscious. Stalking along the top of the sofa back and bearing erect the bushy banner of her magnificent tail, she looked the most ridiculous creature imaginable. She had proceeded half-way on this pilgrimage towards me when suddenly, with the rapidity of lightning, as her ear caught the sound of the hiss and her eyes fell upon the Blue Dryad, her whole civilized "play-acting" demeanour vanished, and her body stiffened and contracted to the form of a watchful wild beast with the ferocious and instinctive antipathy to a natural enemy blazing from its eyes. No change of a shaken kaleidoscope could have been more complete or more striking. In one light bound she was on the floor in a compressed, defensive attitude, with all four feet close together, near, but not too near, the unknown but clearly hostile intruder; and to my surprise, the snake turned and made off towards the window. Stoffles trotted lightly after, obviously interested in its method of locomotion. Then she made a long arm and playfully dropped a paw upon its tail. The snake wriggled free in a moment, and coiling its whole length, some three and a half feet, fronted this new and curious antagonist.

At the very first moment, I need hardly say, I expected that one short stroke of that little pointed head against the cat's delicate body would quickly have settled everything. But one is apt to forget that a snake (I suppose because in romances snakes always "dart") can move but slowly and awkwardly over a smooth surface, such as a tiled or wooden floor. The long body, in spite of its wonderful construction, and of the attitudes in which it is frequently drawn, is no less subject to the laws of gravitation than that of a hedgehog. A snake that "darts" when it has nothing secure to hold on by, only overbalances itself. With half or two-thirds of the body firmly coiled against some rough object or surface, the head—of a poisonous snake at least—is indeed a deadly weapon of precision. This particular reptile, perhaps by some instinct, had now wriggled itself onto a large and thick fur rug about twelve feet square, upon which arena took place the extraordinary contest that followed.

The audacity of the cat astonished me from the first. I have no reason to believe she had ever seen a snake before, yet by a sort of instinct she seemed to know exactly what she was doing. As the Dryad raised its head, with glittering eyes and forked tongue, Stoffles crouched with both front paws in the air, sparring as I had seen her do sometimes with a large moth. The first round passed so swiftly that mortal eye could hardly see with distinctness what happened. The snake made a dart, and the cat, all claws, aimed two rapid blows at its advancing head. The first missed, but the second I could see came home, as the brute, shaking its neck and head, withdrew further into the jungle—I mean, of course, the rug. But Stoffles, who had no idea of the match ending in this manner, crept after it, with an air of attractive carelessness which was instantly rewarded. A full two feet of the Dryad's body straightened like a black arrow, and seemed to strike right into the furry side of its antagonist—seemed, I say, to slowgoing human eyes; but the latter shrank, literally *fell* back, collapsing with such suddenness that she seemed to have turned herself inside out, and become the mere skin of a cat. As the serpent recovered itself, she pounced on it like lightning, driving at least half a dozen claws well home, and then, apparently realizing that she had not a good enough hold, sprang lightly into the air from off the body, alighting about a yard off. There followed a minute of sparring in the air; the snake seemingly half afraid to strike, the cat waiting on its every movement.

Now, the poisonous snake when provoked is an irritable animal, and the next attack of the Dryad, maddened by the scratchings of puss and its own unsuccessful exertions, was so furious, and so close to myself, that I shuddered for the result. Before this stage, I might perhaps, with a little effort have escaped, but now panic fear glued me to the spot; indeed I could not have left my position on the sofa without almost treading upon Stoffles, whose bristling back was not a yard from my feet. At last, I thought—as the Blue Dryad, for one second coiled close as a black silk cable, sprang out the next as straight and sharp as the piston-rod of an engine—this lump of feline vanity and conceit is done for, and—I could not help thinking—it will probably be my turn next! Little did I appreciate the resources of Stoffles, who without a change in her vigilant pose, without a wink of her fierce green eyes, sprang backwards and upwards onto the top of me and there confronted the enemy as calm as ever, sitting, if you please, upon my feet! I don't know that any gymnastic performance ever surprised me more than this, though I have seen this very beast drop twenty feet from a windowsill onto a stone pavement without appearing to notice any particular change of level. Cats with so much plumage have probably their own reasons for not flying.

Trembling all over with fright, I could not but observe that she was trembling too—with rage. Whether instinct inspired her with the advantages of a situation so extremely unpleasant to me, I cannot say. The last act of the drama rapidly approached, and no more strategic catastrophe was ever seen.

For a snake, as everybody knows, naturally rears its head when fighting. In that position, though one may hit it with a stick, it is extremely difficult, as this battle had shown, to get hold of. Now, as the Dryad, curled to a capital S, quivering and hissing advanced for the last time to the charge, it was bound to strike across the edge of the sofa on which I lay, at the erect head of Stoffles, which vanished with a juggling celerity that would have dislocated the collarbone of any other animal in creation. From such an exertion the snake recovered itself with an obvious effort, quick beyond question, but not nearly quick enough. Before I could well see that it had missed its aim, Stoffles had launched out like a spring released, and, burying eight or ten claws in the back of its enemy's head, pinned it down against the stiff cushion of the sofa. The tail of the agonized reptile flung wildly in the air and flapped on the arched back of the imperturbable tigress. The whiskered muzzle of Stoffles dropped quietly, and her teeth met once, twice, thrice, like the needle and hook of a sewing-machine, in the neck of the Blue Dryad; and when, after much deliberation, she let it go, the beast fell into a limp tangle on the floor.

When I saw that the thing was really dead I believe I must have fainted. Coming to myself, I heard hurried steps and voices. "Great heavens!" my husband was screaming, "where has the brute got to?" "It's all right," said the Engineer; "just you come and look here, old man. Commend me to the coolness of that cat. After the murder of your priceless specimen, here's Stoffles cleaning her fur in one of her serenest Anglo-Saxon attitudes."

So she was. My husband looked grave as I described the scene. "Didn't I tell you so?" said the Engineer, "and this beast, I take it, is worse than any cobra."

I can easily believe he was right. From the gland of the said beast, as I afterwards learned, they extracted enough poison to be the death of twenty full-grown human beings.

Tightly clasped between its minute teeth was found (what interested me more) a few long hairs, late the property of Stoffles.

Stoffles, however—she is still with us—has a superfluity of long hair, and is constantly leaving it about.

Madame Jolicœur's Cat

Thomas A. Janvier

BEING somewhat of an age, and a widow of dignity—the late Monsieur Jolicœur has held the responsible position under Government of Ingénieur des Ponts et Chaussées—yet being also of a provocatively fresh plumpness, and a Marseillaise, it was of necessity that Madame Veuve Jolicœur, on being left lonely in the world save for the companionship of her adored Shah de Perse, should entertain expectations of the future that were antipodal and antagonistic: on the one hand, of an austere life suitable to a widow of a reasonable maturity and of an assured position; on the other hand, of a life, not austere, suitable to a widow still of a provocatively fresh plumpness and by birth a Marseillaise.

Had Madame Jolicœur possessed a severe temperament and a resolute mind—possessions inherently improbable, in view of her birthplace—she would have made her choice between these equally possible futures with a promptness and with a finality that would have left nothing at loose ends. So endowed, she would have emphasized her not excessive age by a slightly excessive gravity of dress and of deportment; and would have adorned it, and her dignified widowhood, by becoming dévote: and thereafter, clinging with a modest ostentation only to her piety, would have radiated, as time made its marches, an always increasingly exemplary grace. But as Madame Jolicœur did not possess a temperament that even bordered on severity, and as her mind was a sort that made itself up in at least twenty different directions in a single moment—as she was, in short, an entirely typical and therefore an entirely delightful Provençale—the situation was so much too much for her that, by the process of formulating a

124

great variety of irreconcilable conclusions, she left everything at loose ends by not making any choice at all.

In effect, she simply stood attendant upon what the future had in store for her: and meanwhile avowedly clung only, in default of piety, to her adored Shah de Perse—to whom was given, as she declared in disconsolate negligence of her still provocatively fresh plumpness, all of the bestowable affection that remained in the devastated recesses of her withered heart.

To preclude any possibility of compromising misunderstanding, it is but just to Madame Jolicœur to explain at once that the personage thus in receipt of the contingent remainder of her blighted affections—far from being, as his name would suggest, an Oriental potentate temporarily domiciled in Marseille to whom she had taken something more than a passing fancy—was a Persian superb black cat; and a cat of such rare excellencies of character and of acquirements as fully to deserve all of the affection that any heart of the right sort—withered, or otherwise—was disposed to bestow upon him.

Cats of his perfect beauty, of his perfect grace, possibly might be found, Madame Jolicœur grudgingly admitted, in the Persian royal catteries; but nowhere else in the Orient, and nowhere at all in the Occident, she declared with an energetic conviction, possibly could there be found a cat who even approached him in intellectual development, in wealth of interesting accomplishments, and, above all, in natural sweetness of disposition—a sweetness so marked that even under extreme provocation he never had been known to thrust out an angry paw. This is not to say that the Shah de Perse was a characterless cat, a lymphatic nonentity. On occasion—usually in connection with food that was distasteful to him—he could have his resentments; but they were manifested always with a dignified restraint. His nearest approach to ill-mannered abruptness was to bat with a contemptuous paw the offending morsel from his plate; which brusque act he followed by fixing upon the bestower of unworthy food a coldly, but always politely, contemptuous stare. Ordinarily, however, his displeasure—in the matter of unsuitable food, or in other matters—was exhibited by no more overt action than his retirement to a corner—he had his choices in corners, governed by the intensity of his feelings—and there seating himself with his back turned scornfully to an offending world. Even in his kindliest corner, on such occasions, the expression of his scornful back was as a whole volume of wingéd words!

But the rare little cat tantrums of the Shah de Perse—if to his so gentle excesses may be applied so strong a term—were but as sun-spots on the effulgence of his otherwise constant amiability. His regnant desires, by which his worthy little life was governed, were to love and to please. He was the most cuddlesome cat, Madame Jolicœur unhesitatingly asserted, that ever had lived; and he had a purr—softly thunderous and winningly affectionate—that was in keeping with his cuddlesome ways. When, of his own volition, he would jump into her abundant lap and go to burrowing with his little soft round head beneath her soft round elbows, the while gurglingly purring forth his love for her, Madame Jolicœur, quite justifiably, at times was moved to tears. Equally was his sweet nature exhibited in his always eager willingness to show off his little train of cat accomplishments. He would give his paw with a courteous grace to any lady or gentleman—he drew the caste line rigidly—who asked for it. For his mistress, he would spring to a considerable height and clutch with his two soft paws—never by any mistake scratching—her outstretched wrist, and so would remain suspended while he delicately nibbled from between her fingers her edible offering. For her, he would make an almost painfully real pretence of being a dead cat: extending himself upon the rug with an exaggeratedly death-like rigidity—and so remaining until her command to be alive again brought him briskly to rub himself, rising on his hind legs and purring mellowly, against her comfortable knees.

All of these interesting tricks, with various others that may be passed over, he would perform with a lively zest whenever set at them by a mere word of prompting; but his most notable trick was a game in which he engaged with his mistress not at word of command, but—such was his intelligence—simply upon her setting the signal for it. The signal was a close-fitting white cap—to be quite frank, a nightcap—that she tied upon her head when it was desired that the game should be played.

It was of the game that Madame Jolicœur should assume her cap with an air of detachment and aloofness: as though no such entity as the Shah de Perse existed, and with an insisted-upon disregard of the fact that he was watching her alertly with his great golden eyes. Equally was it of the game that the Shah de Perse should affect—save for his alert watching—a like disregard of the doings of Madame Jolicœur: usually by an ostentatious pretence of washing his upraised hind leg, or by a like pretence of scrubbing his ears. These conventions duly having been observed, Madame Jolicœur would seat herself in her especial easy chair, above the relatively high back of which her nightcapped head a little rose. Being so seated, always with the air of aloofness and detachment, she would take a book from the table and make a show of becoming absorbed in its contents. Matters being thus advanced, the Shah de Perse would make a show of becoming absorbed in searchings for an imaginary mouse—but so would conduct his fictitious quest for that supposititious animal as eventually to achieve for himself a strategic position close behind Madame Jolicœur's chair. Then, dramatically, the pleasing end of the game would come: as the Shah de Perse—leaping with the distinguishing grace and lightness of his Persian race—would flash upward and "surprise" Madame Jolicœur by crowning her white-capped head with his small black person, all a-shake with triumphant purrs! It was a charming little comedy—and so well undersood by the Shah de Perse that he never ventured to essay it under other, and more intimate, conditions of nightcap use; even as he never failed to engage in it with spirit when his white lure properly was set for him above the back of Madame Jolicœur's chair. It was as though to the Shah de Perse the

white nightcap of Madame Jolicœur, displayed in accordance
with the rules of the game, were an oriflamme: akin to, but in
minor points differing from, the helmet of Navarre.

Being such a cat, it will be perceived that Madame Jolicœur
had reason in her avowed intention to bestow upon him all of
the bestowable affection remnant in her withered heart's devastated recesses; and, equally, that she would not be wholly
desolate, having such a cat to comfort her, while standing
impartially attendant upon the decrees of fate.

To assert that any woman not conspicuously old and quite
conspicuously of a fresh plumpness could be left in any city
isolate, save for a cat's company, while the fates were spinning
new threads for her, would be to put a severe strain upon credulity. To make that assertion specifically of Madame Jolicœur,
and specifically—of all cities in the world!—of Marseille,
would be to strain credulity fairly to the breaking point. On
the other hand, to assert that Madame Jolicœur, in defence of
her isolation, was disposed to plant machine-guns in the doorway of her dwelling—a house of modest elegance on the Pavé
d'Amour, at the crossing of the Rue Bausset—would be to go
too far. Nor indeed—aside from the fact that the presence of
such engines of destruction would not have been tolerated by
the other residents of the quietly respectable Pavé d'Amour—
was Madame Jolicœur herself, as has been intimated, tem-
peramentally inclined to go to such lengths as machine-guns
in maintenance of her somewhat waveringly desired privacy in
a merely cat-enlivened solitude.

Between these widely separated extremes of conjectural
possibility lay the mediate truth of the matter: which truth—
thus resembling precious gold in its valueless rock matrix—lay
embedded in, and was to be extracted from, the irresponsible
utterances of the double row of loosely hung tongues, always
at hot wagging, ranged along the two sides of the Rue Bausset.

Madame Jouval, a milliner of repute—delivering herself
with the generosity due to a good customer from whom an

order for a trousseau was a not unremote possibility, yet with the acumen perfected by her professional experiences—summed her views of the situation, in talk with Madame Vic, proprietor of the Vic bakery, in these words: "It is of the convenances, and equally is it of her own melancholy necessities, that this poor Madame retires for a season to sorrow in a suitable seclusion in the company of her sympathetic cat. Only in such retreat can she give vent fitly to her desolating grief. But after storm comes sunshine: and I am happily assured by her less despairing appearance, and by the new mourning that I have been making for her, that even now, from the bottomless depth of her affliction, she looks beyond the storm."

"I well believe it!" snapped Madame Vic. "That the appearance of Madame Jolicœur at any time has been despairing is a matter that has escaped my notice. As to the mourning that she now wears, it is a defiance of all propriety. Why, with no more than that of colour in her frock"—Madame Vic upheld her thumb and finger infinitesimally separated—"and with a mere pin-point of a flower in her bonnet, she would be fit for the opera!"

Madame Vic spoke with a caustic bitterness that had its roots. Her own venture in second marriage had been catastrophic—so catastrophic that her neglected bakery had gone very much to the bad. Still more closely to the point, Madame Jolicœur—incident to finding entomologic specimens misplaced in her breakfast rolls—had taken the leading part in an interchange of incivilities with the bakery's proprietor, and had withdrawn from it her custom.

"And even were her mournings not a flouting of her short year of widowhood," continued Madame Vic, with an acrimony that abbreviated the term of widowhood most unfairly—"the scores of eligible suitors who openly come streaming to her door, and are welcomed there, are as trumpets proclaiming her audacious intentions and her indecorous desires. Even Monsieur Brisson is in that outrageous procession! Is it not enough that she should entice a repulsively bald-headed notary and an old rake of a major to make their brazen advances, without suffering this anatomy of a pharmacien to come treading on their heels?—he with his hands imbrued in the lifeblood of the unhappy old woman whom his mismade prescription sent in agony to the tomb! Pah! I have no patience with her! She and her grief and her seclusion and her sympathetic cat, indeed! It all is a tragedy of indiscretion— that shapes itself as a revolting farce!"

It will be observed that Madame Vic, in framing her bill of particulars, practically reduced her alleged scores of Madame Jolicœur's suitors to precisely two—since the bad third was handicapped so heavily by that notorious matter of the mismade prescription as to be a negligible quantity, quite out of the race. Indeed, it was only the preposterous temerity of Monsieur Brisson—despairingly clutching at any chance to retrieve his broken fortunes—that put him in the running at all. With the others, in such slighting terms referred to by Madame Vic—Monsieur Peloux, a notary of standing, and the Major Gontard, of the Twenty-ninth of the Line—the case was different. It had its sides.

"That this worthy lady reasonably may desire again to wed," declared Monsieur Fromagin, actual proprietor of the Épicerie Russe—an establishment liberally patronized by Madame Jolicœur—"is as true as that when she goes to make her choosings between these estimable gentlemen she cannot make a choice that is wrong."

Madame Gauthier, a clear-starcher of position, to whom Monsieur Fromagin thus addressed himself, was less broadly positive. "That is a matter of opinion," she answered; and added: "To go no further than the very beginning, Monsieur should perceive that her choice has exactly fifty chances in the hundred of going wrong: lying, as it does, between a meagre, sallow-faced creature of a death-white baldness, and a fine big pattern of a man, strong and ruddy, with a close-clipped but abundant thatch on his head, and a moustache that admittedly is superb!"

"Ah, there speaks the woman!" said Monsieur Fromagin, with a patronizing smile distinctly irritating. "Madame will recognize—if she will but bring herself to look a little beyond the mere outside—that what I have advanced is not a matter of opinion but of fact. Observe: Here is Monsieur Peloux—to whose trifling leanness and aristocratic baldness the thoughtful give no attention—easily a notary in the very first rank. As we all know, his services are sought in cases of the most exigent importance—"

"For example," interrupted Madame Gauthier, "the case of the insurance solicitor, in whose countless defraudings my own brother was a sufferer: a creature of a vileness, whose deserts were unnumbered ages of dungeons—and who, thanks to the chicaneries of Monsieur Peloux, at this moment walks free as air!"

"It is of the professional duty of advocates," replied Monsieur Fromagin, sententiously, "to defend their clients; on the successful discharge of that duty—irrespective of minor details—depends their fame. Madame neglects the fact that Monsieur Peloux, by his masterly conduct of the case that she specifies, won for himself from his legal colleagues an immense applause."

"The more shame to his legal colleagues!" commented Madame Gauthier curtly.

"But leaving that affair quite aside," continued Monsieur Fromagin airily, but with insistence, "here is this notable advocate who reposes his important homages at Madame Jolicœur's feet: he a man of an age that is suitable, without being excessive; who has in the community an assured position; whose more than moderate wealth is known. I insist, therefore, that should she accept his homages she would do well."

"And I insist," declared Madame Gauthier stoutly, "that should she turn her back upon the Major Gontard she would do most ill!"

"Madame a little disregards my premises," Monsieur Fromagin spoke in a tone of forbearance, "and therefore a little argues—it is the privilege of her sex—against the air. Distinctly, I do not exclude from Madame Jolicœur's choice that gallant Major: whose rank—now approaching him to the command of a regiment, and fairly equalling the position at the bar achieved by Monsieur Peloux—has been won, grade by grade, by deeds of valour in his African campaignings which have made him conspicuous even in the army that stands first in such matters of all the armies of the world. Moreover—although, admittedly, in that way Monsieur Peloux makes a better showing—he is of an easy affluence. On the Camargue he has his excellent estate in vines, from which comes a revenue more than sufficing to satisfy more than modest wants. At Les Martigues he has his charming coquette villa, smothered in the flowers of his own planting, to which at present he makes his agreeable escapes from his military duties; and in which, when his retreat is taken, he will pass softly his sunset years. With these substantial points in his favour, the standing of the Major Gontard in this matter practically is of a parity with the standing of Monsieur Peloux. Equally, both are worthy of Madame Jolicœur's consideration: both being able to continue her in the life of elegant comfort to which she is accustomed; and both being on a social plane—it is of her level accurately—to which the widow of an ingénieur des ponts et chaussées neither steps up nor steps down. Having now made clear, I trust, my reasonings, I repeat the proposition with which Madame took issue: When Madame Jolicœur goes to make her choosings between these estimable gentlemen she cannot make a choice that is wrong."

"And I repeat, Monsieur," said Madame Gauthier, lifting her basket from the counter, "that in making her choosings Madame Jolicœur either goes to raise herself to the heights of a matured happiness, or to plunge herself into bald-headed abysses of despair. Yes, Monsieur, that far apart are her choosings!" And Madame Gauthier added, in communion with herself as she passed to the street with her basket: "As for me, it would be that adorable Major by a thousand times!"

As was of reason, since hers was the first place in the matter, Madame Jolicœur herself carried on debatings—in the portion of her heart that had escaped complete devastation—identical in essence with the debatings of her case which went up and down the Rue Bausset.

Not having become dévote—in the year and more of opportunity open to her for a turn in that direction—one horn of her original dilemma had been eliminated, so to say, by atrophy. Being neglected, it had withered: with the practical result that out of her very indecisions had come a decisive choice. But to her new dilemma, of which the horns were the Major and the Notary—in the privacy of her secret thoughts she made no bones of admitting that this dilemma confronted her—the atrophying process was not applicable; at least, not until it could be applied with a sharp finality. Too long dallied with, it very well might lead to the atrophy of both of them in dudgeon; and thence onward, conceivably, to her being left to cling only to the Shah de Perse for all the remainder of her days.

Therefore, to the avoidance of that too radical conclusion, Madame Jolicœur engaged in her debatings briskly: offering to herself, in effect, the balanced arguments advanced by Monsieur Fromagin in favour equally of Monsieur Peloux and of the Major Gontard; taking as her own, with moderating exceptions and emendations, the views of Madame Gauthier as to the meagreness and pallid baldness of the one and the sturdiness and gallant bearing of the other; considering, from the standpoint of her own personal knowledge in the premises, the Notary's disposition toward a secretive reticence that bordered upon severity, in contrast with the cordially frank and debonair temperament of the Major; and, at the back of all, keeping well in mind the fundamental truths that opportunity ever is evanescent and that time ever is on the wing.

As the result of her debatings, and not less as the result of experience gained in her earlier campaigning, Madame Jolicœur took up a strategic position nicely calculated to inflame the desire for, by assuming the uselessness of, an assault. In set terms, confirming particularly her earlier and more general avowal, she declared equally to the Major and to the Notary that absolutely the whole of her bestowable affection—of the remnant in her withered heart available for distribution—was bestowed upon the Shah de Perse: and so, with an alluring nonchalance, left them to draw the logical conclusion that their strivings to win that desirable quantity were idle—since a definite disposition of it already had been made.

The reply of the Major Gontard to this declaration was in keeping with his known amiability, but also was in keeping with his military habit of command. "Assuredly," he said, "Madame shall continue to bestow, within reason, her affections upon Monsieur le Shah; and with them that brave animal—he is a cat of ten thousand—shall have my affections as well. Already, knowing my feeling for him, we are friends— as Madame shall see to her own convincing," Addressing himself in tones of kindly persuasion to the Shah de Perse, he added: "Viens, Monsieur!"—whereupon the Shah de Perse instantly jumped himself to the Major's knee and broke forth, in response to a savant rubbing of his soft little jowls, into his gurgling purr. "Voilà, Madame!" continued the Major. "It is to be perceived that we have our good understandings, the Shah de Perse and I. That we all shall live happily together tells itself without words. But observe"—of a sudden the voice of the Major thrilled with a deep earnestness, and his style of address changed to a familiarity that only the intensity of his feeling condoned—"I am resolved that to me, above all, shall be given thy dear affections. Thou shalt give me the perfect flower of them—of that fact rest thou assured. In thy heart I am to be the very first—even as in my heart thou thyself art the very first of all the world. In Africa I have had my successes in my conquests and holdings of fortresses. Believe me, I shall have an equal success in conquering and in holding the sweetest fortress in France!"

Certainly, the Major Gontard had a bold way with him. But that it had its attractions, not to say its compellings, Madame Jolicœur could not honestly deny.

On the part of the Notary—whose disposition, fostered by his profession, was toward subtlety rather than toward boldness—Madame Jolicœur's declaration of cat rights was received with no such belligerent blare of trumpets and beat of drums. He met it with a light show of banter—beneath which, to come to the surface later, lay hidden dark thoughts.

"Madame makes an excellent pleasantry," he said with a smile of the blandest. "Without doubt, not a very flattering pleasantry—but I know that her denial of me in favour of her cat is but a jesting at which we both may laugh. And we may laugh together the better because, in the roots of her jesting, we have our sympathies. I also have an intensity of affection for cats"—to be just to Monsieur Peloux, who loathed cats, it must be said that he gulped as he made this flagrantly untruthful statement—"and with this admirable cat, so dear to Madame, it goes to make itself that we speedily become enduring friends."

Curiously enough—a mere coincidence, of course—as the Notary uttered these words so sharply at points with veracity, in the very moment of them, the Shah de Perse stiffly retired into his sulkiest corner and turned what had every appearance of being a scornful back upon the world.

Judiciously ignoring this inopportunely equivocal incident, Monsieur Peloux reverted to the matter in chief and concluded his deliverance in these words: "I well understand, I repeat, that Madame for the moment makes a comedy of herself and of her cat for my amusing. But I persuade myself that her droll fancyings will not be lasting, and that she will be serious with me in the end. Until then—and then most of all—I am at her feet humbly: an unworthy, but a very earnest, suppliant for her goodwill. Should she have the cruelty to refuse my supplication, it will remain with me to die in an unmerited despair!"

Certainly, this was an appeal—of a sort. But even without perceiving the mitigating subtlety of its comminative final clause—so skilfully worded as to leave Monsieur Peloux free to bring off his threatened unmeritedly despairing death quite at his own convenience—Madame Jolicœur did not find it satisfying. In contrast with the Major Gontard's ringingly audacious declarations of his habits in dealing with fortresses, she felt that it lacked force. And, also—this, of course, was a sheer weakness—she permitted herself to be influenced appreciably by the indicated preferences of the Shah de Perse: who had jumped to the knee of the Major with an affectionate alacrity; and who undeniably had turned on the Notary—either by chance or by intention—a back of scorn.

As the general outcome of these several developments, Madame Jolicœur's debatings came to have in them—if I so may state the trend of her mental activities—fewer bald heads and more moustaches; and her never severely set purpose to abide in a loneliness relieved only by the Shah de Perse was abandoned root and branch.

While Madame Jolicœur continued her debatings—which, in their modified form, manifestly were approaching her to conclusions—water was running under bridges elsewhere.

In effect, her hesitancies produced a period of suspense that gave opportunity for, and by the exasperating delay of it stimulated, the resolution of the Notary's dark thoughts into darker deeds. With reason, he did not accept at its face value Madame Jolicœur's declaration touching the permanent bestowal of her remnant affections; but he did believe that there was enough in it to make the Shah de Perse a delaying obstacle to his own acquisition of them. When obstacles got in this gentleman's way it was his habit to kick them out of it—a habit that had not been unduly stunted by half a lifetime of successful practice at the criminal bar.

Because of his professional relations with them, Monsieur Peloux had an extensive acquaintance among criminals of varying shades of intensity—at times, in his dubious doings, they could be useful to him—hidden away in the shadowy nooks and corners of the city; and he also had his emissaries through whom they could be reached. All the conditions thus standing attendant upon his convenience, it was a facile matter for him to make an appointment with one of these disreputables at a cabaret of bad record in the Quartier de la Tourette: a region—bordering upon the north side of the Vieux Port— that is at once the oldest and the foulest quarter of Marseille.

In going to keep this appointment—as was his habit on such occasions, in avoidance of possible spying upon his movements—he went deviously: taking a cab to the Bassin de Carènage, as though some maritime matter engaged him, and thence making the transit of the Vieux Port in a bateau mouche. It was while crossing in the ferryboat that a sudden shuddering beset him: as he perceived with horror—but without repentance—the pit into which he descended. In his previous, always professional, meetings with criminals his position had been that of unassailable dominance. In his pending meeting—since he himself would be not only a criminal but an inciter to crime—he would be, in the essence of the matter, the under dog. Beneath his seemly black hat his bald head went whiter than even its normal deathly whiteness, and perspiration started from its every pore. Almost with a groan, he removed his hat and dried with his handkerchief what were in a way his tears of shame.

Over the interview between Monsieur Peloux and his hireling—cheerfully moistened, on the side of the hireling, with absinthe of a vileness in keeping with its place of purchase— decency demands the partial drawing of a veil. In brief, Monsieur Peloux—his guilty eyes averted, the shame-tears streaming afresh from his bald head—presented his criminal demand and stated the sum that he would pay for its gratification. This sum—being in keeping with his own estimate of what it paid for—was so much in excess of the hireling's views concerning the value of a mere cat-killing that he fairly jumped at it.

"Be not disturbed, Monsieur!" he replied, with the fervour of one really grateful, and with the expansive extravagance of a Marseillais keyed up with exceptionally bad absinthe. "Be not disturbed in the smallest! In this very coming moment this camel of a cat shall die a thousand deaths; and in but another moment immeasurable quantities of salt and ashes shall obliterate his justly despicable grave! To an instant accomplishment of Monsieur's wishes I pledge wholeheartedly the word of an honest man."

Actually—barring the number of deaths to be inflicted on the Shah de Perse, and the needlessly defiling concealment of his burial-place—this radical treatment of the matter was precisely what Monsieur Peloux desired; and what, in terms of innuendo and euphuism, he had asked for. But the brutal frankness of the hireling, and his evident delight in sinning for good wages, came as an arousing shock to the enfeebled remnant of the Notary's better nature—with a resulting vacillation of purpose to which he would have risen superior had he been longer habituated to the ways of crime.

"No! No!" he said weakly. "I did not mean that—by no means all of that. At least—that is to say—you will understand me, my good man, that enough will be done if you remove the cat from Marseille. Yes, that is what I mean—take it somewhere. Take it to Cassis, to Aries, to Avignon—where you will—and leave it there. The railway ticket is my charge—and, also, you have an extra napoleon for your refreshment by the way. Yes, that suffices. In a bag, you know—and soon!"

Returning across the Vieux Port in the bateau mouche, Monsieur Peloux no longer shuddered in dread of crime to be committed—his shuddering was for accomplished crime. On his bald head, unheeded, the gushing tears of shame accumulated in pools.

When leaves of absence permitted him to make retirements to his coquette little estate at Les Martigues, the Major Gontard was as another Cincinnatus: with the minor differences that the lickerish cookings of the brave Marthe—his old femme de ménage: a veritable protagonist among cooks, even in Provence—checked him on the side of severe simplicity; that he would have welcomed with effusion lictors, or others, come to announce his advance to a regiment; and that he made no use whatever of a plow.

In the matter of the plow, he had his excuses. His two or three acres of land lay on a hillside banked in tiny terraces—quite unsuited to the use of that implement—and the whole of his agricultural energies were given to the cultivation of flowers. Among his flowers, intelligently assisted by old Michel, he worked with a zeal bred of his affection for them; and after his workings, when the cool of evening was come, smoked his pipe refreshingly while seated on the vine-bowered estrade before his trim villa on the crest of the slope: the while sniffing with a just interest at the fumes of old Marthe's cookings, and placidly delighting in the ever-new beauties of the sunsets above the distant mountains and their nearby reflected beauties in the waters of the Étang de Berre.

Save in his professional relations with recalcitrant inhabitants of Northern Africa, he was of a gentle nature, this amiable warrior: ever kindly, when kindliness was deserved, in all his dealings with mankind. Equally, his benevolence was extended to the lower orders of animals—that it was understood, and reciprocated, the willing jumping of the Shah de Perse to his friendly knee made manifest—and was exhibited in practical ways. Naturally, he was a liberal contributor to the funds of the Société protectrice des animaux; and, what was more to the purpose, it was his well-rooted habit to do such protecting as was necessary, on his own account, when he chanced upon any suffering creature in trouble or in pain.

Possessing these commendable characteristics, it follows that the doings of the Major Gontard in the railway station at Pas de Lanciers—on the day sequent to the day on which Monsieur Peloux was the promoter of a criminal conspiracy—could not have been other than they were. Equally does it follow that his doings produced the doings of the man with the bag.

Pas de Lanciers is the little station at which one changes trains in going from Marseille to Les Martigues. Descending from a first-class carriage, the Major Gontard awaited the Martigues train—his leave was for two days, and his thoughts were engaged pleasantly with the breakfast that old Marthe would have ready for him and with plans for his flowers. From a third-class carriage descended the man with the bag, who also awaited the Martigues train. Presently—the two happening to come together in their saunterings up and down the platform—the Major's interest was aroused by observing that within the bag went on a persistent wriggling; and his interest was quickened into characteristic action when he heard from its interior, faintly but quite distinctly, a very pitiful half-strangled little mew!

"In another moment," said the Major, addressing the man sharply, "that cat will be suffocated. Open the bag instantly and give it air!"

"Pardon, Monsieur," replied the man, starting guiltily. "This excellent cat is not suffocating. In the bag it breathes freely with all its lungs. It is a pet cat, having the habitude to travel in this manner; and, because it is of a friendly disposition, it is accustomed thus to make its cheerful little remarks." By way of comment upon this explanation, there came from the bag another half-strangled mew that was not at all suggestive of cheerfulness. It was a faint miserable mew—that told of cat despair!

At that juncture a down train came in on the other side of the platform, a train on its way to Marseille.

"Thou art a brute!" said the Major, tersely. "I shall not suffer thy cruelties to continue!" As he spoke, he snatched away the bag from its uneasy possessor and applied himself to untying its confining cord. Oppressed by the fear that goes with evil-doing, the man hesitated for a moment before attempting to retrieve what constructively was his property.

In that fateful moment the bag opened and a woebegone little black cat-head appeared; and then the whole of a delighted little black cat-body emerged—and cuddled with joy-purrs of recognition in its deliverer's arms! Within the sequent instant the recognition was mutual. "Thunder of guns!" cried the Major. "It is the Shah de Perse!"

Being thus caught red-handed, the hireling of Monsieur Peloux cowered. "Brigand!" continued the Major. "Thou hast ravished away this charming cat by the foulest of robberies. Thou art worse than the scum of Arab camp-followings. And if I had thee to myself, over there in the desert," he added grimly, "thou shouldst go the same way!"

All overawed by the Major's African attitude, the hireling took to whining. "Monsieur will believe me when I tell him that I am but an unhappy tool—I, an honest man whom a rich tempter, taking advantage of my unmerited poverty, has betrayed into crime. Monsieur himself shall judge me when I have told him all!" And then—with creditably imaginative variations on the theme of a hypothetical dying wife in combination with six supposititious starving children—the man came close enough to telling all to make clear that his backer in cat-stealing was Monsieur Peloux!

With a gasp of astonishment, the Major again took the word. "What matters it, animal, by whom thy crime was prompted? Thou art the perpetrator of it—and to thee comes punishment! Shackles and prisons are in store for thee! I shall—"

But what the Major Gontard had in mind to do toward assisting the march of retributive justice is immaterial—since he did not do it. Even as he spoke—in these terms of doom that qualifying conditions rendered doomless—the man suddenly dodged past him, bolted across the platform, jumped to the foot-board of a carriage of the just-starting train, cleverly bundled himself through an open window, and so was gone: leaving the Major standing lonely, with impotent rage filling his heart, and with the Shah de Perse all a purring cuddle in his arms!

Acting on a just impulse, the Major Gontard sped to the telegraph office. Two hours must pass before he could follow the miscreant; but the departed train ran express to Marseille, and telegraphic heading-off was possible. To his flowers, and to the romance of a breakfast that old Marthe by then was in the very act of preparing for him, his thoughts went in bitter relinquishment: but his purpose was stern! Plumping the Shah de Perse down anyway on the telegraph table, and seizing a pen fiercely, he began his writings. And then, of a sudden, an inspiration came to him that made him stop in his writings—and that changed his flames of anger into flames of joy.

His first act under the influence of this new and better emotion was to tear his half-finished dispatch into fragments. His second act was to assuage the needs, physical and psychical, of the Shah de Perse—near to collapse for lack of food and drink, and his little cat feelings hurt by his brusque deposition on the telegraph table—by carrying him tenderly to the buffet; and there—to the impolitely over-obvious amusement of the buffetière—purchasing cream without stint for the allaying of his famishings. To his feasting the Shah de Perse went with the avid energy begotten of his bag-compelled long fast. Dipping his little red tongue deep into the saucer, he lapped with a vigour that all cream-splattered his little black nose. Yet his admirable little cat manners were not forgotten: even in the very thick of his eager lappings—pathetically eager, in view of the cause of them—he purred forth gratefully, with a gurgling chokiness, his earnest little cat thanks.

As the Major Gontard watched this pleasing spectacle his heart was all aglow within him and his face was of a radiance comparable only with that of an Easter-morning sun. To himself he was saying: "It is a dream that has come to me! With the disgraced enemy in retreat, and with the Shah de Perse for my banner, it is that I hold victoriously the whole universe in the hollow of my hand!"

While stopping appreciably short of claiming for himself a clutch upon the universe, Monsieur Peloux also had his satisfactions on the evening of the day that had witnessed the enlévement of the Shah de Perse. By his own eyes he knew certainly that that iniquitous kidnapping of a virtuous cat had been effected. In the morning the hireling had brought to him in his private office the unfortunate Shah de Perse—all unhappily bagged, and even then giving vent to his pathetic complainings—and had exhibited him, as a pièce justificatif, when making his demand for railway fare and the promised extra napoleon. In the mid-afternoon the hireling had returned, with the satisfying announcement that all was accomplished: that he had carried the cat to Pas de Landers, of an adequate remoteness, and there had left him with a person in need of a cat who received him willingly. Being literally true, this statement had in it so convincing a ring of sincerity that Monsieur Peloux paid down in full the blood money and dismissed his bravo with commendation. Thereafter, being alone, he rubbed his hands— gladly thinking of what was in the way to happen in sequence to the permanent removal of this cat stumbling block from his path. Although professionally accustomed to consider the possibilities of permutation, the known fact that petards at times are retroactive did not present itself to his mind.

And yet—being only an essayist in crime, still unhardened— certain compunctions beset him as he approached himself, on the to-be eventful evening of that eventful day, to the door of Madame Jolicœur's modestly elegant dwelling on the Pavé d'Amour. In the back of his head were justly self-condemnatory thoughts, to the general effect that he was a blackguard and deserved to be kicked. In the dominant front of his head, how- ever, were thoughts of a more agreeable sort: of how he would find Madame Jolicœur all torn and rent by the bitter sorrow of her bereavement; of how he would pour into her harried heart a flood of sympathy by which that injured organ would be soothed and mollified; of how she would be lured along gently to requite his tender condolence with a softening gratitude— that presently would merge easily into the yet softer phrase of love! It was a well-made program, and it had its kernel of rea- son in his recognized ability to win bad causes—as that of the insurance solicitor—by emotional pleadings which in the same breath lured to lenience and made the intrinsic demerits of the cause obscure.

"Madame dines," was the announcement that met Monsieur Peloux when, in response to his ring, Madame Jolicœur's door was opened for him by a trim maidservant. "But Madame already has continued so long her dining," added the maid-servant, with a glint in her eyes that escaped his preoccupied attention, "that in but another instant must come the end. If M'sieu' will have the amiability to await her in the salon, it will be for but a point of time!"

Between this maidservant and Monsieur Peloux no love was lost. Instinctively he was aware of, and resented, her views—practically identical with those expressed by Madame Gauthier to Monsieur Fromagin—touching his deserts as compared with the deserts of the Major Gontard. Moreover, she had personal incentives to take her revenges. From Monsieur Peloux, her only vail had been a miserable two-franc Christmas box. From the Major, as from a perpetually verdant Christmas tree, boxes of bonbons and five-franc pieces at all times descended upon her in showers.

Without perceiving the curious smile that accompanied this young person's curiously cordial invitation to enter, he accepted the invitation and was shown into the salon: where he seated himself—a left-handedness of which he would have been incapable had he been less perturbed—in Madame Jolicœur's own special chair. An anatomical vagary of the Notary's meagre person was the undue shortness of his body and the undue length of his legs. Because of this eccen-tricity of proportion, his bald head rose above the back of the chair to a height approximately identical with that of its nor-mal occupant.

His waiting time—extending from its promised point to what seemed to him to be a whole geographical meridian—went slowly. To relieve it, he took a book from the table, and in a desultory manner turned the leaves. While thus perfunc-torily engaged, he heard the clicking of an opening door, and then the sound of voices: of Madame Jolicœur's voice, and of a man's voice—which latter, coming nearer, he recognized beyond all doubting as the voice of the Major Gontard. Of other voices there was not a sound: whence the compromising fact was obvious that the two had gone through that long dinner together, and alone! Knowing, as he did, Madame Jolicœur's habitual disposition toward the convenances—willingly to be boiled in oil rather than in the smallest particular to abrade them—he perceived that only two explanations of the situation were possible: either she had lapsed of a sudden into madness; or—the thought was petrifying—the Major Gontard had won out in his French campaigning on his known conquering African lines. The cheerfully sane tone of the lady's voice forbade him to clutch at the poor solace to be found in the first alternative—and so forced him to accept the second. Yielding for a moment to his emotions, the death-whiteness of his bald head taking on a still deathlier pallor, Monsieur Peloux buried his face in his hands and groaned.

In that moment of his obscured perception a little black personage trotted into the salon on soundless paws. Quite possibly, in his then overwrought condition, had Monsieur Peloux seen this personage enter he would have shrieked—in the confident belief that before him was a cat ghost! Pointedly, it was not a ghost. It was the happy little Shah de Perse himself—all a-frisk with the joy of his blessed homecoming and very much alive! Knowing, as I do, many of the mysterious ways of little cat souls, I even venture to believe that his overbubbling gladness largely was due to his sympathetic perception of the gladness that his homecoming had brought to two human hearts.

Certainly, all through that long dinner the owners of those hearts had done their best, by their pettings and their pamperings of him, to make him a participant in their deep happiness; and he, gratefully respondent, had made his affectionate thankings by going through all of his repertory of tricks—with one exception—again and again. Naturally, his great trick, while unexhibited, repeatedly had been referred to. Blushing delightfully, Madame Jolicœur had told about the night cap that was a necessary part of it; and had promised—blushing still more delightfully—that at sometime, in the very remote future, the Major should see it performed. For my own part, because of my knowledge of little cat souls, I am persuaded that the Shah de Perse, while missing the details of this love-laughing talk, did get into his head the general trend of it; and therefore did trot on in advance into the salon with his little cat mind full of the notion that Madame Jolicœur immediately would follow him—to seat herself, duly night capped, book in hand, in signal for their game of surprises to begin.

Unconscious of the presence of the Shah de Perse, tortured by the gay tones of the approaching voices, clutching his book vengefully as though it were a throat, his bald head beaded with the sweat of agony and the pallor of it intensified by his poignant emotion, Monsieur Peloux sat rigid in Madame Jolicœur's chair!

"It is declared," said Monsieur Brisson, addressing himself to Madame Jouval, for whom he was in the act of preparing what was spoken of between them as "the tonic," a courteous euphuism, "that that villain Notary, aided by a bandit hired to his assistance, was engaged in administering poison to the cat; and that the brave animal, freeing itself from the bandit's holdings, tore to destruction the whole of his bald head—and then triumphantly escaped to its home!"

"A sight to see is that head of his!" replied Madame Jouval. "So swathed is it in bandages, that the turban of the Grand Turk is less!" Madame Jouval spoke in tones of satisfaction that were of reason—already she had held conferences with Madame Jolicœur in regard to the trousseau.

"And all," continued Monsieur Brisson, with rancour, "because of his jealousies of the cat's place in Madame Jolicœur's affections—the affections which he so hopelessly hoped, forgetful of his own repulsiveness, to win for himself!"

"Ah, she has done well, that dear lady," said Madame Jouval warmly. "As between the Notary—repulsive, as Monsieur justly terms him—and the charming Major, her instincts rightly have directed her. To her worthy cat, who aided in her choosing, she has reason to be grateful. Now her cruelly wounded heart will find solace. That she should wed again, and happily, was Heaven's will."

"It was the will of the baggage herself!" declared Monsieur Brisson with bitterness. "Hardly had she put on her travesty of a mourning than she began her oglings of whole armies of men!"

Aside from having confected with her own hands the mourning to which Monsieur Brisson referred so disparagingly, Madame Jouval was not one to hear calmly the ascription of the term baggage—the word has not lost in its native French, as it has lost in its naturalized English, its original epithetical intensity—to a patroness from whom she was in the very article of receiving an order for an exceptionally rich trousseau. Naturally, she bristled. "Monsieur must admit at least," she said sharply, "that her oglings did not come in his direction;" and with an irritatingly smooth sweetness added: "As to the dealings of Monsieur Peloux with the cat, Monsieur doubtless speaks with an assured knowledge. Remembering, as we all do, the affair of the unhappy old woman, it is easy to perceive that to Monsieur, above all others, anyone in need of poisonings would come!"

The thrust was so keen that for the moment Monsieur Brisson met it only with a savage glare. Then the bottle that he handed to Madame Jouval inspired him with an answer. "Madame is in error," he said with politeness. "For poisons it is possible to go variously elsewhere—as, for example, to Madame's tongue." Had he stopped with that retort courteous, but also searching, he would have done well. He did ill by adding to it the retort brutal: "But that old women of necessity come to me for their hair dyes is another matter. That much I grant to Madame with all goodwill."

Admirably restraining herself, Madame Jouval replied in tones of sympathy: "Monsieur receives my commiserations in his misfortunes." Losing a large part of her restraint, she continued, her eyes glittering: "Yet Monsieur's temperament clearly is over-sanguine. It is not less than a miracle of absurdity that he imagined: that he, weighted down with his infamous murderings of scores of innocent old women, had even a chance the most meagre of realizing his ridiculous aspirations of Madame Jolicœur's hand!" Snatching up her bottle and making for the door, without any restraint whatever she added: "Monsieur and his aspirations are a tragedy of stupidity—and equally are abounding in all the materials for a farce at the Palais de Cristal!"

Monsieur Brisson was cut off from opportunity to reply to this outburst by Madame Jouval's abrupt departure. His loss of opportunity had its advantages. An adequate reply to her discharge of such a volley of home truths would have been difficult to frame.

In the Vic bakery, between Madame Vic and Monsieur Fromagin, a discussion was in hand akin to that carried on between Monsieur Brisson and Madame Jouval—but marked with a somewhat nearer approach to accuracy in detail. Being sequent to the settlement of Monsieur Fromagin's monthly bill—always a matter of nettling dispute—it naturally tended to develop its own asperities.

"They say," observed Monsieur Fromagin, "that the cat—it was among his many tricks—had the habitude to jump on Madame Jolicœur's head when, for that purpose, she covered it with a nightcap. The use of the cat's claws on such a covering, and, also, her hair being very abundant—"

"*Very* abundant!" interjected Madame Vic; and added: "She, she is of a richness to buy wigs by the scores!"

"It was his custom, I say," continued Monsieur Fromagin with insistence, "to steady himself after his leap by using lightly his claws. His illusion in regard to the bald head of the

Notary, it would seem, led to the catastrophe. Using his claws at first lightly, according to his habit, he went on to use them with a truly savage energy—when he found himself as on ice on that slippery eminence and verging to a fall."

"They say that his scalp was peeled away in strips and strings!" said Madame Vic. "And all the while that woman and that reprobate of a Major standing by in shrieks and roars of laughter—never raising a hand to save him from the beast's ferocities! The poor man has my sympathies. He, at least, in all his doings—I do not for a moment believe the story that he caused the cat to be stolen—observed rigidly the convenances: so recklessly shattered by Madame Jolicœur in her most compromising dinner with the Major alone!"

"But Madame forgets that their dinner was in celebration of their betrothal—following Madame Jolicœur's glad yielding, in just gratitude, when the Major heroically had rescued her deserving cat from the midst of its enemies and triumphantly had restored it to her arms."

"It is the man's part," responded Madame Vic, "to make the best of such matters. In the eyes of all right-minded women her conduct has been of a shamelessness from first to last: tossing and balancing the two of them for months upon months; luring them, and countless others with them, to her feet; declaring always that for her disgusting cat's sake she will have none of them; and ending by pretending brazenly that for her cat's sake she bestows herself—second-hand remnant that she is—on the handsomest man for his age, concerning his character it is well to be silent; that she could find for herself in all Marseille! On such actions, on such a woman, Monsieur, the saints in heaven look down with an agonized scorn!"

"Only those of the saints, Madame," said Monsieur Fromagin, warmly taking up the cudgels for his best customer, "as in the matter of second marriages, prior to their arrival in heaven, have had regrettable experiences. Equally, I venture to assert, a like qualification applies to a like attitude on earth.

That Madame has her prejudices, incident to her misfortunes, is known."

"That Monsieur has his brutalities, incident to his regrettable bad breeding, also is known. His present offensiveness, however, passes all limits. I request him to remove himself from my sight." Madame Vic spoke with dignity.

Speaking with less dignity, but with conviction—as Monsieur Fromagin left the bakery—she added: "Monsieur, effectively, is a camel! I bestow upon him my disdain!"

Calvin
Charles Dudley Warner

CALVIN is dead. His life, long to him, but short for the rest of us, was not marked by startling adventures, but his character was so uncommon and his qualities were so worthy of imitation, that I have been asked by those who personally knew him to set down my recollections of his career.

His origin and ancestry were shrouded in mystery; even his age was a matter of pure conjecture. Although he was of the Maltese race, I have reason to suppose that he was American by birth as he certainly was in sympathy. Calvin was given to me eight years ago by Mrs. Stowe, but she knew nothing of his age or origin. He walked into her house one day out of the great unknown and became at once at home, as if he had been always a friend of the family. He appeared to have artistic and literary tastes, and it was as if he had inquired at the door if that was the residence of the author of *Uncle Tom's Cabin*, and, upon being assured that it was, had decided to dwell there. This is, of course, fanciful, for his antecedents were wholly unknown, but in his time he could hardly have been in any household where he would not have heard *Uncle Tom's Cabin* talked about. When he came to Mrs. Stowe, he was as large as he ever was, and apparently as old as he ever became. Yet there was in him no appearance of age; he was in the happy maturity of all his powers, and you would rather have said in that maturity he had found the secret of perpetual youth. And it was as difficult to believe that he would ever be aged as it was to imagine that he had ever been in immature youth. There was in him a mysterious perpetuity. After some years, when Mrs. Stowe made her winter home in Florida, Calvin came to live with us. From the first moment, he fell into the ways of the house and assumed a recognized position in the family—I say recognized, because after he became known he was always inquired for by visitors, and in the letters to the other members of the family he always received a message. Although the least obstrusive of beings, his individuality always made itself felt.

His personal appearance had much to do with this, for he was of royal mould, and had an air of high breeding. He was large, but he had nothing of the fat grossness of the celebrated Angora family; though powerful, he was exquisitely proportioned, and as graceful in every movement as a young leopard. When he stood up to open a door—he opened all the doors with old-fashioned latches—he was portentously tall, and when stretched on the rug before the fire he seemed too long for this world—as indeed he was. His coat was the finest and softest I have ever seen, a shade of quiet Maltese; and from his throat downward, underneath, to the white tips of his feet, he wore the whitest and most delicate ermine; and no person was ever more fastidiously neat. In his finely formed head you saw something of his aristocratic character; the ears were small and cleanly cut, there was a tinge of pink in the nostrils, his face was handsome, and the expression of his countenance exceedingly intelligent—I should call it even a sweet expression if the term were not inconsistent with his look of alertness and sagacity.

It is difficult to convey a just idea of his gaiety in connection with his dignity and gravity, which his name expressed. As we know nothing of his family, of course it will be understood that Calvin was his Christian name. He had times of relaxation into utter playfulness, delighting in a ball of yarn, catching sportively at stray ribbons when his mistress was at her toilet, and pursuing his own tail, with hilarity, for lack of anything better. He could amuse himself by the hour, and he did not care for children; perhaps something in his past was present to his memory. He had absolutely no bad habits, and his disposition was perfect. I never saw him exactly angry, though I have seen his tail grow to an enormous size when a strange cat appeared upon his lawn. He disliked cats, evidently regarding them as feline and treacherous, and he had no association with them. Occasionally there would be heard a night concert in the shrubbery. Calvin would ask to have the door opened, and then you would hear a rush and a "pestzt," and the concert would explode, and Calvin would quietly come in and resume his seat on the hearth. There was no trace of anger in his manner, but he wouldn't have any of that about the house. He had the rare virtue of magnanimity. Although he had fixed notions about his own rights, and extraordinary persistency in getting them, he never showed temper at a repulse; he simply and firmly persisted till he had what he wanted. His diet was one point; his idea was that of the scholars about dictionaries—to "get the best." He knew as well as anyone what was in the house, and would refuse beef if turkey was to be had; and if there were oysters, he would wait over the turkey to see if the oysters would not be forthcoming. And yet he was not a gross gourmand; he would eat bread if he saw me eating it, and thought he was not being imposed on. His habits of feeding, also, were refined; he never used a knife, and he would put up his hand and draw the fork down to his mouth as gracefully as a grown person. Unless necessity compelled, he would not eat in the kitchen, but insisted upon his meals in the dining room, and would wait patiently, unless a stranger were present; and then he was sure to importune the visitor, hoping that the latter was ignorant of the rule of the house, and would give him something. They used to say that he preferred as his table-cloth on the floor a certain well-known church journal; but this was said by an Episcopalian. So far as I know, he had no religious prejudices, except that he did not like the association with Romanists. He tolerated the servants, because they belonged to the house, and would sometimes linger by the kitchen stove; but the moment visitors came in he arose, opened the door, and marched into the drawing room. Yet he enjoyed the company of his equals, and never withdrew, no matter how many callers—whom he recognized as of his society—might come into the drawing room. Calvin was fond of company, but he wanted to choose it; and I have no doubt that his was an aristocratic fastidiousness rather than one of faith. It is so with most people.

The intelligence of Calvin was something phenomenal, in his rank of life. He established a method of communicating his wants, and even some of his sentiments; and he could help himself in many things. There was a furnace register in a retired room, where he used to go when he wished to be alone, that he always opened when he desired more heat; but never shut it, any more than he shut the door after himself. He could do almost everything but speak; and you would declare sometimes that you could see a pathetic longing to do that in his intelligent face. I have no desire to overdraw his qualities, but if there was one thing in him more noticeable than another, it was his fondness for nature. He could content himself for hours at a low window, looking into the ravine and at the great trees, noting the smallest stir there; he delighted, above all things, to accompany me walking about the garden, hearing the birds, getting the smell of the fresh earth, and rejoicing in the sunshine. He followed me and gambolled like a dog, rolling over on the turf and exhibiting his delight in a hundred ways. If I worked, he sat and watched me, or looked off over the bank, and kept his ear open to the twitter in the cherry trees. When it stormed, he was sure to sit at the window, keenly watching the rain or the snow, glancing up and down at its falling; and a winter tempest always delighted him. I think he was genuinely fond of birds, but, so far as I know, he usually confined himself to one a day; he never killed, as some sportsmen do, for the sake of killing, but only as civilized people do—from necessity. He was intimate with the flying squirrels who dwell in the chestnut trees—too intimate, for almost every day in the summer he would bring in one, until he nearly discouraged them. He was, indeed, a superb hunter, and would have been a devastating one, if his bump of destructiveness had not been offset by a bump of moderation. There was very little of the brutality of the lower animals about him; I don't think he enjoyed rats for themselves, but he knew his business, and for the first few months of his residence with us he waged an awful campaign against the horde, and after that his simple presence was sufficient to deter them from coming on the premises. Mice amused him, but he usually considered them too small game to be taken seriously; I have seen him play for an hour with a mouse, and then let him go with a royal condescension. In this whole matter of "getting a living," Calvin was a great contrast to the rapacity of the age in which he lived.

I hesitate a little to speak of his capacity for friendship and the affectionateness of his nature, for I know from his own reserve that he would not care to have it much talked about. We understood each other perfectly, but we never made any fuss about it; when I spoke his name and snapped my fingers, he came to me; when I returned home at night, he was pretty sure to be waiting for me near the gate, and would rise and saunter along the walk, as if his being there were purely accidental—so shy was he commonly of showing feeling; and when I opened the door he never rushed in, like a cat, but loitered, and lounged, as if he had had no intention of going in, but would condescend to. And yet, the fact was, he knew dinner was ready, and he was bound to be there. He kept the run of dinnertime. It happened sometimes, during our absence in the summer, that dinner would be early, and Calvin walking about the grounds, missed it and came in late. But he never made a mistake the second day. There was one thing he never did—he never rushed through an open doorway. He never forgot his dignity. If he had asked to have the door opened, and was eager to go out, he always went deliberately; I can see him now, standing on the sill, looking about at the sky as if he was thinking whether it were worthwhile to take an umbrella, until he was near having his tail shut in.

His friendship was rather constant than demonstrative. When we returned from an absence of nearly two years,

Calvin welcomed us with evident pleasure, but showed his satisfaction rather by tranquil happiness than by fuming about. He had the faculty of making us glad to get home. It was his constancy that was so attractive. He liked companionship, but he wouldn't be petted, or fussed over, or sit in anyone's lap a moment; he always extricated himself from such familiarity with dignity and with no show of temper. If there was any petting to be done, however, he chose to do it. Often he would sit looking at me, and then, moved by a delicate affection, come and pull at my coat and sleeve until he could touch my face with his nose, and then go away contented. He had a habit of coming to my study in the morning, sitting quietly by my side or on the table for hours, watching the pen run over the paper, occasionally swinging his tail round for a blotter, and then going to sleep among the papers by the inkstand. Or, more rarely, he would watch the writing from a perch on my shoulder. Writing always interested him, and, until he understood it, he wanted to hold the pen.

He always held himself in a kind of reserve with his friend, as if he had said, "Let us respect our personality, and not make a 'mess' of friendship." He saw, with Emerson, the risk of degrading it to trivial conveniency. "Why insist on rash personal relations with your friend?" "Leave this touching and clawing." Yet I would not give an unfair notion of his aloofness, his fine sense of the sacredness of the me and the not-me. And, at the risk of not being believed, I will relate an incident, which was often repeated. Calvin had the practice of passing a portion of the night in the contemplation of its beauties, and would come into our chamber over the roof of the conservatory through the open window, summer and winter, and go to sleep on the foot of my bed. He would do this always exactly in this way; he never was content to stay in the chamber if we compelled him to go upstairs and through the door. He had the obstinacy of General Grant. But this is by the way. In the morning, he performed his toilet and went down to breakfast with the rest of the family. Now, when the mistress was absent from home, and at no other time, Calvin would come in the morning, when the bell rang, to the head of the bed, put up his feet and look into my face, follow me about when I rose, "assist" at the dressing, and in many purring ways show his fondness, as if he had plainly said, "I know that she has gone away, but I am here." Such was Calvin in rare moments.

He had his limitations. Whatever passion he had for nature, he had no conception of art. There was sent to him once a fine and very expressive cat's head in bronze, by Frémiet. I placed it on the floor. He regarded it intently, approached it cautiously and crouchingly, touched it with his nose, perceived the fraud, turned away abruptly, and never would notice it afterward. On the whole, his life was not only a successful one, but a happy one. He never had but one fear, so far as I know: he had a mortal and a reasonable terror of plumbers. He would never stay in the house when they were here. No coaxing could quiet him. Of course he didn't share our fear about their charges, but he must have had some dreadful experience with them in that portion of his life which is unknown to us. A plumber was to him the devil, and I have no doubt that, in his scheme, plumbers were foreordained to do him mischief.

In speaking of his worth, it has never occurred to me to estimate Calvin by the worldly standard. I know that it is customary now, when anyone dies, to ask how much he was worth, and that no obituary in the newspapers is considered complete without such an estimate. The plumbers in our house were one day overheard to say that, "They say that *she* says that *he* says that he wouldn't take a hundred dollars for him." It is unnecessary to say that I never made such a remark, and that, so far as Calvin was concerned, there was no purchase in money.

As I look back upon it, Calvin's life seems to me a fortunate one, for it was natural and unforced. He ate when he was hungry, slept when he was sleepy, and enjoyed existence to the very tips of his toes and the end of his expressive and slow-moving tail. He delighted to roam about the garden, and stroll among the trees, and to lie on the green grass and luxuriate in all the sweet influences of summer. You could never accuse him of idleness, and yet he knew the secret of repose. The poet who wrote so prettily of him that his little life was rounded with a sleep, understated his felicity; it was rounded with a good many. His conscience never seemed to interfere with his slumbers. In fact, he had good habits and a contented mind. I can see him now walk in at the study door, sit down by my chair, bring his tail artistically about his feet, and look up at me with unspeakable happiness in his handsome face. I often thought that he felt the dumb limitation which denied him the power of language. But since he was denied speech, he scorned the inarticulate mouthings of the lower animals. The vulgar mewing and yowling of the cat species was beneath him; he sometimes uttered a sort of articulate and well-bred ejaculation, when he wished to call attention to something that he considered remarkable, or to some want of his, but he never went whining about. He would sit for hours at a closed window, when he desired to enter, without a murmur, and when it was opened he never admitted that he had been impatient by "bolting" in. Though speech he had not, and the unpleasant kind of utterance given to his race he would not use, he had a mighty power of purr to express his measureless content with congenial society. There was in him a musical organ with stops of varied power and expression, upon which I have no doubt he could have performed Scarlatti's celebrated cat's-fugue.

Whether Calvin died of old age, or was carried off by one of the diseases incident to youth, it is impossible to say; for his departure was as quiet as his advent was mysterious. I only know that he appeared to us in this world in his perfect stature and beauty, and that after a time, like Lohengrin, he withdrew. In his illness there was nothing more to be regretted than in all his blameless life. I suppose there never was an illness that had more of dignity and sweetness and resignation in it. It came on gradually, in a kind of listlessness and want of appetite. An alarming symptom was his preference for the warmth of a furnace register to the lively sparkle of the open wood fire. Whatever pain he suffered, he bore it in silence, and seemed only anxious not to obtrude his malady. We tempted him with the delicacies of the season, but it soon became impossible for him to eat, and for two weeks he ate or drank scarcely anything. Sometimes he made an effort to take something, but it was evident that he made the effort to please us. The neighbours—and I am convinced that the advice of neighbours is never good for anything—suggested catnip. He wouldn't even smell it. We had the attendance of an amateur practitioner of medicine, whose real office was the cure of souls, but nothing touched his case. He took what was offered, but it was with the air of one to whom the time for pellets was past. He sat or lay day after day almost motionless, never once making a display of those vulgar convulsions or contortions of pain which are so disagreeable to society. His favourite place was on the brightest spot of a Smyrna rug by the conservatory, where the sunlight fell and he could hear the fountain play. If we went to him and exhibited our interest in his condition, he always purred in recognition of our sympathy. And when I spoke his name, he looked up with an expression that said, "I understand it, old fellow, but it's no use." He was to all who came to visit him a model of calmness and patience in affliction.

I was absent from home at the last, but heard by daily postal card of his failing condition; and never again saw him alive. One sunny morning, he rose from his rug, went into the conservatory (he was very thin then), walked around it deliberately, looking at all the plants he knew, and then went to the bay window in the dining room, and stood a long time looking out upon the little field, now brown and sere, and toward the garden, where perhaps the happiest hours of his life had been spent. It was a last look. He turned and walked away, laid himself down upon the bright spot in the rug, and quietly died.

It is not too much to say that a little shock went through the neighbourhood when it was known that Calvin was dead, so marked was his individuality; and his friends, one after another, came in to see him. There was no sentimental nonsense about his obsequies; it was felt that any parade would have been distasteful to him. John, who acted as undertaker, prepared a candle box for him, and I believe assumed a professional decorum; but there may have been the usual levity underneath, for I heard that he remarked in the kitchen that it was the "dryest wake he ever attended." Everybody, however, felt a fondness for Calvin, and regarded him with a certain respect. Between him and Bertha there existed a great friendship, and she apprehended his nature; she used to say that sometimes she was afraid of him, he looked at her so intelligently; she was never certain that he was what he appeared to be.

When I returned, they had laid Calvin on a table in an upper chamber by an open window. It was February. He reposed in a candle box, lined about the edge with evergreen, and at his head stood a little wineglass with flowers. He lay with his head tucked down in his arms—a favourite position of his before the fire—as if asleep in the comfort of his soft and exquisite fur. It was the involuntary exclamation of those who saw him, "How natural he looks!" As for myself, I said nothing. John buried him under the twin hawthorn trees— one white and the other pink—in a spot where Calvin was fond of lying and listening to the hum of summer insects and the twitter of birds.

Perhaps I have failed to make appear the individuality of character that was so evident to those who knew him. At any rate, I have set down nothing concerning him but the literal truth. He was always a mystery. I did not know whence he came; I do not know whither he has gone. I would not weave one spray of falsehood in the wreath I lay upon his grave.

The Queen's Cat
Peggy Bacon

ONCE there was a great and powerful King who was as good as gold and as brave as a lion, but he had one weakness, which was a horror of cats. If he saw one through an open window he shuddered so that his medals jangled together and his crown fell off; if anyone mentioned a cat at the table he instantly spilled his soup all down the front of his ermine; and if by any chance a cat happened to stroll into the audience chamber, he immediately jumped onto his throne, gathering his robes around him and shrieking at the top of his lungs.

Now this King was a bachelor and his people didn't like it; so being desirous of pleasing them, he looked around among the neighbouring royal families and hit upon a very sweet and beautiful princess, whom he asked in marriage without any delay, for he was a man of action.

Her parents giving their hearty consent, the pair were married at her father's palace; and after the festivities were over, the King sped home to see to the preparation of his wife's apartments. In due time she arrived, bringing with her a cat. When he saw her mounting the steps with the animal under her arm, the King, who was at the door to meet her, uttering a horrid yell, fell in a swoon and had to be revived with spirits of ammonia. The courtiers hastened to inform the Queen of her husband's failing, and when he came to, he found her in tears.

"I cannot exist without a cat!" she wept.

"And I, my love," replied the King, "cannot exist with one!"

"You must learn to bear it!" said she.

"You must learn to live without it!" said he.

"But life would not be worth living without a cat!" she wailed.

"Well, well, my love, we will see what we can do," sighed the King.

"Suppose," he went on, "you kept it in the round tower over there. Then you could go to see it."

"Shut up my cat that has been used to running around in the open air?" cried the Queen. "Never!"

"Suppose," suggested the King again, "we made an enclosure for it of wire netting."

"My dear," cried the Queen, "a good strong cat like mine could climb out in a minute."

"Well," said the King once more, "suppose we give it the palace roof, and I will keep out of the way."

"That is a good scheme," said his wife, drying her eyes.

And they immediately fitted up the roof with a cushioned shelter, and a bed of catnip, and a bench where the Queen might sit. There the cat was left; and the Queen went up three times a day to feed it, and twice as many times to visit it, and for almost two days that seemed the solution of the problem. Then the cat discovered that by making a spring to the limb of an overhanging oak tree, it could climb down the trunk and go where it liked. This it did, making its appearance in the throne room, where the King was giving audience to an important ambassador. Much to the amazement of the latter, the monarch leapt up screaming, and was moreover so upset, that the affairs of state had all to be postponed till the following day. The tree was, of course, cut down; and the next day the cat found crawling down the gutter to be just as easy, and jumped in the window while the court was at breakfast. The King scrambled onto the breakfast table, skilfully overturning the cream and the coffee with one foot, while planting the other in the poached eggs, and wreaking untold havoc among the teacups. Again the affairs of state were postponed while the gutter was ripped off the roof, to the fury of the head gardener, who had just planted his spring seeds in the beds around the palace walls. Of course the next rain washed them all away.

This sort of thing continued. The wistaria vine which had covered the front of the palace for centuries, was ruthlessly torn down, the trellises along the wings soon followed; and finally an ancient grape arbour had perforce to be removed as it proved a sure means of descent for that invincible cat. Even then, he cleverly utilized the balconies as a ladder to the ground; but by this time the poor King's nerves were quite shattered and the doctor was called in. All he could prescribe was a total abstinence from cat; and the Queen, tearfully finding a home for her pet, composed herself to live without one. The King, well cared for, soon revived and was himself again, placidly conducting the affairs of state, and happy in the society of his beloved wife. Not so the latter.

Before long it was noticed that the Queen grew wan, was often heard to sniff, and seen to wipe her eyes, would not eat, could not sleep—in short, the doctor was again called in.

"Dear, dear," he said disconsolately, combing his long beard with his thin fingers. "This is a difficult situation indeed. There must not be a cat on the premises, or the King will assuredly have nervous prostration. Yet the Queen must have a cat or she will pine quite away with nostalgia."

"I think I had best return to my family," sobbed the poor Queen, dejectedly. "I bring you nothing but trouble, my own."

"That is impossible, my dearest love," said the King decidedly—"Here my people have so long desired me to marry, and now that I am at last settled in the matrimonial way, we must not disappoint them. They enjoy a Queen so much. It gives them something pretty to think about. Besides, my love, I am attached to you, myself, and could not possibly manage without you. No, my dear, there may be a way out of our difficulties, but that certainly is not it." Having delivered which speech the King lapsed again into gloom, and the doctor who was an old friend of the King's went away sadly.

He returned, however, the following day with a smile tangled somewhere in his long beard. He found the King sitting mournfully by the Queen's bedside.

"Would your majesty," began the doctor, turning to the Queen, "object to a cat that did not look like a cat?"

"Oh, no," cried she, earnestly, "just so it's a *cat!*"

"Would your majesty," said the doctor again, turning to the King, "object to a cat that did not look like a cat?"

"Oh, no," cried he, "just so it doesn't *look* like a cat!"

"Well," said the doctor, beaming, "I have a cat that is a cat and that doesn't look any more like a cat than a skillet, and I should be only too honoured to present it to the Queen if she would be so gracious as to accept it."

Both the King and the Queen were overjoyed and thanked the doctor with tears in their eyes. So the cat—for it was a cat though you never would have known it—arrived and was duly presented to the Queen, who welcomed it with open arms and felt better immediately.

It was a thin, wiry, long-legged creature, with no tail at all, and large ears like sails, a face like a lean isosceles triangle with the nose as a very sharp apex, eyes small and yellow like flat buttons, brown fur short and coarse, and large floppy feet. It had a voice like a steam siren and its name was Rosamund.

The King and Queen were both devoted to it; she because it was a cat, he because it seemed anything but a cat. No one indeed could convince the King that it was not a beautiful animal, and he had made for it a handsome collar of gold and amber—"to match," he said, sentimentally, "its lovely eyes." In sooth so ugly a beast never had such a pampered and luxurious existence, certainly never so royal a one. Appreciating its wonderful good fortune, it never showed any inclination to depart; and the King, the Queen, and Rosamund lived happily ever after.

Plato: The Story of a Cat
A. S. Downs

ONE day last summer a large handsome black cat walked gravely up one side of Main Street, crossed, and went halfway down the other. He stopped at a house called The Den, went up the piazza steps, and paused by an open window.

A lady sitting inside saw and spoke to him; but without taking any notice, he put his paws on the sill, looked around the room as if wondering if it would suit him, and finally gazed into her face.

After thinking a minute he went in, and from that hour took his place as an important member of the family. Civil to all, he gives his love only to the lady whom he first saw; and it is odd to see, as he lies by the fire, how he listens to all conversation, but raises his head only when she speaks, and drops it again when she has finished, with a pleased air.

No other person in the house is so wise, for he alone never makes a mistake. The hours he selects for his exercise are the sunniest; the carpets he lies upon the softest, and he knows the moment he enters the room whether his friend will let him lie in her lap, or whether because of her best gown she will have none of him. No one at The Den can tell how he came to be called Plato. It is a fact that he answers to the name, and when asked if so known before he came there, smiles wisely. "What matters it," the smile says, "how I was called, or where I came from, since I am Plato, and am here?"

He dislikes noise, and entirely disapproves sweeping. A broom and dustpan fill him with anxiety, and he seeks the soft cushions of the big lounge; but when these in their turn are beaten and tossed about, he retreats to the study table.

However, as soon as he learned that once a week his favorite room was turned into chaos, he sought another refuge, and refuses to get up that day until noon.

Many were the speculations as to Plato's Christmas present. All were satisfied with a rattan basket just large enough for him to lie in, with a light, open canopy, cushions of cardinal chintz, and a cardinal satin bow to which was fastened a lovely card.

It was set down before Plato, and although it is probable it was the first he had ever seen, he showed neither surprise nor curiosity, but looked at it loftily as if such a retreat should have been given him long ago, for could not any discerning person see he was accustomed to luxury? He stepped in carefully and curled himself gracefully upon the soft cushions, the glowing tints of which were very becoming to his sable beauty.

It was soon seen that Plato was very fond of his basket, and was unwilling to share it in the smallest degree. When little Bessie put her doll in, "just to see if cardinal was becoming to her," he looked so stern and walked so fiercely toward them that dolly's heart sank within her, and Bessie said, "Please excuse us, Plato." If balls and toys were carelessly dropped there he would push them out without delay, and if visitors took up the basket to examine it, he would fix his eyes upon them, thinking, "O yes, you would pick pockets or steal the spoons if I did not watch you."

As his conduct can never be predicted, great was the curiosity when one cold afternoon he was noticed walking up the avenue while a miserable yellow kitten dragged herself after him. She was so thin you could count her bones, and she had been so pulled and kicked that there seemed to be nothing of her but length and—dirt.

When Lord Plato chooses, he enters the front doors, but as he waits no man's pleasure, unless it pleases him first, he has a way of getting in on his own account. Upon one of the shed doors is an old-fashioned latch, which by jumping he can reach and lift with his paw. Having opened the door, he pushed his poor yellow straggler in and followed himself. She laid down at once on the floor, and Plato began washing her with his rough tongue, while the lookers-on assisted his hospitality by bringing a saucer of milk. While she ate, Plato rested, looking as pleased as if he were her mother at her enjoyment. The luncheon finished, the washing was resumed, and as the waif was now able to help, she soon looked more respectable. But Plato had not finished his work of mercy. He looked at the door leading to the parlor, then at her; and finally bent down tenderly to her little torn ears, as if whispering, but she would not move. Perhaps in all her wretched life she had never been so comfortable, and believed in letting well enough alone. Reason and persuasion alike useless, Plato concluded to try force and, taking her by the back of the neck, carried her through the house and dropped her close to his dainty cherished basket.

Then he appeared a little uncertain what to do. The basket was nice and warm; he was tired and cold; it had been a present to him; the street wanderer was dirty still; and the rug would be a softer bed than she had ever known. Were these his thoughts, and was it selfishness he conquered when at last he lifted the shivering homeless creature into his own beautiful nest?

Frisk's First Rat
Charles W. Chesnutt

FRISK was Rosy's kitten. One day when she was coming home from school, she saw a boy at the creek, tying a string round a little kitten's neck.

"Boy, what are you going to do with that kitten?" said she.

"Drown," was the laconic response.

"O, don't," said Rosy. "Please give him to me."

"What'll you gi'me?" said the boy who had an eye to trade.

"Oh dear," said Rosy, "I haven't got any money."

"Gi'me that apple you got?"

"Oh, yes," said she.

The bargain was made, and Rosy hurried home with her new acquisition, which, after being displayed to the whole household, was put to bed in an old basket and became a household institution.

Frisk, for so he was named, in a few months had vastly increased in size and had explored the cellar, closets, house, and garden; had caught several mice but had not yet arrived at the height of his ambition—this was to catch a rat. He had heard of them from Tom, the big cat over the way, but had never met with one. There were no rats in the cellar, but there was an old garret in the house Frisk had not explored, because he could not get in it.

But he watched his chance, and one evening when Patsy, the maid, went up to the garret to deposit some plunder, of which it was a time honored receptacle, he slipped in and hid 'til she went out.

There was an old corn bin in one corner, which had still a few grains of corn in it, and near it Frisk stationed himself, as he had had some experience in the mouse line.

In a little while, a large rat emerged from a hole in the wall nearby and came toward the bin. This was a trying moment to Frisk. His emotions were indescribable, his breast heaved, his back rose, his tail moved slowly from side to side; his eyes flashed fire, and in his bosom burned a desire to distinguish himself. He gave a spring and seized him. There ensued a terrific struggle, the like of which was never heard of in feline tradition. Over old crockery, among the old tinware, in old baskets, and over a good portion of the garret they rolled. The racket brought Patsy, Rosy, and Mamma from below just as Frisk had achieved a glorious victory. Sitting by the body of his fallen foe, with one bloody paw on his neck, he eyed him with the greatest satisfaction and was highly applauded by Rosy and Patsy.

When he had eaten enough rat, he was carried in triumph downstairs, the blood was washed off him by Patsy, and he was installed in state on the sitting-room rug for the rest of the evening.

And now my young friend, don't you think that Frisk was a pretty smart kitten?

Aunt Cynthia's Persian Cat
L. M. Montgomery

MAX always blesses the animal when it is referred to; and I don't deny that things have worked together for good after all. But when I think of the anguish of mind which Ismay and I underwent on account of that abominable cat, it is not a blessing that arises uppermost in my thoughts.

I never was fond of cats, although I admit they are well enough in their place, and I can worry along comfortably with a nice, matronly old tabby who can take care of herself and be of some use in the world. As for Ismay, she hates cats and always did.

But Aunt Cynthia, who adored them, never could bring herself to understand that anyone could possibly dislike them. She firmly believed that Ismay and I really liked cats deep down in our hearts, but that, owing to some perverse twist in our moral natures, we would not own up to it, but willfully persisted in declaring we didn't.

Of all cats I loathed that white Persian cat of Aunt Cynthia's. And, indeed, as we always suspected and finally proved, Aunt herself looked upon the creature with more pride than affection. She would have taken ten times the comfort in a good, common puss than she did in that spoiled beauty. But a Persian cat with a recorded pedigree and a market value of one hundred dollars tickled Aunt Cynthia's pride of possession to such an extent that she deluded herself into believing that the animal was really the apple of her eye.

It had been presented to her when a kitten by a missionary nephew who had brought it all the way home from Persia; and for the next three years Aunt Cynthia's household existed to wait on that cat, hand and foot. It was snow-white, with a bluish-grey

spot on the tip of its tail; and it was blue-eyed and deaf and delicate. Aunt Cynthia was always worrying lest it should take cold
and die. Ismay and I used to wish that it would—we were so
tired of hearing about it and its whims. But we did not say so to
Aunt Cynthia. She would probably never have spoken to us again
and there was no wisdom in offending Aunt Cynthia. When you
have an unencumbered aunt, with a fat bank account, it is just as
well to keep on good terms with her, if you can. Besides, we really
liked Aunt Cynthia very much—at times. Aunt Cynthia was one
of those rather exasperating people who nag at and find fault with
you until you think you are justified in hating them, and who then
turn round and do something so really nice and kind for you that
you feel as if you were compelled to love them dutifully instead.

So we listened meekly when she discoursed on Fatima—the
cat's name was Fatima—and, if it was wicked of us to wish for
the latter's decease, we were well punished for it later on.

One day, in November, Aunt Cynthia came sailing out to
Spencervale. She really came in a phaeton, drawn by a fat
grey pony, but somehow Aunt Cynthia always gave you the
impression of a full-rigged ship coming gallantly on before a
favorable wind.

That was a Jonah day for us all through. Everything had gone
wrong. Ismay had spilled grease on her velvet coat, and the fit
of the new blouse I was making was hopelessly askew, and the
kitchen stove smoked and the bread was sour. Moreover,
Huldah Jane Keyson, our tried and trusty old family nurse and
cook and general "boss," had what she called the "realagy" in
her shoulder; and, though Huldah Jane is as good an old creature as ever lived, when she has the "realagy" other people who
are in the house want to get out of it and, if they can't, feel
about as comfortable as St. Lawrence on his gridiron.

And on the top of this came Aunt Cynthia's call and request.

"Dear me," said Aunt Cynthia, sniffing, "don't I smell
smoke? You girls must manage your range very badly. Mine
never smokes. But it is no more than one might expect when
two girls try to keep house without a man about the place."

"We get along very well without a man about the place," I said loftily. Max hadn't been in for four whole days and, though nobody wanted to see him particularly, I couldn't help wondering why. "Men are nuisances."

"I dare say you would like to pretend you think so," said Aunt Cynthia, aggravatingly. "But no woman ever does really think so, you know. I imagine that pretty Anne Shirley, who is visiting Ella Kimball, doesn't. I saw her and Dr. Irving out walking this afternoon, looking very well satisfied with themselves. If you dillydally much longer, Sue, you will let Max slip through your fingers yet."

That was a tactful thing to say to *me*, who had refused Max Irving so often that I had lost count. I was furious, and so I smiled most sweetly on my maddening aunt.

"Dear Aunt, how amusing of you," I said, smoothly. "You talk as if I wanted Max."

"So you do," said Aunt Cynthia.

"If so, why should I have refused him time and again?" I asked, smilingly. Right well Aunt Cynthia knew I had. Max always told her.

"Goodness alone knows why," said Aunt Cynthia, "but you may do it once too often and find yourself taken at your word. There is something very fascinating about this Anne Shirley."

"Indeed there is," I assented. "She has the loveliest eyes I ever saw. She would be just the wife for Max, and I hope he will marry her."

"Humph," said Aunt Cynthia. "Well, I won't entice you into telling any more fibs. And I didn't drive out here today in all this wind to talk sense into you concerning Max. I'm going to Halifax for two months and I want you to take charge of Fatima for me, while I am away."

"Fatima!" I exclaimed.

"Yes. I don't dare to trust her with the servants. Mind you always warm her milk before you give it to her, and don't on any account let her run out of doors."

I looked at Ismay and Ismay looked at me. We knew we were in for it. To refuse would mortally offend Aunt Cynthia. Besides, if I betrayed any unwillingness, Aunt Cynthia would be sure to put it down to grumpiness over what she had said about Max, and rub it in for years. But I ventured to ask, "What if anything happens to her while you are away?"

"It is to prevent that, I'm leaving her with you," said Aunt Cynthia. "You simply must not let anything happen to her. It will do you good to have a little responsibility. And you will have a chance to find out what an adorable creature Fatima really is. Well, that is all settled. I'll send Fatima out tomorrow."

"You can take care of that horrid Fatima beast yourself," said Ismay, when the door closed behind Aunt Cynthia. "I won't touch her with a yardstick. You had no business to say we'd take her."

"Did I say we would take her?" I demanded, crossly. "Aunt Cynthia took our consent for granted. And you know, as well as I do, we couldn't have refused. So what is the use of being grouchy?"

"If anything happens to her Aunt Cynthia will hold us responsible," said Ismay darkly.

"Do you think Anne Shirley is really engaged to Gilbert Blythe?" I asked curiously.

"I've heard that she was," said Ismay, absently. "Does she eat anything but milk? Will it do to give her mice?"

"Oh, I guess so. But do you think Max has really fallen in love with her?"

"I dare say. What a relief it will be for you if he has."

"Oh, of course," I said, frostily. "Anne Shirley or Anne Anybody Else, is perfectly welcome to Max if she wants him. I certainly do not. Ismay Meade, if that stove doesn't stop smoking I shall fly into bits. This is a detestable day. I hate that creature!"

"Oh, you shouldn't talk like that, when you don't even know her," protested Ismay. "Everyone says Anne Shirley is lovely—"

"I was talking about Fatima," I cried in a rage.

"Oh!" said Ismay.

Ismay is stupid at times. I thought the way she said "Oh" was inexcusably stupid.

Fatima arrived the next day. Max brought her out in a covered basket, lined with padded crimson satin. Max likes cats and Aunt Cynthia. He explained how we were to treat Fatima and when Ismay had gone out of the room—Ismay always went out of the room when she knew I particularly wanted her to remain—he proposed to me again. Of course I said no, as usual, but I was rather pleased. Max had been proposing to me about every two months for two years. Sometimes, as in this case, he went three months, and then I always wondered why. I concluded that he could not be really interested in Anne Shirley, and I was relieved. I didn't want to marry Max but it was pleasant and convenient to have him around, and we would miss him dreadfully if any other girl snapped him up. He was so useful and always willing to do anything for us—nail a shingle on the roof, drive us to town, put down carpets—in short, a very present help in all our troubles.

So I just beamed on him when I said no. Max began counting on his fingers. When he got as far as eight he shook his head and began over again.

"What is it?" I asked.

"I'm trying to count up how many times I have proposed to you," he said. "But I can't remember whether I asked you to marry me that day we dug up the garden or not. If I did it makes—"

"No, you didn't," I interrupted.

"Well, that makes it eleven," said Max reflectively. "Pretty near the limit, isn't it? My manly pride will not allow me to propose to the same girl more than twelve times. So the next time will be the last, Sue darling."

"Oh," I said, a trifle flatly. I forgot to resent his calling me darling. I wondered if things wouldn't be rather dull when Max gave up proposing to me. It was the only excitement I had. But of course it would be best—and he couldn't go on at it forever, so, by the way of gracefully dismissing the subject, I asked him what Miss Shirley was like.

"Very sweet girl," said Max. "You know I always admired those grey-eyed girls with that splendid Titian hair."

I am dark, with brown eyes. Just then I detested Max. I got up and said I was going to get some milk for Fatima.

I found Ismay in a rage in the kitchen. She had been up in the garret, and a mouse had run across her foot. Mice always get on Ismay's nerves.

"We need a cat badly enough," she fumed, "but not a useless, pampered thing, like Fatima. That garret is literally swarming with mice. You'll not catch me going up there again."

Fatima did not prove such a nuisance as we had feared. Huldah Jane liked her, and Ismay, in spite of her declaration that she would have nothing to do with her, looked after her comfort scrupulously. She even used to get up in the middle of the night and go out to see if Fatima was warm. Max came in every day and, being around, gave us good advice.

Then one day, about three weeks after Aunt Cynthia's departure, Fatima disappeared—just simply disappeared as if she had been dissolved into thin air. We left her one afternoon, curled up asleep in her basket by the fire, under Huldah Jane's eye, while we went out to make a call. When we came home Fatima was gone.

Huldah Jane wept and was as one whom the gods had made mad. She vowed that she had never let Fatima out of her sight the whole time, save once for three minutes when she ran up to the garret for some summer savory. When she came back the kitchen door had blown open and Fatima had vanished.

Ismay and I were frantic. We ran about the garden and through the outhouses, and the woods behind the house, like wild creatures, calling Fatima, but in vain. Then Ismay sat down on the front doorsteps and cried.

"She has got out and she'll catch her death of cold and Aunt Cynthia will never forgive us."

"I'm going for Max," I declared. So I did, through the spruce woods and over the field as fast as my feet could carry me, thanking my stars that there was a Max to go to in such a predicament.

Max came over and we had another search, but without result. Days passed, but we did not find Fatima. I would certainly have gone crazy had it not been for Max. He was worth his weight in gold during the awful week that followed. We did not dare advertise, lest Aunt Cynthia should see it; but we inquired far and wide for a white Persian cat with a blue spot on its tail, and offered a reward for it; but nobody had seen it, although people kept coming to the house, night and day, with every kind of a cat in baskets, wanting to know if it was the one we had lost.

"We shall never see Fatima again," I said hopelessly to Max and Ismay one afternoon. I had just turned away an old woman with a big, yellow tommy which she insisted must be ours—"cause it kem to our place, mem, a-yowling fearful, mem, and it don't belong to nobody not down Grafton way, mem."

"I'm afraid you won't," said Max. "She must have perished from exposure long ere this."

"Aunt Cynthia will never forgive us," said Ismay, dismally. "I had a presentiment of trouble the moment that cat came to this house."

We had never heard of this presentiment before, but Ismay is good at having presentiments—after things happen.

"What shall we do?" I demanded, helplessly. "Max, can't you find some way out of this scrape for us?"

"Advertise in the Charlottetown papers for a white Persian cat," suggested Max. "Someone may have one for sale. If so, you must buy it, and palm it off on your good Aunt as Fatima. She's very shortsighted, so it will be quite possible."

"But Fatima has a blue spot on her tail," I said.

"You must advertise for a cat with a blue spot on its tail," said Max.

"It will cost a pretty penny," said Ismay dolefully. "Fatima was valued at one hundred dollars."

"We must take the money we have been saving for our new furs," I said, sorrowfully. "There is no other way out of it. It will cost us a good deal more if we lose Aunt Cynthia's favor. She is quite capable of believing that we have made away with Fatima deliberately and with malice aforethought."

So we advertised. Max went to town and had the notice inserted in the most important daily. We asked anyone who had a white Persian cat, with a blue spot on the tip of its tail, to dispose of, to communicate with M. I., care of the *Enterprise.*

We really did not have much hope that anything would come of it, so we were surprised and delighted over the letter Max brought home from town four days later. It was a type-written screed from Halifax stating that the writer had for sale a white Persian cat answering to our description. The price was a hundred and ten dollars and, if M. I. cared to go to Halifax and inspect the animal, it would be found at 110 Hollis Street, by inquiring for "Persian."

"Temper your joy, my friends," said Ismay, gloomily. "The cat may not suit. The blue spot may be too big or too small or not in the right place. I consistently refuse to believe that any good thing can come out of this deplorable affair."

Just at this moment there was a knock at the door and I hurried out. The postmaster's boy was there with a telegram. I tore it open, glanced at it, and dashed back into the room.

"What is it now?" cried Ismay, beholding my face.

I held out the telegram. It was from Aunt Cynthia. She had wired us to send Fatima to Halifax by express immediately.

For the first time Max did not seem ready to rush into the breach with a suggestion. It was I who spoke first.

"Max," I said, imploringly, "you'll see us through this, won't you? Neither Ismay nor I can rush off to Halifax at once. You must go tomorrow morning. Go right to 110 Hollis Street and ask for 'Persian.' If the cat looks enough like Fatima, buy it and take it to Aunt Cynthia. If it doesn't—but it must! You'll go, won't you?"

"That depends," said Max.

I stared at him. This was so unlike Max.

"You are sending me on a nasty errand," he said, coolly. "How do I know that Aunt Cynthia will be deceived after all, even if she be shortsighted. Buying a cat in a joke is a huge risk. And if she should see through the scheme I shall be in a pretty mess."

"Oh, Max," I said, on the verge of tears.

"Of course," said Max, looking meditatively into the fire, "if I were really one of the family, or had any reasonable prospect of being so, I would not mind so much. It would be all in the day's work then. But as it is—"

Ismay got up and went out of the room.

"Oh, Max, please," I said.

"Will you marry me, Sue?" demanded Max sternly. "If you will agree, I'll go to Halifax and beard the lion in his den unflinchingly. If necessary, I will take a black street cat to Aunt Cynthia, and swear that it is Fatima. I'll get you out of the scrape, if I have to prove that you never had Fatima, that she is safe in your possession at the present time, and that there never was such an animal as Fatima anyhow. I'll do anything, say anything—but it must be for my future wife."

"Will nothing else content you?" I said helplessly.

"Nothing."

I thought hard. Of course Max was acting abominably — but—but—he was really a dear fellow—and this was the twelfth time—and there was Anne Shirley! I knew in my secret soul that life would be a dreadfully dismal thing if Max were not around somewhere. Besides, I would have married him long ago had not Aunt Cynthia thrown us so pointedly at each other's heads ever since he came to Spencervale.

"Very well," I said crossly.

Max left for Halifax in the morning. Next day we got a wire saying it was all right. The evening of the following day he was back in Spencervale. Ismay and I put him in a chair and glared at him impatiently.

Max began to laugh and laughed until he turned blue.

"I am glad it is so amusing," said Ismay severely. "If Sue and I could see the joke it might be more so."

"Dear little girls, have patience with me," implored Max. "If you knew what it cost me to keep a straight face in Halifax you would forgive me for breaking out now."

"We forgive you—but for pity's sake tell us all about it," I cried.

"Well, as soon as I arrived in Halifax I hurried to 110 Hollis Street, but—see here! Didn't you tell me your Aunt's address was 10 Pleasant Street?"

"So it is."

"'Tisn't. You look at the address on a telegram next time you get one. She went a week ago to visit another friend who lives at 110 Hollis."

"Max!"

"It's a fact. I rang the bell, and was just going to ask the maid for 'Persian' when your Aunt Cynthia herself came through the hall and pounced on me.

"'Max,' she said, 'have you brought Fatima?'

"'No,' I answered, trying to adjust my wits to this new development as she towed me into the library. 'No, I—I—just came to Halifax on a little matter of business.'

"'Dear me,' said Aunt Cynthia, crossly, 'I don't know what those girls mean. I wired them to send Fatima at once. And she has not come yet and I am expecting a call every minute from someone who wants to buy her.'

"'Oh!' I murmured, mining deeper every minute.

"'Yes,' went on your aunt, 'there is an advertisement in the Charlotteville *Enterprise* for a Persian cat, and I answered it. Fatima is really quite a charge, you know—and so apt to die and be a dead loss'—did your aunt mean a pun, girls?—'and so, although I am considerably attached to her, I have decided to part with her.'

"By this time I had got my second wind, and I promptly decided that a judicious mixture of the truth was the thing required.

"'Well, of all the curious coincidences,' I exclaimed. 'Why, Miss Ridley, it was I who advertised for a Persian cat—on Sue's behalf. She and Ismay have decided that they want a cat like Fatima for themselves.'

"You should have seen how she beamed. She said she knew you always really liked cats, only you would never own up to it. We clinched the dicker then and there. I passed her over your hundred and ten dollars—she took the money without turning a hair—and now you are the joint owners of Fatima. Good luck to your bargain!"

"Mean old thing," sniffed Ismay. She meant Aunt Cynthia, and, remembering our shabby furs, I didn't disagree with her.

"But there is no Fatima," I said, dubiously. "How shall we account for her when Aunt Cynthia comes home?"

"Well, your aunt isn't coming home for a month yet. When she comes you will have to tell her that the cat—is lost—but you needn't say *when* it happened. As for the rest, Fatima is your property now, so Aunt Cynthia can't grumble. But she will have a poorer opinion than ever of your fitness to run a house alone."

When Max left I went to the window to watch him down the path. He was really a handsome fellow, and I was proud of him. At the gate he turned to wave me good-bye, and, as he did, he glanced upward. Even at that distance I saw the look of amazement on his face. Then he came bolting back.

"Ismay, the house is on fire!" I shrieked, as I flew to the door.

"Sue," cried Max, "I saw Fatima, or her ghost, at the garret window a moment ago!"

"Nonsense!" I cried. But Ismay was already half way up the stairs and we followed. Straight to the garret we rushed. There sat Fatima, sleek and complacent, sunning herself in the window.

Max laughed until the rafters rang.

"She can't have been up here all this time," I protested, half tearfully. "We would have heard her meowing."

"But you didn't," said Max.

"She would have died of the cold," declared Ismay.

"But she hasn't," said Max.

"Or starved," I cried.

"The place is alive with mice," said Max. "No, girls, there is no doubt the cat has been here the whole fortnight. She must have followed Huldah Jane up here, unobserved, that day. It's a wonder you didn't hear her crying — if she did cry. But perhaps she didn't, and, of course, you sleep downstairs. To think you never thought of looking here for her!"

"It has cost us over a hundred dollars," said Ismay, with a malevolent glance at the sleek Fatima.

"It has cost me more than that," I said, as I turned to the stairway.

Max held me back for an instant, while Ismay and Fatima pattered down.

"Do you think it has cost too much, Sue?" he whispered.

I looked at him sideways. He was really a dear. Niceness fairly exhaled from him.

"No-o-o," I said, "but when we are married you will have to take care of Fatima, I won't."

"Dear Fatima," said Max gratefully.

How a Cat Played Robinson Crusoe
Charles G. D. Roberts

THE island was a mere sandbank off the low, flat coast. Not a tree broke its bleak levels—not even a shrub. But the long, gritty stalks of the marsh grass clothed it everywhere above tidemark; and a tiny rivulet of sweet water, flowing from a spring at its centre, drew a ribbon of inland herbage and tenderer green across the harsh and sombre yellow grey of the grass. Few would have chosen the island as a place to live, yet at its seaward end, where the changing tides were never still, stood a spacious, one-storied, wide-verandaed cottage, with a low shed behind it. The virtue of this lone plot of sand was coolness. When the neighbour mainland would be sweltering day and night alike under a breathless heat, out here on the island there was always a cool wind blowing. Therefore a wise city dweller had appropriated the sea waif and built his summer home thereon, where the tonic airs might bring back the rose to the pale cheeks of his children.

The family came to the island toward the end of June. In the first week of September they went away, leaving every door and window of house and shed securely shuttered, bolted or barred against the winter's storms. A roomy boat, rowed by two fishermen, carried them across the half mile of racing tides that separated them from the mainland. The elders of the household were not sorry to get back to the world of men, after two months of mere wind, and sun, and waves, and waving grass tops. But the children went with tear-stained faces. They were leaving behind them their favourite pet, the accustomed comrade of their migrations, a handsome, moonfaced cat, striped like a tiger. The animal had mysteriously disappeared two days before, vanishing from the face of the island without leaving a trace behind. The only reasonable explanation seemed to be that she had been snapped up by a passing eagle. The cat, meanwhile, was a fast prisoner at the other end of the island, hidden beneath a broken barrel and some hundredweight of drifted sand.

The old barrel, with the staves battered out of one side, had stood, half buried, on the crest of a sand ridge raised by a long prevailing wind. Under its lee the cat had found a sheltered hollow, full of sun, where she had been wont to lie curled up for hours at a time, basking and sleeping. Meanwhile the sand had been steadily piling itself higher and higher behind the unstable barrier. At last it had piled too high; and suddenly, before a stronger gust, the barrel had come toppling over beneath a mass of sand, burying the sleeping cat out of sight and light. But at the same time the sound half of the barrel had formed a safe roof to her prison, and she was neither crushed nor smothered. When the children in their anxious search all over the island chanced upon the mound of fine, white sand they gave it but one careless look. They could not hear the faint cries that came, at intervals, from the close darkness within. So they went away sorrowfully, little dreaming that their friend was imprisoned almost beneath their feet.

For three days the prisoner kept up her appeals for help. On the third day the wind changed and presently blew up a gale. In a few hours it had uncovered the barrel. At one corner a tiny spot of light appeared.

Eagerly the cat stuck her paw through the hole. When she withdrew it again the hole was much enlarged. She took the hint and fell to scratching. At first her efforts were rather aimless; but presently, whether by good luck or quick sagacity, she learned to make her scratching more effective. The opening rapidly enlarged, and at last she was able to squeeze her way out.

The wind was tearing madly across the island, filled with flying sand. The seas hurled themselves trampling up the beach, with the uproar of a bombardment. The grasses lay bowed flat in long quivering ranks. Over the turmoil the sun stared down from a deep, unclouded blue. The cat, when first she met the full force of the gale, was fairly blown off her feet. As soon as she could recover herself she crouched low and darted into the grasses for shelter. But there was little shelter there, the long stalks being held down almost level. Through their lashed lines, however, she sped straight before the gale, making for the cottage at the other end of the island, where she would find, as she fondly imagined, not only food and shelter but also loving comfort to make her forget her terrors.

Still and desolate in the bright sunshine and the tearing wind, the house frightened her. She could not understand the tight-closed shutters, the blind, unresponding doors that would no longer open to her anxious appeal. The wind swept her savagely across the naked veranda. Climbing with difficulty to the dining-room windowsill, where so often she had been let in, she clung there a few moments and yowled heart-brokenly. Then, in a sudden panic, she jumped down and ran to the shed. That, too, was closed. Never before had she seen the shed doors closed, and she could not understand it. Cautiously she crept around the foundations—but those had been built honestly: there was no such thing as getting in that way. On every side it was nothing but a blank, forbidding face that the old familiar house confronted her with.

The cat had always been so coddled and pampered by the children that she had had no need to forage for herself; but, fortunately for her, she had learned to hunt the marsh mice and grass sparrows for amusement. So now, being ravenous from her long fast under the sand, she slunk mournfully away from the deserted house and crept along under the lee of a sand ridge to a little grassy hollow which she knew. Here the gale caught only the tops of the grasses; and here, in the warmth and comparative calm, the furry little marsh folk, mice and shrews, were going about their business undisturbed.

The cat, quick and stealthy, soon caught one and eased her hunger. She caught several. And then, making her way back to the house, she spent hours in heartsick prowling around it and around, sniffing and peering, yowling piteously on the threshold and windowsill; and every now and then being blown ignominiously across the smooth, naked expanse of the veranda floor. At last, hopelessly discouraged, she curled herself up beneath the children's window and went to sleep.

In spite of her loneliness and grief the life of the island prisoner during the next two or three weeks was by no means one of hardship. Besides her abundant food of birds and mice she quickly learned to catch tiny fish in the mouth of the rivulet, where saltwater and freshwater met. It was an exciting game, and she became expert at dashing the grey tomcod and blue-and-silver sand lance far up the slope with a sweep of her armed paw. But when the equinoctial storms roared down upon the island, with furious rain, and low, black clouds torn to shreds, then life became more difficult for her. Game all took to cover, where it was hard to find. It was difficult to get around in the drenched and lashing grass; and, moreover, she loathed wet. Most of the time she went hungry, sitting sullen and desolate under the lee of the house, glaring out defiantly at the rush and battling tumult of the waves.

The storm lasted nearly ten days before it blew itself clean out. On the eighth day the abandoned wreck of a small Nova Scotia schooner drove ashore, battered out of all likeness to a ship. But hulk as it was it had passengers of a sort. A horde of rats got through the surf and scurried into the hiding of the grass roots. They promptly made themselves at home, burrowing under the grass and beneath old, half-buried timbers, and carrying panic into the ranks of the mice and shrews.

When the storm was over the cat had a decided surprise in her first long hunting expedition. Something had rustled the grass heavily and she trailed it, expecting a particularly large, fat marsh mouse. When she pounced and alighted upon an immense old ship's rat, many-voyaged and many-battled, she got badly bitten. Such an experience had never before fallen to her lot. At first she felt so injured that she was on the point of backing out and running away. Then her latent pugnacity awoke, and the fire of far-off ancestors. She flung herself into the fight with a rage that took no accounting of the wounds she got; and the struggle was soon over. Her wounds, faithfully licked, quickly healed themselves in that clean and tonic air; and after that, having learned how to handle such big game, she no more got bitten.

During the first full moon after her abandonment—the first week in October—the island was visited by still weather with sharp night frosts. The cat discovered then that it was most exciting to hunt by night and do her sleeping in the daytime. She found that now, under the strange whiteness of the moon, all her game was astir—except the birds, which had fled to the mainland during the storm, gathering for the southward flight. The blanched grasses, she found, were now everywhere a-rustle; and everywhere dim little shapes went darting with thin squeaks across ghostly-white sands. Also she made the acquaintaince of a new bird, which she regarded at first uneasily and then with vengeful wrath. This was the brown marsh owl, which came over from the mainland to do some autumn mouse hunting. There were two pairs of these big, downy-winged, round-eyed hunters, and they did not know there was a cat on the island.

The cat, spying one of them as it swooped soundlessly hither and thither over the silvered grass tops, crouched with flattened ears. With its wide spread of wing it looked bigger than herself; and the great round face, with hooked beak and wild, staring eyes, appeared extremely formidable. However, she was no coward; and presently, though not without reasonable caution, she went about her hunting. Suddenly the owl caught a partial glimpse of her in the grass—probably of her ears or head. He swooped; and at the same instant she sprang upward to meet the assault, spitting and growling harshly and striking with unsheathed claws. With a frantic flapping of his great wings the owl checked himself and drew back into the air, just escaping the clutch of those indignant claws. After that the marsh owls were careful to give her a wide berth. They realized that the black-striped animal with the quick spring and the clutching claws was not to be interfered with. They perceived that she was some relation to that ferocious prowler, the lynx.

In spite of all this hunting, however, the furry life of the marsh grass was so teeming, so inexhaustible, that the depredations of cat, rats and owls were powerless to make more than a passing impression upon it. So the hunting and the merrymaking went on side by side under the indifferent moon.

As the winter deepened—with bursts of sharp cold and changing winds that forced the cat to be continually changing her refuge—she grew more and more unhappy. She felt her homelessness keenly. Nowhere on the whole island could she find a nook where she might feel secure from both wind and rain. As for the old barrel, the first cause of her misfortunes, there was no help in that. The winds had long ago turned it completely over, open to the sky, then drifted it full of sand and reburied it. And in any case the cat would have been afraid to go near it again. So it came about that she alone of all the island dwellers had no shelter to turn to when the real winter arrived, with snows that smothered the grass tops out of sight, and frosts that lined the shore with grinding ice cakes. The rats had their holes under the buried fragments of wreckage; the mice and shrews had their deep, warm tunnels; the owls had nests in hollow trees far away in the forests of the mainland. But the cat, shivering and frightened, could do nothing but crouch against the blind walls of the unrelenting house and let the snow whirl itself and pile itself about her.

And now, in her misery, she found her food cut off. The mice ran secure in their hidden runways, where the grass roots on each side of them gave them easy and abundant provender. The rats, too, were out of sight—digging burrows

themselves in the soft snow in the hope of intercepting some
of the tunnels of the mice, and now and then snapping up an
unwary passerby. The ice fringe, crumbling and heaving
under the ruthless tide, put an end to her fishing. She would
have tried to capture one of the formidable owls in her hunger, but the owls no longer came to the island. They would
return, no doubt, later in the season when the snow had hard-
ened and the mice had begun to come out and play on the
surface. But for the present they were following an easier
chase in the deeps of the upland forest.

When the snow stopped falling and the sun came out again
there fell such keen cold as the cat had never felt before. The
day, as it chanced, was Christmas; and if the cat had had any
idea as to the calendar she would certainly have marked the
day in her memory as it was an eventful one for her. Starving
as she was she could not sleep, but kept ceaselessly on the
prowl. This was fortunate, for had she gone to sleep without
any more shelter than the wall of the house she would never
have wakened again. In her restlessness she wandered to the
farther side of the island where, in a somewhat sheltered and
sunny recess of the shore facing the mainland, she found a
patch of bare sand, free of ice cakes and just uncovered by the
tide. Opening upon this recess were the tiny entrances to several of the mouse tunnels.

Close beside one of these holds in the snow the cat crouched,
quiveringly intent. For ten minutes or more she waited, never
so much as twitching a whisker. At last a mouse thrust out its
little pointed head. Not daring to give it time to change its
mind or take alarm, she pounced. The mouse, glimpsing the
doom ere it fell, doubled back upon itself in the narrow runway.
Hardly realizing what she did in her desperation the cat
plunged head and shoulders into the snow, reaching blindly
after the vanished prize. By great good luck she caught it.

It was her first meal in four bitter days. The children had
always tried to share with her their Christmas cheer and
enthusiasm, and had usually succeeded in interesting her by

an agreeable lavishness in the matter of cream; but never before had she found a Christmas feast so good.

Now she had learned a lesson. Being naturally clever and her wits sharpened by her fierce necessities, she had grasped the idea that it was possible to follow her prey a little way into the snow. She had not realized that the snow was so penetrable. She had quite wiped out the door of this particular runway; so she went and crouched beside a similar one, but here she had to wait a long time before an adventurous mouse came to peer out. But this time she showed that she had grasped her lesson. It was straight at the side of the entrance that she pounced, where instinct told her that the body of the mouse would be. One outstretched paw thus cut off the quarry's retreat. Her tactics were completely successful; and as her head went plunging into the fluffy whiteness she felt the prize between her paws.

Her hunger now fairly appeased, she found herself immensely excited over this new fashion of hunting. Often before had she waited at mouse holes, but never had she found it possible to break down the walls and invade the holes themselves. It was a thrilling idea. As she crept toward another hole a mouse scurried swiftly up the sand and darted into it. The cat, too late to catch him before he disappeared, tried to follow him. Scratching clumsily but hopefully she succeeded in forcing the full length of her body into the snow. She found no sign of the fugitive, which was by this time racing in safety down some dim transverse tunnel. Her eyes, mouth, whiskers and fur full of the powdery white particles, she backed out, much disappointed. But in that moment she had realized that it was much warmer in there beneath the snow than out in the stinging air. It was a second and vitally important lesson; and though she was probably unconscious of having learned it she instinctively put the new lore into practice a little while later.

Having succeeded in catching yet another mouse for which her appetite made no immediate demand, she carried it back to the house and laid it down in tribute on the veranda steps while she meowed and stared hopefully at the desolate, snow-draped door. Getting no response she carried the mouse down with her to the hollow behind the drift which had been caused by the bulging front of the bay window on the end of the house. Here she curled herself up forlornly, thinking to have a wink of sleep.

But the still cold was too searching. She looked at the sloping wall of snow beside her and cautiously thrust her paw into it. It was very soft and light. It seemed to offer practically no resistance. She pawed away in an awkward fashion till she had scooped out a sort of tiny cave. Gently she pushed herself into it, pressing back the snow on every side till she had room to turn around.

Then turn around she did several times, as dogs do in getting their beds arranged to their liking. In this process she not only packed down the snow beneath her, but she also rounded out for herself a snug chamber with a comparatively narrow doorway. From this snowy retreat she gazed forth with a solemn air of possession; then she went to sleep with a sense of comfort, of "homeyness," such as she had never before felt since the disappearance of her friends.

Having thus conquered misfortune and won herself the freedom of the winter wild, her life though strenuous was no longer one of any terrible hardship. With patience at the mouse holes she could catch enough to eat; and in her snowy den she slept warm and secure. In a little while, when a crust had formed over the surface, the mice took to coming out at night and holding revels on the snow. Then the owls, too, came back; and the cat, having tried to catch one, got sharply bitten and clawed before she realized the propriety of letting it go. After this experience she decided that owls, on the whole, were meant to be let alone. But for all that she found it fine hunting, out there on the bleak, unfenced, white reaches of the snow.

Thus, mistress of the situation, she found the winter slipping by without further serious trials. Only once, toward the end of January, did Fate send her another bad quarter of an hour. On the heels of a peculiarly bitter cold snap a huge white owl from the Arctic Barrens came one night to the island. The cat, taking observations from the corner of the veranda, caught sight of him. One look was enough to assure her that this was a very different kind of visitor from the brown marsh owls. She slipped inconspicuously down into her burrow; and until the great white owl went away, some twenty-four hours later, she kept herself discreetly out of sight.

When spring came back to the island, with the nightly shrill chorus of fluting frogs in the shallow, sedgy pools and the young grass alive with nesting birds, the prisoner's life became almost luxurious in its easy abundance. But now she was once more homeless, since her snug den had vanished with the snow. This did not much matter to her, however, for the weather grew warmer and more tranquil day by day; and moreover, she herself, in being forced back upon her instincts, had learned to be as contented as a tramp. Nevertheless, with all her capacity for learning and adapting herself she had not forgotten anything. So when, one day in June, a crowded boat came over from the mainland, and children's voices, clamouring across the grass tops, broke the desolate silence of the island, the cat heard and sprang up out of her sleep on the veranda steps.

For one second she stood, listening intently. Then, almost as a dog would have done, and as few of her supercilious tribe ever condescend to do, she went racing across to the landing place—to be snatched up into the arms of four happy children at once, and to have her fine fur ruffled to a state which it would cost her an hour's assiduous toilet to put in order.

From the Diary of a Cat
Edwina Stanton Babcock

MONDAY.—Very uncertain and lamentable conditions of the weather, much dampness and discomfort. This morning I was forced to rise early, as it appeared that the cook at the house where I occasionally stay wished to use the coal scuttle in which I passed the night. I conveyed to her that she might have it and welcome, that its usefulness to me was, for the time being, over; and intimated that I should be obliged to her if she could furnish me with any suggestions as to where I might obtain a breakfast. She thrust me out of the gate. I turned and surveyed the cook with a look of reproach; the cook had not a graceful foot—yet I determined to accept it as an omen, and I kept on in the same direction in which I had been, as it were, impelled. Thus a calamity often saves us indecision. Being impelled in any direction is better than no progress at all. I proceeded with some deliberation around the edges of many puddles towards an ash barrel which I could dimly make out through the grey dawn. I saw very little that was worthy of my attention, but after acute search, walking slowly around the rim of the barrel, I at last descried a small chicken bone half embedded in the ashes. With some degree of exertion I drew it forth and made a delicious repast. My breakfast completed, and my personal appearance all that I could render it, the weather being so unpropitious, I spent the day in short excursions up and down fire escapes and in an observing ramble down Back Fence Boulevard. At last the sun came out, and I found a convenient porch step, and passed the remainder of the day in quiet reflections.

Tuesday.— . . . For a long while I have been very curious about a garden with a spiked fence enclosing it, which I pass daily on my promenades over the roofs. I often pause to look down upon it, and I have three times had the same dream about it. In the dream I thought that I had somehow obtained access to the garden, and that I dwelt there amid scenes of luxury and content. I did not lack for adventure and sport, for there were droves of entrancing white mice tripping here and there; enticing birds flew from tree to tree and played rarely at my favorite game of catching and eating; and besides all this there was a fountain of milk spinning high in the sunlight, with tender goldfish roving about in the great basin and endeavoring to attract my eye. It is not surprising that since my vivid dream I have used every device to effect an entrance into the garden, but I have not discovered a crack nor a crevice where I can creep in. Always, on my tours over the roofs, I have kept this object in mind. I have surveyed the situation carefully and accurately from every possible viewpoint, making estimates and measuring, and at last I think I can gain an entrance to the garden in four jumps. The first three I have essayed and found practicable, but the fourth jump is a feat of peculiar requirements. What agility I command has not yet proved equal to it, yet I am determined to accomplish it.

This fourth jump I have failed in repeatedly. Friends of mine who have unfailingly achieved well-nigh impossible leaps have warned me against the dangers attending this one. But it seems to me that what may not be crawled under must be jumped over, and so far in practising the jump, though I have invariably fallen, I have invariably alighted upon my feet.

Wednesday.— . . . Today I went in to see the grocer to consult with him as to my using one of the barrels in his cellar as a winter habitation. I offered to pay him in dead mice. I produced one as a sample. He asked what he could do with a dead mouse. I thought it a stupid question, for I have observed that he was never able to put live mice to any use, and I suggested that he should sell them, as he had been so successful in selling dead fish. What there was in my bearing that should so have offended the grocer I do not know. As he has no tail,

I could not be aware of his rising wrath. I was, therefore, not a little surprised when he seized me by the neck and hurled me into the street. I had no time to remonstrate. My sensations were indescribable. Flying through the air in a revolving manner does away with apperception. It is well-nigh impossible to record one's impressions when one is in doubt as to whether he is upside down or side wise over, and keeps on revolving in a maze of successive inversions. I obtained some exceedingly curious views of my surroundings, and I regret that I cannot recall them more clearly. But as I remember my swift and shameful transit, I see how much we have to depend upon our own uprightness to judge correctly the position of others. The grocer, as I left his grasp, appeared to me to be standing on his head, but it was in reality I who stood upon nothing who mistook his attitude.

As I say, my speed was great, and, though I alighted upon my feet, my distance from the grocer was incredibly long. Fortunately, I retained my presence of mind, and I turned, surveying the grocer with intense disapproval. I conveyed to him that from my point of view he had acted with undue haste and under grave error, and that I should trouble him no further. I then went down a side street, regretting that I had left the sample mouse where the grocer would be sure to see it and appropriate it.

Friday.— . . . For some time I have been interested in the cultivation of my voice. There are certain tones that I find I can produce with ease, and I have developed them into sounds of extraordinary power. Of late, in the evenings, I have taken up a comfortable position on Back Fence Avenue and practised these tones; I keep to simple exercises, striving for a certain quality of great beauty and sweetness. One or two friends having a like ambition, we have formed an agreeable custom of meeting at the same spot every night and comparing our progress. Our exertions have caused intense curiosity in the inmates of the houses about us, and exclamations of wonder and awe are often heard. We expect to combine our several tones of excellence into a chord which will express great emotion. It will be called the "Yearn Chord," or the "Song of Unnumbered Woes," and will be of a plaintive, pleading character, with rising and falling cadences and inflections of great depth and resonance.

Monday.— . . . After practising the fourth jump and being unsuccessful, I repaired to the butcher's to try and obtain a portion of meat. I walked in upon him early, and with a brisk manner, as one who should say, "It is necessary that I should eat to live." "Are you sure that you do not live to eat?" retorted the butcher.

The butcher is a brief and caustic man. The shortness of his speech is due to the influence of his pursuits upon his character. There is nothing quicker and shorter than a chop or a cut. A butcher might, with great success, found a school of expression for preciseness and brevity. I jumped upon his broad back where he could not reach me.

"Get off, you brute!" cried the butcher, but I dug my claws deeper into his soft, fat flesh. Then he bribed me, and when he tempted me with something worth my while, a red and juicy bit of steak, down I came, and, seizing the meat in my mouth, ran out of the shop and ate the steak behind a garbage can. Poverty, it is said, sharpens the wits, but it is hard to keep the wits as sharp as the hunger, which poverty also grinds out to a pretty point.

Tuesday.— . . . After many failures, I have at last discovered a most desirable place in which to sleep. I have adopted one of the large white urns on the gateway of the entrance to the park. It is a commodious, elegant affair, sheltered by the great oak tree that spreads its branches over the gateway, and I can drop into it from the oak boughs as softly and lightly as a snowflake. There I have solitude and shadowed gloom; the moonlight reveals the cold statues glimmering in the groves and bathes the dead fountain in white streams. Not wishing to be selfish, and sensible of the lack of sleeping-places, I invited a chance acquaintance, Speckle Devil by name, to occupy the other urn. He refused in a sullen, dogged manner, saying in a shamefaced way that "he didn't want to sleep in no Symbol"; but Speckle is of a rough and superstitious nature, given to foolish and groundless prejudices. He and two friends of his, Stealthy Rake and Smutty Sneak, make a strange trio. Careless of appearances, rough and defiant in manner, theirs seem to be characters of intense swagger and bravado; but their adventures and their conversation I find highly interesting. I detect a certain eloquence and clear-cutness in their expressions. I find that their lack of conventionality renders them at once picturesque and convincing. Hence I ask the question— can it be that it is only the vagabond and the social outcast to whom it has been given to utter plain truths? Is it only a rake that can call a spade a spade?

Tuesday.— . . . Mild weather. Perhaps spring is coming. I spent the morning wandering through some empty sewer pipes. It is a stealthy mode of travel, and one that much pleases me. Things that I wish to eat I often secret in these pipes until such time as I can enjoy them. The only difficulty is that the pipes are all very much alike, and are placed end to end in long lines down the different streets, so that it is often hard for me to remember in which pipe I placed the bone or bacon rind that I wished to preserve. I sometimes wander on through miles and miles of pipe in search of the treasure, only to discover at last that I have entered the wrong line of pipes. However, my travels are entertaining, and often bring me out to interesting places. This morning, as I stepped out of the end of the pipe tunnel into the open sunlight, I found myself facing a dog kennel, which I concluded was empty. There was a saucer of milk by the door. I stopped to quench my thirst, when immediately I was set upon by an old blind creature, who flew out of the kennel and hurled furious invective at me. I drew back. "Madam," said I, "there is some mistake here."

"You are the mistake!" retorted the old creature. "Get out of here!"—uttering horrible imprecations. This unpleasant exhibition of feminine temper completely unnerved me.

Though I wished to explain that my interest in the milk had been merely that of endeavoring to test the accuracy of casual observation, I refrained, and, completely disgusted, moved rapidly back into the sewer pipe.

Wednesday.— . . . I was in an ailantus tree in Pigeon Place the other day, devoting my leisure to nature study. I was endeavoring to concentrate upon the innocent gambols of a flock of sparrows, one of whom, by her artless coquetries, particularly engaged my attention. Her fascination for me was exceedingly pleasant, and I cast about for some means of drawing nearer to her, for nothing could have been more coy and retiring than the little sparrows. As I gently advanced along the limb upon which she perched, gazing at me with a pretty shyness, I was startled to perceive someone else climbing the tree. Looking down, I recognized my acquaintance, Speckle Devil, who rapidly ascended. I concealed myself, but the astute Speckle soon discovered me. When he approached, the sparrows ceased their interesting sports, and flew away. I was disappointed, and could not conceal my chagrin from the clumsy Speckle. He stopped and surveyed me.

"Chasing dickey birds, hey?" he volunteered, in his coarse way.

I was irritated, and did not hesitate to show it. I climbed farther out on the limb. Speckle followed me. "Don't be mad," he whined, teasingly.

I faced him and surveyed him with cool scorn. "You look like a shattered ideal, Speckle," I said, trying to make him sensible of his uncouth appearance, for nothing could have been filthier or more shocking than his entire person.

He turned and sharpened his claws on the limb, saying, defiantly: "Oh, get gay, then—wot do I care? You look like an animal cracker, you do. Gee! You look like a leopard that's lost his spots."

I saw then that the honest fellow was hurt, and in a milder tone I asked him his reason for disturbing me. Speckle chewed a twig or two in silence, then he replied, "Fight."

I was interested at once. I hesitated. I had some idea of going to practise the fourth jump, and I disliked the society of Rat Alley. Speckle watched me disdainfully, narrowing his yellow eyes. Finally I said:

"No, Speckle, I think I shall stay here. You must understand that is a principle of mine—not to witness a fight."

Speckle, having reached the ground, turned up his face and eyed me scornfully. "Principle?" he sneered. "Principle! Won't witness a fight, hey? Sits on a limb and witnesses dickey birds, but he's too good to witness a fight. Oh, Lord!" and he swore violently. Then saying, with intense scorn, "Yes, you're full of principle, you are!" he ran along the fence towards Rat Alley.

Thursday.— . . . Had an interesting debate this morning with an old family friend who used to know my mother. Our talk drifted to serious things, and I asked her if she believed in the theory of nine lives. She replied that she did, that she knew for certain that she had lived through seven lives, and warned me against such rash ventures as the fourth jump without making sure of at least one life to spare.

Saturday.— . . . I spent yesterday afternoon and evening at the home of a young child, whom I followed because she bore a paper of codfish which attracted me. The house where the child lives was exceedingly warm and pleasant, and I reclined in front of the glowing fire and made myself agreeable and attractive, considering meanwhile the advantages of such a home. It has often occurred to me that sometime in my life I must have been owned. I can recall the feeling of caresses and the scent of soft garments worn by some gentle person who felt solicitude and affection for me. I think I can remember, though but dimly, the look of delicate white hands that cuddled me, and the warmth and sweetness of a breast to which I was pressed. How I ever became dissevered from all those comfortable conditions I do not know, but it was long ago, and has no part in my present life, for now I become restless in any close environment, and invariably after a short stay by some hearth of friendliness I feel the spell of the streets—a spell that draws me away from mere ease and plenty to the thrill and mystery of a roving life. And so it was yesterday. Half slumbering on the little girl's lap after a delicious refreshment of custard and cold liver, I heard suddenly, or thought I heard, a voice that called me; and an old desire for vast lonely spaces, for the Desert of the Roofs, for silent cobbled streets, seized me. I thought of the vague gutters stretching away into solitude and night, and the old hungry haunting, the strong longing to go out and look for something, possessed me. I got down from the little girl's lap and went out of the door that led to the street.

A Black Affair
W. W. *Jacobs*

"I didn't want to bring it," said Captain Gubson, regarding somewhat unfavorably a grey parrot whose cage was hanging against the mainmast, "but my old uncle was so set on it I had to. He said a sea voyage would set its 'elth up."

"It seems to be all right at present," said the mate, who was tenderly sucking his forefinger. "Best of spirits, I should say."

"It's playful," assented the skipper. "The old man thinks a rare lot of it. I think I shall have a little bit in that quarter, so keep your eye on the beggar."

"Scratch Poll!" said the parrot, giving its bill a preliminary strop on its perch. "Scratch poor Polly!"

It bent its head against the bars, and waited patiently to play off what it had always regarded as the most consummate practical joke in existence. The first doubt it had ever had about it occurred when the mate came forward and obligingly scratched it with the stem of his pipe. It was a wholly unforeseen development, and the parrot ruffling its feathers, edged along its perch and brooded darkly at the other end of it.

Opinion before the mast was also against the new arrival, the general view being that the wild jealousy which raged in the bosom of the ship's cat would sooner or later lead to mischief.

"Old Satan don't like it," said the cook, shaking his head. "The blessed bird hadn't been aboard ten minutes before Satan was prowling around. The blooming image waited till he was about a foot off the cage, and then he did the perlite and asked him whether he'd like a glass o' beer. *I* never see a cat so took aback in all my life. Never."

"There'll be trouble between 'em," said old Sam, who was the cat's special protector, "mark my words."

"I'd put my money on the parrot," said one of the men confidently. "It's 'ad a crool bit out of the mate's finger. Where 'ud the cat be agin that beak?"

"Well, you'd lose your money," said Sam. "If you want to do the cat a kindness, every time you see him near that cage cuff his 'ed."

The crew being much attached to the cat, which had been presented to them when a kitten by the mate's wife, acted upon the advice with so much zest that for the next two days the indignant animal was like to have been killed with kindness. On the third day, however, the parrot's cage being on the cabin table, the cat stole furtively down, and, at the pressing request of the occupant itself, scratched its head for it.

The skipper was the first to discover the mischief, and he came on deck and published the news in a voice which struck a chill to all hearts.

"Where's that black devil got to!" he yelled.

"Anything wrong, sir?" asked Sam anxiously.

"Come and look here," said the skipper. He led the way to the cabin, where the mate and one of the crew were already standing, shaking their heads over the parrot.

"What do you make of that?" demanded the skipper fiercely.

"Too much dry food," repeated Sam firmly. "A parrot—a grey parrot—wants plenty o' sop. If it don't get it, it molts."

"It's had too much *cat*," the skipper said fiercely, "and you know it, and overboard it goes."

"I don't believe it was the cat, sir," interposed the other man. "It's too softhearted to do a thing like that."

"You can shut your jaw," said the skipper, reddening. "Who asked you to come down here at all?"

"Nobody saw the cat do it," urged the mate.

The skipper said nothing, but, stooping down, picked up a tail feather from the floor, and laid it on the table. He then went on deck, followed by the others, and began calling, in seductive tones, for the cat. No reply forthcoming from the sagacious animal, which had gone into hiding, he turned to Sam, and bade him call it.

"No, sir, I won't 'ave no 'and in it," said the old man. "Putting aside my liking for the animal, *I'm* not going to 'ave anything to do with the killing of a black cat."

"Rubbish!" said the skipper.

"Very good, sir," said Sam, shrugging his shoulders. "You know best, best o' course. You're educated and I'm not, an' p'r'aps you can afford to make a laugh o' such things. I knew one man who killed a black cat an' he went mad. There's something very pecooliar about that cat o' ours."

"It knows more than we do," said one of the crew, shaking his head. "That time you—I mean we—ran the smack down, that cat was expecting of it 'ours before. It was like a wild thing."

"Look at the weather we've 'ad—look at the trips we've made since he's been aboard," said the old man. "Tell me it's chance if you like, but I *know* better."

The skipper hesitated. He was a superstitious man even for a sailor, and his weakness was so well known that he had become a sympathetic receptacle for every ghost story which, by reason if its crudeness or lack of corroboration, had been rejected by other experts. He was a perfect reference library for omens, and his interpretations of dreams had gained for him a widespread reputation.

"That's all nonsense," he said, pausing uneasily. "Still, I only want to be just. There's nothing vindictive about me, and I'll have no hand in it myself. Joe, just tie a lump of coal to that cat and heave it overboard."

"Not me," said the cook, following Sam's lead, and working up a shudder. "Not for fifty pun in gold. I don't want to be haunted."

"The parrot's a little better now, sir," said one of the men, taking advantage of his hesitation. "He's opened one eye."

"Well, I only want to be just," repeated the skipper. "I won't do anything in a hurry, but, mark my words, if the parrot dies that cat goes overboard."

Contrary to expectations, the bird was still alive when London was reached, though the cook, who from his connection with the cabin had suddenly reached a position of unusual importance, reported great loss of strength and irritability of temper. It was still alive, but failing fast on the day they were put to sea again; and the fo'c'sle, in preparation for the worst, stowed their pet away in the paint locker, and discussed the situation.

Their council was interrupted by the mysterious behavior of the cook, who, having gone out to lay in a stock of bread, suddenly broke in upon them more in the manner of a member of a secret society than a humble but useful unit of a ship's company.

"Where's the cap'n?" he asked in a hoarse whisper, as he took a seat on the locker with the sack of bread between his knees.

"In the cabin," said Sam, regarding his antics with some disfavor. "What's wrong, cookie?"

"What d' yer think I've got in here?" asked the cook, patting the bag.

The obvious reply to this question was, of course, bread; but as it was known that the cook had departed specially to buy some, and that he could hardly ask a question involving such a simple answer, nobody gave it.

"It come to me all of a sudden," said the cook, in a thrilling whisper. "I'd just bought the bread and left the shop, when I see a big black cat, the very image of ours, sitting on a doorstep. I just stooped down to stroke its 'ed, when it come to me."

"They will sometimes," said one of the seamen.

"I don't mean that," said the cook, with the contempt of genius. "I mean the idea did. Says I to myself, 'You might be old Satan's brother by the look of you; an' if the cap'n wants to kill a cat, let it be you,' I says. And with that, before it could say Jack Robinson, I picked it up by the scruff o' the neck and shoved it in the bag."

"What, all in along of our bread?" said the previous interrupter, in a pained voice.

"Some of yer are 'ard ter please," said the cook, deeply offended.

"Don't mind him, cook," said the admiring Sam. "You're a masterpiece, that's what you are."

"Of course, if any of you've got a better plan—" said the cook generously.

"Don't talk rubbish, cook," said Sam. "Fetch the two cats out and put 'em together."

"Don't mix 'em," said the cook warningly, "for you'll never know which is which agin if you do."

He cautiously opened the top of the sack and produced his captive, and Satan having been relieved from his prison, the two animals were carefully compared.

"They're as like as two lumps o' coal," said Sam slowly. "Lord, what a joke on the old man. I must tell the mate o' this; he'll enjoy it."

"It'll be all right if the parrot don't die," said the dainty pessimist, still harping on his pet theme. "All that bread spoilt, and two cats aboard."

"Don't mind what he says," said Sam; "you're a brick, that's what you are. I'll just make a few holes on the lid o' the boy's chest, and pop old Satan in. You don't mind, do you, Billy?"

"Of course he don't," said the other men indignantly.

Matters being thus agreeably arranged, Sam got a gimlet, and prepared the chest for the reception of its tenant, who, convinced that he was being put out of the way to make room for a rival, made a frantic fight for freedom.

"Now get something 'eavy and put on the top of it," said Sam, having convinced himself that the lock was broken; "and, Billy, put the new cat in the paint locker till we start; it's homesick."

The boy obeyed, and the understudy was kept in durance vile until they were off Limehouse, when he came on deck and nearly ended his career there and then by attempting to jump over the bulwark into the next garden. For some time he paced the deck in a perturbed fashion, and then, leaping on the stern, mewed plaintively as his native city receded farther and farther from his view.

"What's the matter with old Satan?" said the mate, who had been let into the secret. "He seems to have something on his mind."

"He'll have something round his neck presently," said the skipper grimly.

The prophecy was fulfilled some three hours later, when he came up on deck ruefully regarding the remains of a bird whose vocabulary had once been the pride of its native town. He threw it on board without a word, and then, seizing the innocent cat, who had followed him under the impression that it was about to lunch, produced half a brick attached to a string, and tied it round his neck. The crew, who were enjoying the joke immensely, raised a howl of protest.

"The *Skylark*'ll never have another like it, sir," said Sam solemnly. "That cat was the luck of the ship."

"I don't want any of your old woman's yarns," said the skipper brutally. "If you want the cat, go and fetch it."

He stepped aft as he spoke, and sent the gentle stranger hurtling through the air. There was a "plomp" as it reached the water, a bubble or two came to the surface, and all was over.

"That's the last o' that," he said, turning away.

The old man shook his head. "You can't kill a black cat for nothing," said he, "mark my words!"

The skipper, who was in a temper at the time, thought little of them, but they recurred to him vividly the next day. The wind had freshened during the night, and rain was falling heavily. On deck the crew stood about in oilskins, while below, the boy, in his new capacity of gaoler, was ministering to the wants of an ungrateful prisoner, when the cook, happening to glance that way, was horrified to see the animal emerge from the fo'c'sle. It eluded easily the frantic clutch of the boy as he sprang up the ladder after it, and walked leisurely along the deck in the direction of the cabin. Just as the crew had given it up for lost it encountered Sam, and the next moment, despite its cries, was caught up and huddled away beneath his stiff, clammy oilskins. At the noise the skipper, who was talking to the mate, turned as though he had been shot, and gazed wildly round him.

"Dick," said he, "can you hear a cat?"

"Cat!" said the mate, in accents of great astonishment.

"I thought I heard it," said the puzzled skipper.

"Fancy sir," said Dick firmly, as a mewing, appalling in its wrath, came from beneath Sam's coat.

"Did you hear it, Sam?" called the skipper, as the old man was moving off.

"Hear what, sir?" inquired Sam respectfully, without turning round.

"Nothing," said the skipper, collecting himself. "Nothing. All right."

The old man, hardly able to believe in his good fortune, made his way forward, and, seizing a favorable opportunity, handed his ungrateful burden back to the boy.

"Fancy you heard a cat just now?" inquired the mate casually.

"Well, between you an' me, Dick," said the skipper, in a mysterious voice, "I did, and it wasn't fancy neither. I heard that cat as plain as if it was alive."

"Well, I've heard of such things," said the other, "but I don't believe 'em. What a lark if the old cat comes back climbing up over the side out of the sea tonight, with the brick hanging round its neck."

The skipper stared at him for some time without speaking. "If that's your idea of a lark," he said at length, in a voice which betrayed traces of some emotion. "It ain't mine."

"Well, if you hear it again," said the mate cordially, "you might let me know. I'm rather interested in such things."

The skipper, hearing no more of it that day, tried hard to persuade himself that he was the victim of imagination, but, in spite of this, he was pleased at night, as he stood at the wheel, to reflect on the sense of companionship afforded by the lookout in the bows. On his part the lookout was quite charmed with the unwonted affability of the skipper, as he yelled out to him two or three times on matters only faintly connected with the progress of the schooner.

The night, which had been dirty, cleared somewhat, and the bright crescent of the moon appeared above a heavy bank of clouds as the cat, which had by dint of using its back as a lever at length got free from that cursed chest, licked its shapely limbs, and came up on deck. After its stifling prison, the air was simply delicious.

"Bob!" yelled the skipper suddenly.

"Ay, ay, sir!" said the lookout, in a startled voice.

"Did you mew?" inquired the skipper.

"Did I *wot,* sir?" cried the astonished Bob.

"Mew," said the skipper sharply, "like a cat?"

"No, sir," said the offended seaman. "What 'ud I want to do that for?"

"I don't know what you want to for," said the skipper, looking round him uneasily. "There's some more rain coming, Bob."

"Ay, ay, sir," said Bob.

"Lot o' rain we've had this summer," said the skipper, in a meditative bawl.

"Ay, ay, sir," said Bob. "Sailing ship on the port bow, sir."

The conversation dropped, the skipper, anxious to divert his thoughts, watching the dark mass of sail as it came plunging out of the darkness into the moonlight until it was abreast of his own craft. His eyes followed it as it passed his quarter, so that he saw not the stealthy approach of the cat which came from behind the companion, and sat down close by him. For

over thirty hours the animal had been subjected to the gross-
est indignities at the hands of every man on board the ship
except one. That one was the skipper, and there is no doubt
but that its subsequent behavior was a direct recognition of
that fact. It rose to its feet, and crossing over to the unconscious skipper, rubbed its head affectionately and vigorously
against his leg.

From simple causes great events do spring. The skipper
sprang four yards, and let off a screech which was the subject
of much comment on the bark which had just passed. When
Bob, who came shuffling up at the double, reached him he
was leaning against the side, incapable of speech, and shaking
all over.

"Anything wrong, sir?" inquired the seaman anxiously, as he
ran to the wheel.

The skipper pulled himself together a bit, and got closer to
his companion.

"Believe me or not, Bob," he said at length, in trembling
accents, "just as you please, but the ghost of that—cat, I mean
the ghost of that poor affectionate animal which I drowned,
and which I wish I hadn't, came and rubbed itself up against
my leg."

"Which leg?" inquired Bob, who was ever careful about
details.

"What the blazes does it matter which leg?" demanded the
skipper, whose nerves were in a terrible state. "Ah, look—look
there!"

The seaman followed his outstretched finger, and his heart
failed him as he saw the cat, with its back arched, gingerly
picking its way along the side of the vessel.

"I can't see nothing," he said doggedly.

"I don't suppose you can, Bob," said the skipper in a melancholy voice, as the cat vanished in the bows. "It's evidently
only meant for me to see. What it means I don't know. I'm
going down to turn in. I ain't fit for duty. You don't mind being
left alone till the mate comes up, do you?"

"I ain't afraid," said Bob.

His superior officer disappeared below, and, shaking the sleepy mate, who protested strongly against the proceedings, narrated in trembling tones his horrible experiences.

"If I were you—" said the mate.

"Yes?" said the skipper, waiting a bit. Then he shook him again, roughly.

"What were you going to say?" he inquired.

"Say?" said the mate, rubbing his eyes. "Nothing."

"About the cat?" suggested the skipper.

"Cat?" said the mate, nestling lovingly down in the blankets again. "What—ca'—goo'ni'—"

Then the skipper drew the blankets from the mate's sleepy clutches, and, rolling him backward and forward in the bunk, patiently explained to him that he was very unwell, that he was going to have a drop of whiskey neat, and turn in, and that he, the mate, was to take the watch. From this moment the joke lost much of its savor for the mate.

"You can have a nip too, Dick," said the skipper, proffering him the whiskey, as the other sullenly dressed himself.

"It's all rot," said the mate, tossing the spirits down his throat, "and it's no use either; you can't run away from a ghost; it's just as likely to be in your bed as anywhere else. Good night."

He left the skipper pondering over his last words, and dubiously eyeing the piece of furniture in question. Nor did he retire until he had subjected it to an analysis of the most searching description, and then, leaving the lamp burning, he sprang hastily in, and forgot his troubles in sleep.

It was day when he awoke, and went on deck to find a heavy sea running, and just sufficient sail set to keep the schooner's head before the wind as she bobbed about on the waters. An exclamation from the skipper, as a wave broke against the side and flung a cloud of spray over him, brought the mate's head round.

"Why, you ain't going to get up?" he said, in tones of insincere surprise.

"Why not?" inquired the other gruffly.

"You go and lay down agin," said the mate, "and have a cup o' nice hot tea an' some toast."

"Clear out," said the skipper, making a dash for the wheel, and reaching it as the wet deck suddenly changed his angle. "I know you didn't like being woke up, Dick; but I got the horrors last night. Go below and turn in."

"All right," said the mollified mate.

"You didn't see anything?" inquired the skipper, as he took the wheel from him.

"Nothing at all," said the other.

The skipper shook his head thoughtfully, then shook it again vigorously, as another shower bath put its head over the side and saluted him.

"I wish I hadn't drowned that cat, Dick," he said.

"You won't see it agin," said Dick, with the confidence of a man who had taken every possible precaution to render the prophecy a safe one.

He went below, leaving the skipper at the wheel idly watching the cook as he performed marvelous feats of jugglery, between the galley and the fo'c'sle, with the men's breakfast.

A little while later, leaving the wheel to Sam, he went below himself and had his own, talking freely, to the discomfort of the conscience-stricken cook, about his weird experiences of the night before.

"You won't see it no more, sir, I don't expect," he said faintly. "I believe it come and rubbed itself up agin your leg to show it forgave you."

"Well, I hope it knows it's understood," said the other. "I don't want it to take any more trouble."

He finished the breakfast in silence, and then went on deck again. It was still blowing hard, and he went over to superintend the men who were attempting to lash together some empties which were rolling about in all directions amidships. A violent roll set them free again, and at the same time separated two chests in the fo'c'sle, which were standing one on top of the other. This enabled Satan, who was crouching in the lower one, half crazed with terror, to come flying madly up on deck and give his feelings full vent. Three times in full view of the horrified skipper he circled the deck at racing speed, and had just started on the fourth when a heavy packing case, which had been temporarily set on end and abandoned by the men at his sudden appearance, fell over and caught him by the tail. Sam rushed to the rescue.

"Stop!" yelled the skipper.

"Won't I put it up, sir?" inquired Sam.

"Do you see what's beneath it?" said the skipper, in a husky voice.

"Beneath it, sir?" said Sam, whose ideas were in a whirl.

"The cat, can't you see the cat?" said the skipper, whose eyes had been riveted on the animal since its first appearance on deck.

Sam hesitated a moment, and then shook his head.

"The case has fallen on the cat," said the skipper, "I can see it distinctly."

He might have said "heard it," too, for Satan was making frenzied appeals to his sympathetic friends for assistance.

"Let me put the case back, sir," said one of the men, "then p'r'aps the wision'll disappear."

"No, stop where you are," said the skipper. "I can stand it better by daylight. It's the most wonderful and extraordinary thing I've ever seen. Do you mean to say you can't see anything, Sam?"

"I can see a case, sir," said Sam, speaking slowly and carefully, "with a bit of rusty iron band sticking out from it. That's what you're mistaking for the cat, p'r'aps, sir."

"Can't you see anything, cook?" demanded the skipper.

"It may be fancy, sir," faltered the cook, lowering his eyes, "but it does seem to me as though I can see a little misty sort o' thing there. Ah, now it's gone."

"No, it ain't," said the skipper. "The ghost of Satan's sitting there. The case seems to have fallen on its tail. It appears to be howling something dreadful."

The men made a desperate effort to display the astonishment suitable to such a marvel, while Satan, who was trying all he knew to get his tail out, cursed freely. How long the superstitious captain of the *Skylark* would have let him remain there will never be known for just then the mate came on deck and caught sight of it before he was quite aware of the part he was expected to play.

"Why the devil don't you lift the thing off the poor brute," he yelled, hurrying up toward the case.

"What, can *you* see it, Dick?" said the skipper impressively, laying his hand on his arm.

"*See* it?" retorted the mate. "D'ye think I'm blind? Listen to the poor brute. I should—oh!"

He became conscious of the concentrated significant gaze of the crew. Five pairs of eyes speaking as one, all saying "idiot" plainly, the boy's eyes conveying an expression too great to be translated.

Turning, the skipper saw the byplay, and a light slowly dawned upon him. But he wanted more, and he wheeled suddenly to the cook for the required illumination.

The cook said it was a lark. Then he corrected himself and said it wasn't a lark, then he corrected himself again and became incoherent. Meantime the skipper eyed him stonily, while the mate released the cat and good-naturedly helped to straighten its tail.

It took fully five minutes of unwilling explanation before the skipper could grasp the situation. He did not appear to fairly understand it until he was shown the chest with the ventilated lid; then his countenance cleared, and, taking the unhappy Billy by the collar, he called sternly for a piece of rope.

By this statesmanlike handling of the subject a question of much delicacy and difficulty was solved, discipline was preserved, and a practical illustration of the perils of deceit afforded to a youngster who was at an age best suited to receive such impressions. That he should exhaust the resources of a youthful but powerful vocabulary upon the crew in general, and Sam in particular, was only to be expected. They bore him no malice for it, but, when he showed signs of going beyond his years, held a hasty consultation, and then stopped his mouth with sixpence-halfpenny and a broken jackknife.

The Yellow Terror
W. L. *Alden*

"SPEAKING of cats," said Captain Foster, "I'm free to say that I don't like 'em. I don't care to be looked down on by any person, whether he be man or cat. I know I ain't the President of the United States, nor yet a millionaire, nor yet the Boss of New York, but all the same I calculate that I'm a man, and entitled to be treated as such. Now, I never knew a cat yet that didn't look down on me, same as cats do on everybody. A cat considers that men are just dirt under his or her paws, as the case may be. I can't see what it is that makes a cat believe that he is so everlastingly superior to all the men that have ever lived, but there's no denying the fact that such is his belief, and he acts accordingly. There was a Professor here one day, lecturing on all sorts of animals, and I asked him if he could explain this aggravating conduct of cats. He said that it was because cats used to be gods, thousands of years ago in the land of Egypt; but I didn't believe him. Egypt is a Scripture country, and consequently we ought not to believe anything about it that we don't read in the Bible. Show me anywhere in the Bible that Egyptian cats are mentioned as having practised as gods, and I'll believe it. Till you show it to me, I'll take the liberty of disbelieving any worldly statement that Professors or anybody else may make about Egypt.

"The most notorious cat I ever met was old Captain Smedley's Yellow Terror. His real legal name was just plain Tom: but being yellow, and being a holy terror in many respects, it got to be the fashion among his acquaintances to call him 'The Yellow Terror.' He was a tremendous big cat, and he had been with Captain Smedley for five years before I saw him.

"Smedley was one of the best men I ever knew. I'll admit that he was a middling hard man on his sailors, so that his ship got the reputation of being a slaughter-house, which it didn't really deserve. And there is no denying that he was a very religious man, which was another thing which made him unpopular with the men. I'm a religious man myself, even when I'm at sea, but I never held with serving out religion to a crew, and making them swallow it with belaying pins. That's what old Smedley used to do. He was in command of the barque *Medford*, out of Boston, when I knew him. I mean the city of Boston in Massachusetts, and not the little town that folks over in England call Boston: and I must say that I can't see why they should copy the names of our cities, no matter how celebrated they may be. Well! The *Medford* used to sail from Boston to London with grain, where she discharged her cargo and loaded again for China. On the outward passage we used to stop at Madeira, and the Cape, and generally Bangkok, and so on to Canton, where we filled up with tea, and then sailed for home direct.

"Now thishyer Yellow Terror had been on the ship's books for upwards of five years when I first met him. Smedley had him regularly shipped, and signed his name to the ship articles, and held a pen in his paw while he made a cross. . . . You see, in those days the underwriters wouldn't let a ship go to sea without a cat, so as to keep the rats from getting at the cargo. I don't know what a land cat may do, but there ain't a seafaring cat that would look at a rat. What with the steward, and the cook and the men forrard, being always ready to give the ship's cat a bite, the cat is generally full from kelson to deck, and wouldn't take the trouble to speak to a rat, unless one was to bite her tail. But, then, underwriters never know anything about what goes on at sea, and it's a shame that a sailorman should be compelled to give in to their ideas. The Yellow Terror had the general idea that the *Medford* was his private yacht, and that all hands were there to wait on him. And Smedley sort of confirmed him in that idea, by treating

him with more respect than he treated his owners, when he
was ashore. I don't blame the cat, and after I got to know what
sort of a person the cat really was, I can't say as I blamed
Smedley to any great extent.

"Tom, which I think I told you was the cat's real name, was
far and away the best fighter of all cats in Europe, Asia,
Africa, and America. Whenever we sighted land he would get
himself up in his best fur, spending hours brushing and polishing it, and biting his claws so as to make sure that they
were as sharp as they could be made. As soon as the ship was
made fast to the quay, or anchored in the harbour, the Yellow
Terror went ashore to look for trouble. He always got it too,
though he had such a reputation as a fighter, that whenever
he showed himself, every cat that recognised him broke for
cover. Why, the gatekeeper at the London Docks—I mean
the one at the Shadwell entrance—told me that he always
knew when the *Medford* was warping into dock, by the stream
of cats that went out of the gate, as if a pack of hounds were
after them. You see that as soon as the *Medford* was reported,
and word passed among the cats belonging to the ships in
dock that the Yellow Terror had arrived, they judged that it
was time for them to go ashore, and stop till the *Medford*
should sail. Whitechapel used to be regularly overflowed with
cats, and the newspapers used to have letters from scientific
chaps trying to account for what they called the wave of cats
that had spread over East London.

"I remember that once we laid alongside of a Russian brig,
down in the basin by Old Gravel Lane. There was a tremendous big black cat sitting on the poop, and as soon as he
caught sight of our Tom, he sung out to him, remarking that
he was able and ready to wipe the deck up with him at any
time. We all understood that the Russian was a new arrival
who hadn't ever heard of the Yellow Terror, and we knew that
he was, as the good book says, rushing on his fate. Tom was
sitting on the rail near the mizzen rigging when the Russian
made his remarks, and he didn't seem to hear them. But

presently we saw him going slowly aloft till he reached our crossjack yard. He laid out on the yardarm till he was near enough to jump onto the mainyard of the Russian, and the first thing that the Russian cat knew Tom landed square on his back. The fight didn't last more than one round, and at the end of that, the remains of the Russian cat sneaked behind a water cask, and the Yellow Terror came back by the way of the crossjack yard and went on fur brushing, as if nothing had happened.

"When Tom went ashore in a foreign port he generally stopped ashore till we sailed. A few hours before we cast off hawsers, Tom would come aboard. He always knew when we were going to sail, and he never once got left. I remember one time when we were just getting up anchor in Cape Town harbour, and we all reckoned that this time we should have to sail without Tom, he having evidently stopped ashore just a little too long. But presently alongside comes a boat, with Tom lying back at full length in the sternsheets, for all the world like a drunken sailor who has been delaying the ship, and is proud of it. The boatman said that Tom had come down to the pier and jumped into his boat, knowing that the man would row him off to the ship, and calculating that Smedley would be glad to pay the damage. It's my belief that if Tom hadn't found a boatman, he would have chartered the government launch. He had the cheek to do that or anything else.

"Fighting was really Tom's only vice; and it could hardly be called a vice, seeing as he always licked the other cat, and hardly ever came out of a fight with a torn ear or a black eye. Smedley always said that Tom was religious. I used to think that was rubbish; but after I had been with Tom for a couple of voyages I began to believe what Smedley said about him. Every Sunday when the weather permitted, Smedley used to hold service on the quarterdeck. He was a Methodist, and when it came to ladling out Scripture, or singing a hymn, he could give odds to almost any preacher. All hands, except the man at the wheel, and the lookout, were required to attend

service on Sunday morning, which naturally caused considerable grumbling, as the watch below considered they had a
right to sleep in peace, instead of being dragged aft for service. But they had to knock under, and what they considered
even worse, they had to sing, for the old man kept a bright
lookout while the singing was going on, and if he caught any
man malingering and not doing his full part of the singing he
would have a few words to say to that man with a belaying pin,
or a rope's end, after the service was over.

"Now Tom never failed to attend service, and to do his level
best to help. He would sit somewhere near the old man and
pay attention to what was going on better than I've seen some
folks do in first-class churches ashore. When the men sang,
Tom would start in and let out a yell here and there, which
showed that he meant well even if he had never been to a
singing school, and didn't exactly understand singing according to Gunter. First along, I thought that it was all an accident
that the cat came to service, and I calculated that his yelling
during the singing meant that he didn't like it. But after a
while I had to admit that Tom enjoyed the Sunday service as
much as the Captain himself, and I agreed with Smedley that
the cat was a thoroughgoing Methodist.

"Now after I'd been with Smedley for about six years, he
got married all of a sudden. I didn't blame him, for in the first
place it wasn't any of my business; and, in the next place, I
hold that a ship's captain ought to have a wife, and the underwriters would be a sight wiser if they insisted that all captains
should be married, instead of insisting that all ships should
carry cats. You see that if a ship's captain has a wife, he is naturally anxious to get back to her, and have his best clothes
mended, and his food cooked to suit him. Consequently he
wants to make good passages and he don't want to run the risk
of drowning himself, or of getting into trouble with his owners, and losing his berth. You'll find, if you look into it, that
married captains live longer, and get on better than unmarried
men, as it stands to reason that they ought to do.

"But it happened that the woman Smedley married was an Agonyostic, which is a sort of person that doesn't believe in anything, except the multiplication table, and suchlike human vanities. She didn't lose any time in getting Smedley round to her way of thinking, and instead of being the religious man he used to be, he chucked the whole thing, and used to argue with me by the hour at a time, to prove that religion was a waste of time, and that he hadn't any soul, and had never been created, but had just descended from a family of seafaring monkeys. It made me sick to hear a respectable sailorman talking such rubbish, but of course, seeing as he was my commanding officer, I had to be careful about contradicting him. I wouldn't ever yield an inch to his arguments, and I told him as respectfully as I could, that he was making the biggest mistake of his life. 'Why, look at the cat,' I used to say, 'he's got sense enough to be religious, and if you was to tell him that he was descended from a monkey, he'd consider himself insulted.' But it wasn't any use. Smedley was full of his new agonyostical theories, and the more I disagreed with him, the more set he was in his way.

"Of course he knocked off holding Sunday morning services; and the men ought to have been delighted, considering how they used to grumble at having to come aft and sing hymns, when they wanted to be below. But there is no accounting for sailors. They were actually disappointed when Sunday came and there wasn't any service. They said that we should have an unlucky voyage, and that the old man, now that he had got a rich wife, didn't consider sailors good enough to come aft on the quarterdeck, and take a hand in singing. Smedley didn't care for their opinion, but he was some considerable worried about the Yellow Terror. Tom missed the Sunday morning service, and he said so as plain as he could. Every Sunday, for three or four weeks, he came on deck, and took his usual seat near the captain, and waited for the service to begin. When he found out that there was no use in waiting for it, he showed that he disapproved of Smedley's conduct in the strongest way. He gave up being intimate with the old man, and once when Smedley tried to pat him, and be friendly, he swore at him, and bit him on the leg—not in an angry way, you understand, but just to show his disapproval of Smedley's irreligious conduct.

"When we got to London, Tom never once went ashore, and he hadn't a single fight. He seemed to have lost all interest in worldly things. He'd sit on the poop in a melancholy sort of way, never minding how his fur looked, and never so much as answering if a strange cat sang out to him. After we left London he kept below most of the time, and finally, about the time that we were crossing the line, he took to his bed, as you might say, and got to be as thin and weak as if he had been living in the forecastle of a lime-juicer. And he was that melancholy that you couldn't get him to take an interest in anything. Smedley got to be so anxious about him that he read up in his medical book to try and find out what was the matter with him; and finally made up his mind that the cat had a first-class disease with a big name something like spinal menagerie. That was some little satisfaction to Smedley, but it didn't benefit the cat any; for nothing that Smedley could do would induce Tom to take medicine. He wouldn't so much as sniff at salts, and when Smedley tried to poultice his neck, he considered himself insulted, and roused up enough to take a piece out of the old man's ear.

"About that time we touched at Funchal, and Smedley sent ashore to lay in another tomcat, thinking that perhaps a fight would brace Tom up a little. But when the new cat was put down alongside of Tom, and swore at him in the most impudent sort of way, Tom just turned over on his other side, and pretended to go asleep. After that we all felt that the Yellow Terror was done for. Smedley sent the new cat ashore again, and told me that Tom was booked for the other world, and that there wouldn't be any more luck for us on that voyage.

"I went down to see the cat, and though he was thin and weak, I couldn't see any signs of serious disease about him. So I says to Smedley that I didn't believe the cat was sick at all.

"'Then what's the matter with him?' says the old man. 'You saw yourself that he wouldn't fight, and when he's got to that point I consider that he is about done with this world and its joys and sorrows.'

"'His nose is all right,' said I. 'When I felt it just now it was as cool as a teetotaller's.'

"'That does look as if he hadn't any fever to speak of,' says Smedley, 'and the book says that if you've got spinal menagerie you're bound to have a fever.'

"'The trouble with Tom,' says I, 'is mental: that's what it is. He's got something on his mind that is wearing him out.'

"'What can he have on his mind?' says the captain. 'He's got everything to suit him aboard this ship. If he was a millionaire he couldn't be better fixed. He won all his fights while we were in Boston, and hasn't had a fight since, which shows that he can't be low-spirited on account of a licking. No, sir! You'll find that Tom's mind is all right.'

"'Then what gives him such a mournful look out of his eyes?' says I. 'When you spoke to him this morning he looked at you as if he was on the point of crying over your misfortunes—that is to say, if you've got any. Come to think of it, Tom begun to go into thishyer decline just after you were married. Perhaps that's what's the matter with him.'

"But there was no convincing Smedley that Tom's trouble was mental, and he was so sure that the cat was going to die, that he got to be about as low-spirited as Tom himself. 'I begin to wish,' says Smedley to me one morning, 'that I was a Methodist again, and believed in a hereafter. It does seem kind of hard that a first-class cat-fighter like Tom shouldn't have a chance when he dies. He was a good religious cat if ever there was one, and I'd like to think that he was going to a better world.'

"Just then an idea struck me. 'Captain Smedley,' says I, 'you remember how Tom enjoyed the meetings that we used to have aboard here on Sunday mornings!'

"'He did so,' said Smedley. 'I never saw a person who took more pleasure in his Sunday privileges than Tom did.'

"'Captain Smedley,' says I, putting my hand on the old man's sleeve. 'All that's the matter with Tom is seeing you deserting the religion that you was brought up in, and turning agonyostical, or whatever you call it. I call it turning plain infidel. Tom's mourning about your soul, and he's miserable because you don't have any more Sunday morning meetings. I told you the trouble was mental, and now you know it is.'

"'Mebbe you're right,' says Smedley, taking what I'd said in a peaceable way, instead of flying into a rage, as I expected he would. 'To tell you the truth, I ain't so well satisfied in my own mind as I used to be, and I was thinking last night, when I started in to say "Now I lay me"—just from habit you know— that if I'd stuck to the Methodist persuasion I should be a blamed sight happier than I am now.'

"'Tomorrow's Sunday,' says I, 'and if I was you, Captain, I should have the bell rung for service, same as you used to do, and bring Tom up on deck, and let him have the comfort of hearing the rippingest hymns you can lay your hand to. It can't hurt you, and it may do him a heap of good. Anyway, it's worth trying, if you really want the Yellow Terror to get well.'

"'I don't mind saying,' says Smedley, 'that I'd do almost anything to save his life. He's been with me now going on for seven years, and we've never had a hard word. If a Sunday morning meeting will be any comfort to him, he shall have it. Mebbe if it doesn't cure him, it may sort of smooth his hatchway to the tomb.'

"Now the very next day was Sunday, and at six the Captain had the bell rung for service, and the men were told to lay aft. The bell hadn't fairly stopped ringing, when Tom comes up the companionway, one step at a time, looking as if he was on his way to his own funeral. He came up to his usual place alongside of the capstan, and lay down on his side at the old man's feet, and sort of looked up at him with what anybody would have said was a grateful look. I could see that Smedley was feeling pretty serious. He understood what the cat wanted to say, and when he started in to give out a hymn, his voice sort

of choked. It was a ripping good hymn, with a regular hurricane chorus, and the men sung it for all they were worth,
hoping that it would meet Tom's views. He was too weak to
join in with any of his old-time yells, but he sort of flopped the
deck with his tail, and you could see he was enjoying it down
to the ground.

"Well, the service went on just as it used to do in old times,
and Smedley sort of warmed up as it went along, and by and
by he'd got the regular old Methodist glow on his face. When
it was all through, and the men had gone forrard again,
Smedley stooped down, and picked up Tom, and kissed him,
and the cat nestled up in the old man's neck and licked his
chin. Smedley carried Tom down into the saloon, and sung
out to the steward to bring some fresh meat. The cat turned
to and ate as good a dinner as he'd ever eaten in his best days,
and after he was through, he went into Smedley's own cabin,
and curled up in the old man's bunk, and went to sleep purring fit to take the deck off. From that day Tom improved
steadily, and by the time we got to Cape Town he was well
enough to go ashore, though he was still considerable weak. I
went ashore at the same time, and kept an eye on Tom, to see
what he would do. I saw him pick out a small measly-looking
cat, that couldn't have stood up to a full-grown mouse, and
lick him in less than a minute. Then I knew that Tom was all
right again, and I admired his judgment in picking out a small
cat that was suited to his weak condition. By the time that we
got to Canton, Tom was as well in body and mind as he had
ever been; and when we sailed, he came aboard with two
inches of his tail missing, and his starboard ear carried away,
but he had the air of having licked all creation, which I don't
doubt he had done, that is to say, so far as all creation could
be found in Canton.

"I never heard any more of Smedley's agonyostical nonsense. He went back to the Methodists again, and he always
said that Tom had been the blessed means of showing him
the error of his ways. I heard that when he got back to

Boston, he gave Mrs. Smedley notice that he expected her to go to the Methodist meeting with him every Sunday, and that if she didn't, he should consider that it was a breach of wedding articles, and equivalent to mutiny. I don't know how she took it, or what the consequences were, for I left the *Medford* just then, and took command of a barque that traded between Boston and the West Indies. And I never heard of the Yellow Terror after that voyage, though I often thought of him, and always held that for a cat he was the ablest cat, afloat or ashore, that any man ever met."

A Talk with Mark Twain's Cat, the Owner Being Invisible
The New York Times

MARK Twain had lost his cat. Consumed with an attack of wanderlust, Bambino had fled from home and roamed for a day and a half. The humorist had offered a reward of $5. Then his secretary, Miss Lyon, had met Bambino on University Place and haled him home.

It was all in the papers.

Failing to understand why it shouldn't be in the papers some more, a woman from the *Times* had called at the Clemens mansion, 21 Fifth Avenue.

A man with china blue eyes and a white waistcoat opened the door for her. He opened it just half way.

Upon her request to see Mr. Clemens, he gave a start of surprise, frowned, and said:

"Mr. Clemens is asleep."

It was then 1:30 in the afternoon.

"When can I see him?" asked the woman.

"I will find out," said the servant, and shut the door upon her while he did so.

By and by he reopened it.

"He may see you," he told her, "if you come back at 5 o'clock."

It was a beautiful sunshiny day, but the woman went home, stayed indoors to rest up for this interview, and at 5 o'clock again sauntered toward the Clemens mansion.

The same man appeared. He wore the same waistcoat. He had, likewise, the same blue eyes.

"Mr. Clemens is not in now," he said, "but his secretary might see you."

"Very well," responded the woman, and stood outside the shut door once more while he searched for the secretary.

As she gazed upon Fifth Avenue, gay in the sunshine with automobiles and carriages and people enjoying themselves, she wondered vaguely if thieves were in the habit of infesting the Clemens mansion; if that was the reason they were so particular about the door.

Then it opened cautiously and the servant said:

"You may come in."

Precious privilege. The woman went in and stood in the hall as if she were a book agent. There were chairs, but she was afraid to sit down.

Presently the secretary, a nice little woman with brown eyes and old-fashioned sleeves, came down the stairs and asked her what she wanted.

"I want to see Mr. Clemens about the cat," replied the woman.

"Mr. Clemens never sees anybody—I mean any newspaper people. Besides, he is not at home."

"Then," said the woman, "may I see the cat?"

"Yes," nodded the secretary, "you may see the cat," and she ran lightly up the long stairway and came down soon with Bambino in her arms, a beautiful black silent cat with long velvety fur and luminous eyes that looked very intelligently into the face of the woman.

The secretary and the woman then sat down on a bench in the hall, and talked about the cat. The cat listened but said nothing.

"We were terribly distressed about him," cooed the secretary. "He is a great pet with Mr. Clemens. He is a year old. It is the first time he has ever run away. He lies curled up on Mr. Clemens's bed all day long."

"Does Mr. Clemens breakfast at five o'clock tea and dine on the following day?" asked the woman.

"Oh, no. He does all his writing before he gets up. That's why he gets up at 5 o'clock. Bambino always stays with him while he writes."

"I should consider it a great privilege," smiled the woman, "to breathe the same atmosphere with Mr. Clemens for about three minutes. Don't you think if I came back at 7 you might arrange it?"

"I will try," promised the secretary, kindly.

At 7, therefore, the woman toiled up the dark red steps and rang the bell. The china-eyed man with the white waistcoat opened the door, disclosed one eye and the half of his face, said abruptly, "Mr. Clemens doesn't wish to see you," and slammed the door.

The woman walked slowly down the red steps and looked up Fifth Avenue, wondering whether she would walk home or take a car.

Fifth Avenue was very beautiful.

Purplish in the dusk, it was gemmed with softly gleaming opalescent electric balls of light.

It was, moreover, admirably bare of people.

She concluded to walk home.

She was about to start forward when she became aware of a furry gentle something rubbing against her skirts.

She looked down, and there was Bambino, purring at her, looking up at her out of his luminous cat eyes.

The man at the door had shut him out, too!

She took him in both hands and lifted him up. He nestled against her shoulder.

"I don't like to prejudice you against the people you have to live with, Bambino," she said. "It seems they will make you live with them. But they weren't so nice. Were they? They might have told me at the start he wouldn't see me. They needn't have made me lose all the sunshine of today. You can't bring back a day and you can't bring back sunshine.

"You wouldn't have treated me like that, would you?"

Bambino purred musically in his earnest assurance that he would not.

"I suppose you heard it all," she went on, "and you sympathized with me. You are awfully tired yourself. I can see that.

If you were a Parisian cat we'd call it *ennui,* that expresses it better, but we'll let it go at tired. You are. Aren't you? Or you wouldn't have run off."

Bambino sighed wearily and half closed his eyes.

"It's a pretty rarefied atmosphere, I imagine, for a cat," she reasoned. "I don't blame you for wanting to get out with the common cats and whoop it up a little. Any self-respecting cat would rather run himself in a gutter or walk the back fence than sit cooped up the livelong day with a humorist. You can't tell me anything about that. It's a deadly thing to see people grind out fun. I used to know a comic artist. I had to sit by and watch him try to match his jokes to pictures!"

She clasped Bambino closer and caught her breath in a sigh.

"I don't blame you one bit for running off," she reiterated. "I can imagine what you must have suffered. Shall we walk along a little on this beautiful street that's so wide and empty now of people?" she asked politely. "I get as tired as you do sometimes of people, Bambino. They are not always so nice. There are a lot of times that I like cats better."

Bambino curled himself up in her arms and laid an affectionate paw on her wrist by way of rewarding her.

She walked on, fondling him.

"I've the greatest notion," she confided presently, "to run off with you and paralyze them. It would serve them right. How would you like, Bambino, to come and live with me in my studio?"

Bambino raised his head and purred loudly against her cheek to show how well he would like it.

"Now, I want to tell you exactly how it will be. I want to be perfectly fair with you. If you come with me you must come with your eyes open. Maybe you won't have half as soft a bed to lie on, but you won't have to lie on it all day long. I'll promise you that. In the first place, it masquerades as a couch full of pillows in the daytime, and in the second place I've got to get out and hustle if I want to eat. Not that I mind hustling. I wouldn't stay in bed all day long out of the sunshine if I could. And you mayn't have as much to eat either, but if you get too hungry there are the goldfish—and the canary wouldn't make half a bad meal. I am pretty fond of both, but I am reckless tonight somehow. You'll be welcome to them."

Bambino licked his chops preparatorily.

"There are a good many little things you are apt to miss. The studio isn't as big as a house by any means, but you'll have all outdoors to roam in. I'll trust to your coming home of nights because you'll like it there," she concluded confidently.

"And you'll be rid of the man at the door for good and all. Tell me, now, doesn't he step on your tail and 'sic' the mice on you when they are all away?"

Bambino groaned slightly, but he was otherwise noncommittal.

"I knew he did. He looks capable of anything. He's not as wise as he looks, though. He may not know it, but I push the pen for the tallest newspaper building in the city, the tallest in the world, I think. I'll take you up to the top of that building of mine, and let you climb the flag pole. Then if there should happen to be another cat on the Flatiron Building there'd be some music, wouldn't there, for the rest of the city? And they couldn't throw that flatiron at you anyway, could they? Want to go?"

Bambino put both paws around her neck, and purred an eloquent assent.

"You talk less than anybody I ever interviewed," remarked the woman, "but I think I know what you mean."

She pressed his affectionate black paws against her neck and hurried up the avenue, looking back over her shoulder to see that nobody followed.

She almost ran until she got to the bridge over the yawning chasm near Sixteenth Street. Then she stopped.

Bambino looked anxiously up to see what was the matter.

But turned deliberately around.

Bambino gave a long-drawn sigh. He looked appealingly up at her out of his luminous eyes.

"I reckon I won't steal you, Bambino," she concluded, sadly. "I'd like to, but it wouldn't be fair.

"In the morning he'd be sorry. Maybe he couldn't work without you there, looking at him out of your beautiful eyes. You don't have to hear him dictate, too, do you, Bambino? If I thought that! *** But no. There is a limit. He's had his troubles, too, you know. He's bound to be a little lenient. The goose hasn't always hung so high for him. Of course you don't remember it, but he had an awful time establishing himself as the great American humorist. Couldn't get a single publisher to believe it. Had to publish his *Innocents Abroad* himself. Just said to the American public, 'Now, you've got to take this. It's humor,' and made them take it. Held their noses. That was a long time ago. Couldn't do it today. Not with *Innocents Abroad.* The American public is getting too well educated. Who ever reads *Innocents Abroad* now? Not the rising generation. You ask any boy of today what is the funniest book, and see if he doesn't say *Alice in Wonderland*?

"Still, for an old back-date book, that wasn't half bad. He has never written anything better. It must give him the heartache to see it laid on the shelf. I suppose you must hear these things discussed, but not this side of them, perhaps. No. Naturally no. They don't make you read their books, they can't, but you must have to hear about them. *** Life is hard! But I must take you back. We mustn't do anything at all to hurt his feelings."

Bambino was fairly limp with disappointment. He had set his heart on the top of the *Times* building flagpole. He had almost tasted the canary, to say nothing of the goldfish. He hadn't the heart to purr any longer. His paws fell from the woman's neck. She had to carry him like that, all four feet hanging lifeless, his head drooping.

"And there's another thing, Bambino," she continued, as they went along. "I don't want anything I said about his having to establish himself as a humorist to disillusion you or make you more dissatisfied than you are. All humorists are like that. They have to establish themselves. Why, wasn't I in London when Nat Goodwin produced his *Cowboy and the Lady* at Daly's? Couldn't I hear people he had planted all over the audience that first night explaining that he was a humorist, and the play was intended to be funny? Certainly. But it didn't work that well. Those English people are more determined than we are. They wouldn't stand for it. He had to take the play off.

"Your master happened to catch us when we were young and innocent. He deserves a lot of credit for bamboozling us. You ought to admire him for it. I do."

They were nearly home by now. Bambino managed to emit another purr. It was like a whimper.

"Don't you cry, Bambino," she soothed. "We all have our troubles. You must be a brave cat and bear up under yours," and she tiptoed up the red steps and set him at the door where they could find him when they missed him.

He sat there, a crumpled, black, discouraged ball, his eyes following her hungrily.

She ran back to him.

"Bear up under it the best you can, Bambino," she implored; "but if it gets so you can't stand it again, you know where to find a friend."

There was a sound of approaching footsteps in the hall.

She pressed her lips to Bambino's ear, whispered her address to him, and fled.

On Cats

Guy de Maupassant

I was sitting, the other day, on a bench outside of my door, with the sun shining full upon me, a basket of blooming anemones in front of me, reading a book that had recently appeared, a good book, a rare thing, and also a delightful book, *Le Tonnelier*, by Georges Duval. A large white cat, which belonged to the gardener, jumped on my knees, by the shock of its impact closing the book, which I laid beside me, to caress the beast.

It was hot; the odor of young flowers, a shy, light, intermittent odor, floated in the air, and I also felt passing breaths of cold coming from those great white peaks that I saw in the distance.

But the sun was scorching, penetrating, with that heat which digs down into the earth and makes it alive, which splits the seeds in order to animate the sleeping germs within, and slits the buds, so that the young leaves may come out. The cat was rolling on its back, on my knees, with its paws extended, clawing the air, showing its pointed teeth inside of its lips, and its green eyes peeping out through the slit of its half-closed lids. I patted and caressed the soft and nervous animal, supple as a piece of silk, gentle, warm, delicious, and dangerous. She was purring delightedly, and ready to bite, for she likes to claw, as well as to be caressed. She stretched and turned her neck, and when I stopped touching her, she sat up and passed her head under my raised hand.

I made her nervous and she made me nervous, too, for I both love and detest these charming and perfidious animals. It gives me pleasure to touch them, to pass my hand over their silky, crackling fur, to feel their warmth through the fine, exquisite texture of their coat. There is nothing softer than the warm and vibrant hair of a cat, and nothing imparts to the skin a more delicate, refined, and rare sensation. But this living coat makes my fingers itch with a strange and fierce desire to strangle the beast that I am caressing. I feel in her the inclination that she has to bite me and to tear me. I feel and I catch this inclination, like a fluid which she communicates to me; I catch it from this warm skin through the tips of my fingers, and it creeps along my nerves, along my limbs, up to my heart, up to my head; it fells me, it runs along my skin, and it makes me clinch my teeth. And all the while I feel at the tips of my ten fingers the light, lively tickling which penetrates and suffuses my body.

And if the beast begins, if she bites me or claws me, I take her by the neck, give a turn, and fling her away like a sling-stone, so quickly and so brutally that she never has the time to get even with me.

I remember that, even as a child, I loved cats, but yet with the brusque desire to strangle them in my little hands. One day I suddenly saw, at the far end of the garden, on the edge of the woods, something grey that was rolling over in the tall grass. I ran down to see; it was a cat caught in a trap, that was strangling, with the death rattle in its throat. It was twisting its body, clawing the earth round it, jumping up, and falling down; and then it began all over again, and its quick, hoarse breathing sounded like the noise of a pump, a dreadful noise that is still ringing in my ears.

I might have taken a spade and cut the trap; I might have run for our manservant, or I might have gone to tell my father. But, no; I did not stir from the spot, and with beating heart and trembling and cruel joy I watched it die; for it was a cat. Had it been a dog I should have cut the wire string with my teeth, rather than let it suffer a moment longer.

And when the cat was dead, quite dead, and still warm, I went up to touch it and pull its tail.

Yet they are delicious, especially when, in caressing them, they rub against our skin, purr, and roll over us, looking at us with their yellow eyes which never seem to see us, and it is then that we feel the insecurity of their caresses, the perfidious egoism of their pleasure.

Women also give us this sensation, charming, gentle women, with clear and false eyes, who have chosen us in order to get a taste of love. With them, when they open their arms, with pursed-up lips, when one presses them close, with beating heart, when one tastes the sweet, sensual joy of their tender caress, one feels very well that one is holding a cat, a cat with claws and nails, a perfidious, sly, amorous, hostile cat, who will bite when she is tired of kissing.

All the poets have loved cats. Baudelaire has sung of them divinely.

"Les amoureux fervents et les savants austere"

One day I had the strange sensation of having lived in the enchanted palace of the White Cat, a magical château, where ruled one of these sinuous, mysterious, troublous beasts, perhaps the only one of all the beings whose footfall one never hears.

It was last summer, on the same coast of the Mediterranean. There was a fierce heat at Nice, and I asked if the people here did not have somewhere in the mountain above a cool valley, where they could go for a breath of fresh air.

They told me of the valley of Thorence. I wanted to see it. I must first go to Grasse, the city of perfumes, of which I shall speak some day, describing how they make those essences and quintessences of flowers, which are worth up to two thousand francs a liter. I passed the evening and the night in an old hotel in the city, a second-class inn, where the quality of the food was as doubtful as the cleanness of the rooms. I left in the morning.

The route lay through the mountains, skirting deep ravines, with sharp, sterile, and wild peaks rising up on the sides. I was wondering to what a curious summer place I had been sent, and I was on the point of turning back to get to Nice that same evening, when I suddenly perceived in front of me, on a mountain which seemed to shut off the entire valley, an immense and splendid ruin, with its towers and crumbled walls outlined against the sky, a curious heap of a dead fortress. It was the remains of an ancient priory of the Knights Templars, who formerly held sway in the country of Thorence.

Skirting this mountain, I suddenly discovered a long green valley, fresh and restful. In the bottom there were meadows, running water, and willows, and on the slope pines were climbing up to the sky.

Opposite the priory, on the further side of the valley, but lower, there stands the Château of Quatre Tours, which was built about 1530, and is still inhabited. Its architecture does not yet show any trace of the Renaissance.

It is a heavy and well-built pile of masonry, very strong in appearance, and flanked by four watchtowers, as its name indicates.

I had a letter of introduction to the owners of this manor, who would not let me go on to the hotel.

The whole valley, which is really delightful, is one of the most charming summer places that one can imagine.

I went first through a kind of salon, the walls of which are covered by old Cordova leather, then through another room, where, by the light of my candle, I caught a glimpse of old portraits of ladies on the walls, those pictures of which Théophile Gautier has said:

> "I love to see you in your oval frames,
> Yellow portraits of the beauties of old,
> Holding withering roses in your hands,
> As is fitting for century-old flowers."

Then I entered the room in which I was to sleep.

I turned to examine it as soon as I was alone. It was hung with old painted tapestries, showing pink towers against blue backgrounds, and large, fantastic birds under foliage of precious stones.

My dressing-room was in one of the towers. The windows, which were cut large into the wall on the inside, sloped through the masonry, narrowing as they went out toward the daylight, being, in fact, nothing more than portholes, openings through which men on the outside were killed. I closed my door, lay down, and went to sleep.

And I dreamed; one always dreams somewhat of that through which he has passed during the day. I was traveling; I entered an inn, where I saw at a table before the fire a servant in gala livery and a mason, a curious fellowship, but which did not astonish me. They were talking of Victor Hugo, who had just died, and I took part in their conversation. I finally went to bed in a room whose door did not close, and suddenly I saw the servant and the mason tiptoeing toward my bed, armed with bricks.

I started out of my sleep, and it took me some minutes to collect myself. Then I recalled the events of the day before my arrival at Thorence, the *châtelain's* amiable reception. . . . I was about to close my eyes when I saw—yes, I saw in the darkness of the night, in the middle of my room, at about the height of a man's head, two fiery eyes looking at me.

I reached for a match, and while I was striking it I heard a noise, a slight, soft noise, like that of the dropping of a damp roll of cloth, and when I had made a light I saw nothing but a large table in the middle of the apartment.

I got up. I went through the two rooms, looked under my bed and into the closets, but found nothing.

I thought, therefore, that I had continued to dream for a few seconds after being awake, and I went to sleep again, not without some difficulty.

Again I began to dream. This time, also, I was traveling, but in the East, the land that I love, and I came to a Turk who was living in the open desert. He was a splendid Turk; not an Arab, but a Turk, large, amiable, charming, dressed in Turkish fashion, with a turban and a whole assortment of silks on his back, a real Turk of the Théâtre Français, who made me compliments in offering me sweets, on a delicious divan.

Then a small negro boy led me to my room—so all my dreams finished there—a perfumed, sky-blue room, with skins on the floor, and before the fire—the idea of fire pursued me even to the desert—sat a scantily clad woman in a low chair, who was expecting me.

She was of the most pure Oriental type, with stars on the cheeks, the forehead, and chin, immense eyes, an admirable body, a little brown but warm and captivating.

She looked at me, and I thought: "This is what I call hospitality. It is not in our stupid land of the North, our land of inept prudishness and odious shamefacedness and imbecile morality, where one would receive a stranger in this fashion."

I went up to her and spoke, but she replied only by signs, not knowing a word of my language, which my Turk, her master, knew so well.

All the more happy in that she would be silent, I took her by the hand and led her to my couch, where I lay down beside her. . . . But one always awakens just at that point! So I woke up, and I was not very much surprised to feel something soft and warm under my hand, which I caressed amorously.

Then, on gathering together my thoughts, I saw that it was a cat, a large cat, snuggled up against my cheek, which slept undisturbed. I let it lie, and, following its example, went to sleep once more.

When day broke it was gone, and I really thought that I had been dreaming, for I did not understand how she could have come into my room and gone out again, the door being locked.

When I told my adventure (not all of it) to my amiable host, he began to laugh, and said: "He came in through the cat-hole," and, lifting up a curtain, he showed me a small, round black hole in the wall.

And I learned that almost all the old habitations in this country have such long, narrow passages through the walls, which go from the cellar to the garret, from the maid servant's room to that of the master, and which constitute the cat the king and the master of the house.

He goes about as he likes, visiting his domain at his pleasure; he can sleep in all the beds, see everything and hear everything, know all the secrets, all the habits, and all the shame of the house. He is everywhere at home, and can enter everywhere, the animal that goes about noiselessly, the silent prowler, the midnight promenader of hollow walls.

And I thought of a stanza of Baudelaire's:

> "He is the homely spirit of the spot;
> As judge he sees us all, and doth inspire
> All things that pass in his domain;
> Perhaps he is a fay—perhaps a god."

The Philanthropist and the Happy Cat
Saki

JOCANTHA Bessbury was in the mood to be serenely and graciously happy. Her world was a pleasant place, and it was wearing one of its pleasantest aspects. Gregory had managed to get home for a hurried lunch and a smoke afterwards in the little snuggery; the lunch had been a good one, and there was just time to do justice to the coffee and cigarettes. Both were excellent in their way, and Gregory was, in his way, an excellent husband. Jocantha rather suspected herself of making him a very charming wife, and more than suspected herself of having a first-rate dressmaker.

"I don't suppose a more thoroughly contented personality is to be found in all Chelsea," observed Jocantha in allusion to herself; "except perhaps Attab," she continued, glancing towards the large tabby-marked cat that lay in considerable ease in a corner of the divan. "He lies there, purring and dreaming, shifting his limbs now and then in an ecstasy of cushioned comfort. He seems the incarnation of everything soft and silky and velvety, without a sharp edge in his composition, a dreamer whose philosophy is sleep and let sleep; and then, as evening draws on, he goes out into the garden with a red glint in his eyes and slays a drowsy sparrow."

"As every pair of sparrows hatches out ten or more young ones in the year, while their food supply remains stationary, it is just as well that the Attabs of the community should have that idea of how to pass an amusing afternoon," said Gregory. Having delivered himself of this sage comment he lit another cigarette, bade Jocantha a playfully affectionate good-bye, and departed into the outer world.

"Remember, dinner's a wee bit earlier tonight, as we're going to the Haymarket," she called after him.

Left to herself, Jocantha continued the process of looking at her life with placid, introspective eyes. If she had not everything she wanted in this world, at least she was very well pleased with what she had got. She was very well pleased, for instance, with the snuggery, which contrived somehow to be cozy and dainty and expensive all at once. The porcelain was rare and beautiful, the Chinese enamels took on wonderful tints in the firelight, the rugs and hangings led the eye through sumptuous harmonies of coloring. It was a room in which one might have suitably entertained an ambassador or an archbishop, but it was also a room in which one could cut out pictures for a scrapbook without feeling that one was scandalizing the deities of the place with one's litter. And as with the snuggery, so with the rest of the house, and as with the house, so with the other departments of Jocantha's life; she really had good reason for being one of the most contented women in Chelsea.

From being in a mood of simmering satisfaction with her lot she passed to the phase of being generously commiserating for those thousands around her whose lives and circumstances were dull, cheap, pleasureless, and empty. Work girls, shop assistants and so forth, the class that have neither the happy-go-lucky freedom of the poor nor the leisured freedom of the rich, came specially within the range of her sympathy. It was sad to think that there were young people who, after a long day's work, had to sit alone in chill, dreary bedrooms because they could not afford the price of a cup of coffee and a sandwich in a restaurant, still less a shilling for a theatre gallery.

Jocantha's mind was still dwelling on this theme when she started forth on an afternoon campaign of desultory shopping; it would be rather a comforting thing, she told herself, if she could do something, on the spur of the moment, to bring a gleam of pleasure and interest into the life of even one or two wistful-hearted, empty-pocketed workers; it would add a good deal to her sense of enjoyment at the theatre that night. She would get two upper circle tickets for a popular play, make her way into some cheap tea shop, and present the tickets to the first couple of interesting work girls with whom she could casually drop into conversation. She could explain matters by saying that she was unable to use the tickets herself and did not want them to be wasted, and, on the other hand, did not want the trouble of sending them back. On further reflection she decided that it might be better to get only one ticket and give it to some lonely-looking girl sitting eating her frugal meal by herself; the girl might scrape acquaintance with her next-seat neighbor at the theatre and lay the foundations of a lasting friendship.

With the Fairy Godmother impulse strong upon her, Jocantha marched into a ticket agency and selected with immense care an upper circle seat for the "Yellow Peacock," a play that was attracting a considerable amount of discussion and criticism. Then she went forth in search of a tea shop and philanthropic adventure, at about the same time that Attab sauntered into the garden with a mind attuned to sparrow stalking. In a corner of an A.B.C. shop she found an unoccupied table, whereat she promptly installed herself, impelled by the fact that at the next table was sitting a young girl, rather plain of feature, with tired, listless eyes, and a general air of uncomplaining forlornness. Her dress was of poor material, but aimed at being in the fashion, her hair was pretty, and her complexion bad; she was finishing a modest meal of tea and scone, and she was not very different in her way from thousands of other girls who were finishing, or beginning, or continuing their teas in London tea shops at that exact moment. The odds were enormously in favor of the supposition that she had never seen the "Yellow Peacock": obviously she supplied excellent material for Jocantha's first experiment in haphazard benefaction.

Jocantha ordered some tea and a muffin, and then turned a friendly scrutiny on her neighbor with a view to catching her eye. At that precise moment the girl's face lit up with sudden pleasure, her eyes sparkled, a flush came into her cheeks, and she looked almost pretty. A young man, whom she greeted with an affectionate "Hullo, Bertie," came up to her table and took his seat in a chair facing her. Jocantha looked hard at the newcomer; he was in appearance a few years younger than herself, very much better looking than Gregory, rather better looking, in fact, than any of the young men of her set. She guessed him to be a well-mannered young clerk in some wholesale warehouse, existing and amusing himself as best he might on a tiny salary, and commanding a holiday of about two weeks in the year. He was aware, of course, of his good looks, but with the shy self-consciousness of the Anglo-Saxon, not the blatant complacency of the Latin. He was obviously on terms of friendly intimacy with the girl he was talking to, prob- ably they were drifting towards a formal engagement. Jocantha pictured the boy's home, in a rather narrow circle, with a tire- some mother who always wanted to know how and where he spent his evenings. He would exchange that humdrum thrall- dom in due course for a home of his own, dominated by a chronic scarcity of pounds, shillings, and pence, and a dearth of most of the things that made life attractive or comfortable. Jocantha felt extremely sorry for him. She wondered if he had seen the "Yellow Peacock": the odds were enormously in favor of the supposition that he had not. The girl had finished her tea and would shortly be going back to her work; when the boy was alone it would be quite easy for Jocantha to say: "My hus- band has made other arrangements for me this evening; would you care to make use of this ticket, which would other- wise be wasted?" Then she could come there again one after- noon for tea, and, if she saw him, ask him how he liked the play. If he was a nice boy and improved on acquaintance he could be given more theatre tickets, and perhaps asked to come one Sunday to tea at Chelsea. Jocantha made up her mind that he would improve on acquaintance, and that Gregory would like him, and that the Fairy Godmother business would prove far more entertaining than she had originally anticipated. The boy was distinctly presentable; he knew how to brush his hair, which was possibly an imitative faculty; he knew what color of tie suited him, which might be intuition; he was exactly the type that Jocantha admired, which of course was accident. Altogether she was rather pleased when the girl looked at the clock and bade a friendly but hurried farewell to her companion. Bertie nodded "good-bye," gulped down a mouthful of tea, and then produced from his overcoat pocket a paper-covered book, bearing the title *Sepoy and Sahib, a Tale of the Great Mutiny.*

The laws of tea shop etiquette forbid that you should offer theatre tickets to a stranger without having first caught the stranger's eye. It is even better if you can ask to have a sugar basin passed to you, having previously concealed the fact that you have a large and well-filled sugar basin on your own table; this is not difficult to manage, as the printed menu is generally nearly as large as the table, and can be made to stand on end. Jocantha set to work hopefully; she had a long and rather high-pitched discussion with the waitress concerning alleged defects in an altogether blameless muffin, she made loud and plaintive inquiries about the tube service to some impossibly remote suburb, she talked with brilliant insincerity to the tea-shop kitten, and as a last resort she upset a milk jug and swore at it daintily. Altogether she attracted a good deal of attention, but never for a moment did she attract the attention of the boy with the beautifully brushed hair, who was some thousands of miles away in the baking plains of Hindostan, amid deserted bungalows, seething bazaars, and riotous barrack squares, listening to the throbbing of tom-toms and the distant rattle of musketry

Jocantha went back to her house in Chelsea, which struck her for the first time as looking dull and over-furnished. She had a resentful conviction that Gregory would be uninteresting at dinner, and that the play would be stupid after dinner. On the whole her frame of mind showed a marked divergence from the purring complacency of Attab, who was again curled up in his corner of the divan with a great peace radiating from every curve of his body

But then he had killed his sparrow.

My Cat
Michel de Montaigne

WHEN my cat and I entertain each other with mutual antics, as playing with a garter, who knows but that I make more sport for her than she makes for me? Shall I conclude her to be simple that has her time to begin or to refuse to play, as freely as I have mine. Nay, who knows but that it a defect of not my understanding her language (for doubtless cats can talk and reason with one another) that we agree no better; and who knows but that she pities me for being no wiser than to play with her; and laughs, and censures my folly in making sport for her, when we two play together.

Tom Quartz
Mark Twain

ONE of my comrades there—another of those victims of eighteen years of unrequited toil and blighted hopes—was one of the gentlest spirits that ever bore its patient cross in a weary exile: grave and simple Dick Baker, pocket miner of Dead-House Gulch. He was forty-six, grey as a rat, thoughtful, slenderly educated, slouchily dressed and clay-soiled, but his heart was finer metal than any gold his shovel ever brought to light—than any, indeed, that ever was mined or minted.

Whenever he was out of luck and a little downhearted, he would fall to mourning over the loss of a wonderful cat he used to own (for where women and children are not, men of kindly impulses take up with pets, for they must love something). And he always spoke of the strange sagacity of that cat with the air of a man who believed in his secret heart that there was something human about it—maybe even supernatural.

I heard him talking about this animal once. He said:

"Gentlemen, I used to have a cat here, by the name of Tom Quartz, which you'd a took an interest in, I reckon—most anybody would. I had him here eight year—and he was the remarkablest cat *I* ever see. He was a large grey one of the Tom specie, an' he had more hard, natchral sense than any man in this camp—'n' a *power* of dignity—he wouldn't let the Guv'nor of Californy be familiar with him. He never ketched a rat in his life—'peared to be above it. He never cared for nothing but mining. He knowed more about mining, that cat did, than any man I ever, ever see. You couldn't tell *him* noth'n' 'bout placer diggin's—'n' as for pocket mining, why, he was just born for it. He would dig out after me an' Jim when

246

we went over the hills, prospect'n', and he would trot along
behind us for as much as five mile, if we went so fur. An' he
had the best judgment about mining ground—why, you never
see anything like it. When we went to work, he'd scatter a
glance around, 'n' if he didn't think much of the indications,
he would give a look as much as to say, 'Well, I'll have to get
you to excuse *me*,' 'n' without another word he'd hyste his
nose into the air 'n' shove for home. But if the ground suited
him, he would lay low 'n' keep dark till the first pan was
washed, 'n' then he would sidle up 'n' take a look, an' if there
was about six or seven grains of gold *he* was satisfied—he
didn't want no better prospect 'n' that—'n' then he would lay
down on our coats and snore like a steamboat till we'd struck
the pocket, an' then get up 'n' superintend. He was nearly
lightnin' on superintending.

"Well, by-an'-bye, up comes this yer quartz excitement.
Everybody was into it—everybody was pick'n' 'n' blast'n'
instead of shovellin' dirt on the hillside—everybody was put'n'
down a shaft instead of scrapin' the surface. Noth'n' would do
Jim but *we* must tackle the ledges, too, 'n' so we did. We com-
menced put'n' down a shaft, 'n' Tom Quartz he begin to wonder what in the Dickens it was all about. *He* hadn't ever seen
any mining like that before, 'n' he was all upset, as you may
say—he couldn't come to a right understanding of it no way—
it was too many for *him.* He was down on it, too, you bet you—
he was down on it powerful—'n' always appeared to consider
it the cussedest foolishness out. But that cat, you know, was
always agin newfangled arrangements—somehow he never
could abide 'em. *You* know how it is with old habits. But by-
an'-bye Tom Quartz begin to git sort of reconciled a little,
though he never *could* altogether understand that eternal
sinkin' of a shaft an' never pannin' out anything. At last he got
to comin' down in the shaft, hisself, to try to cipher it out. An'
when he'd git the blues, 'n' feel kind of scruffy, 'n' aggravated
'n' disgusted—knowin', as he did, that the bills was runnin' up
all the time an' we warn't makin' a cent—he would curl up on

a gunnysack in the corner an' go to sleep. Well, one day when the shaft was down about eight foot, the rock got so hard that we had to put in a blast—the first blast'n' we'd ever done since Tom Quartz was born. An' then we lit the fuse, 'n' climb out 'n' got off 'bout fifty yards—'n' forgot 'n' left Tom Quartz sound asleep on the gunnysack. In 'bout a minute we seen a puff of smoke bust up out of the hole, 'n' then everything let go with an awful crash, 'n' about four million ton of rocks 'n' dirt 'n' smoke 'n' splinters shot up 'bout a mile an' a half into the air, an' by George, right in the dead centre of it was old Tom Quartz a-goin' end over end, an' a snortin' an' a sneez'n', an' a clawin' an' a reachin' for things like all possessed. But it warn't no use, you know, it warn't no use. An' that was the last we see of *him* for about two minutes 'n' a half, an' then all of a sudden it begin to rain rocks and rubbage, an' directly he come down kerwhop about ten foot off f'm where we stood. Well, I reckon he was p'raps the orneriest-lookin' beast you ever see. One ear was sot back on his neck, 'n' his tail was stove up, 'n' his eye-winkers was swinged off, 'n' he was all blacked up with powder an' smoke, an' all sloppy with mud 'n' slush f'm one end to the other. Well, sir, it warn't no use to try to apologize—we couldn't say a word. He took a sort of a disgusted look at hisself, 'n' then he looked at us—an' it was just exactly the same as if he had said—'Gents, maybe *you* think it's smart to take advantage of a cat that 'ain't had no experience of quartz minin', but *I* think *different*'—an' then he turned on his heel 'n' marched off home without ever saying another word.

"That was jest his style. An' maybe you won't believe it, but after that you never see a cat so prejudiced agin quartz mining as what he was. An' by-an'-bye when he *did* get to goin' down in the shaft agin, you'd a been astonished at his sagacity. The minute we'd tetch off a blast 'n' the fuse'd begin to sizzle, he'd give a look as much as to say, 'Well, I'll have to git you to excuse *me*,' an' it was surpris'n' the way he'd shin out of that hole 'n' go f'r a tree. Sagacity? It ain't no name for it. 'Twas *inspiration!*"

I said, "Well, Mr. Baker, his prejudice against quartz mining *was* remarkable, considering how he came by it. Couldn't you ever cure him of it?"

"*Cure him!* No! When Tom Quartz was sot once, he was *always* sot—and you might a blowed him up as much as three million times 'n' you'd never a broken him of his cussed prejudice agin quartz mining."

The affection and the pride that lit up Baker's face when he delivered this tribute to the firmness of his humble friend of other days will always be a vivid memory with me.